C000303907

About the author

Susan Parry began writing when she was a university professor at Imperial College. Her work included forensic studies and archaeological investigations that form the basis for her writing. She lives with her husband in Swaledale, where the views from her house provide inspiration.

website: www.susanparry.co.uk
facebook/instagram: susanparryauthor
twitter: @susan_parry

GRAND DEPART

A YORKSHIRE DALES MYSTERY

SUSAN PARRY

Viridian Publishing

This edition first published in the United Kingdom in 2014 by
Viridian Publishing

Reprinted in 2021

Copyright © Susan Parry

The right of Susan Parry to be identified as the author of this work has
been asserted by her in accordance with the Copyright, Designs and
Patents Act, 1988

This novel is a work of fiction. Names and characters are the product of
the authors imagination and any resemblance to actual persons, living or
dead, is entirely coincidental

Viridian Publishing
PO Box 594
Dorking
Surrey
RH4 9HU

www.viridian-publishing.co.uk
e-mail: enquiries@viridian-publishing.co.uk

ISBN 978-0-9567891-4-3

For Paul

Chapter 1

'What the hell is going on?' shouted Mills, flinging the door open.

She'd heard the commotion down the corridor, as soon as she'd turned the corner. Above the general background chatter there were cries and an occasional shriek.

There were twenty third-year students in her class; a few of them were seated in their places looking on but most were in a cluster at the front of the lecture room. Some were shouting and several of the girls looked distressed. The group parted quickly when they saw Mills, revealing two lads who'd obviously been fighting. One had the other pinned to the floor with his knees while a girl was trying to pull him away. She was in tears.

'Jack! Matthew! Here, now!' Mills screeched.

She stormed out and waited in the corridor. After a minute, Jack appeared, red in the face and breathing heavily. He leaned back against the wall rubbing his elbow and stared at the floor. Another minute and Matthew came out, clutching a handkerchief to his face. When he removed it, there was blood on his nose and his eye was half-closed.

Some of the students were hovering by the door, waiting to see what would happen next, so Mills ordered the pair to her office, hoping that Jake was out of the way. She didn't want an audience.

'What on earth was going on?' she demanded, once she'd shut the door.

They stood in front of her like two small children, hanging their heads and shuffling their feet.

'What was it?' she asked more gently this time, hoping for an adequate explanation. She was aware that she would have to report the incident.

'Sorry,' said Matthew.

'Yes, sorry,' Jack mumbled.

'An apology is good but I'd rather know the reason why you two were fighting,' Mills said.

'You'll have to ask him,' said Jack. 'Can I go now?'

Once he'd left the room, Mills told Matthew to sit down. She was uncertain what the university procedures were in these circumstances and needed time to think.

'It was my fault,' he offered, touching his nose gingerly and studying his hand.

Mills waited.

'I shouldn't have said anything. It was stupid.'

'You upset him?'

'Yes.'

'Are you going to tell me what it was about?'

'I'd rather not.' The handkerchief was turning red as he held it to his nose.

There wasn't time to go into details and Mills was reticent to get involved. She'd ask Jake what was to be done but meanwhile she had a class to teach.

'Go and clean yourself up. I need to get back to the lecture theatre. Go on.'

He shuffled off in the opposite direction as she hurried

along the corridor. The students were standing around chatting quietly but quickly resumed their places when she arrived. Looking round she satisfied herself that the rest of the class had calmed down sufficiently for her to continue the lecture, although she'd certainly been shaken by the experience. The students were unusually subdued and no-one had any questions at the end.

As she was leaving, a quiet voice behind her asked, 'Are they OK?'

Mills turned to see the girl who had been trying to pull Jack off Matthew. Her eyes were red and swollen.

'Will they be in trouble Dr Sanderson?'

'I'm sure they're both fine, May.'

The girl turned but Mills called her back. 'Do you know what it was about?'

She shrugged and played with her long strands of thick black hair, shaking her whole body from side to side as if to emphasise her ignorance. Mills was sure she knew exactly what had caused the fight and suspected it might have been May herself.

When Jake was back in the office, she asked what the official line was on fighting in the lecture rooms. He was amused by the incident and insisted on having the full story, including every detail.

'Jack Bassett and Matthew Watson?' Jake seemed as surprised by their behaviour as she had been.

She scanned the university intranet for the appropriate form to report the incident to the Academic Tutor. According to the information, it would be fully investigated and could lead to disciplinary action.

'It looks like it will be a reprimand,' she said, leafing through the instructions for completing the incident form.

'Worst case scenario – a suspension.'

'I hope not,' said Jake vehemently. 'They're both in UNYCYCLE.'

'What's that?' Mills asked.

'The University of North Yorkshire Cycling Team,' he answered with a grin. 'Didn't you know that? They're the best road racers we've got at the moment,' Jake continued. 'Jack's fastest but Matthew Watson's not far behind. Let's hope this incident doesn't affect their places in the team.'

Mills settled down to complete the form online, hesitating as she pressed the send button, hoping there would be no serious repercussions.

Jake looked up from his desk as she was preparing to leave.

'Are you going to this freshers' evening that's being given by the alumnus next week?' he asked.

'I wasn't planning to.'

She hadn't wanted to subject Alex to an evening of university chat when they'd only just started dating and she didn't fancy going by herself, in case there weren't any of her colleagues there.

'I'm going. It might be a laugh.'

'I'll think about it,' she said as she left.

'More wine Madam?'

The waiter winked at Mills and filled her glass to the top. She recognised him as a second-year student from her forensics course. She smiled and sipped cautiously as she surveyed the group. Nige was the centre of attention, in full flow explaining the rules of rugby to anyone who would listen. She looked past the circle and across the marquee packed full of new students, or at least those who had bothered to come along to meet graduates of the university. Jake had eventually persuaded her to attend and Nige was happy to join them with the promise of free booze.

'Did you ever find out what Matthew and Jack were arguing about?' Jake asked Mills when there was a lull in the conversation.

'It's being dealt with by the Academic Tutor. She came to see me yesterday but she didn't discuss the details – just wanted my side of events.'

'But you think they were fighting over a woman, don't you?' Nige asked.

'They wouldn't tell me but I wouldn't be surprised,' Mills said. She was pretty sure that May was at the root of the trouble.

'Ask Will Humphreys, he knows them better than anyone. They're at training nearly every day.'

'He's their coach,' explained Nige. 'That tall guy over there.' He pointed across the room.

As she turned to look, her eye was caught by Professor Green. He acknowledged her with a nod and began moving in their direction.

'Don't look now but Sydney's coming over,' she warned and they exchanged glances.

'Is it too late to run?' asked Jake with a grin.

'I'm glad I caught you, Dr Sanderson,' he began when he was within speaking distance. 'I wanted to have a word about young Jack Bassett.'

Nige and Jake dissolved into the crowd, leaving Mills alone with him.

'He's a bright lad and I've selected him to work with me on his research project this year. He's going to be involved in some important forensic work for the prosecution of a case I'm involved with.'

'That's interesting.'

'Indeed. So any disruption of that work would be most unfortunate. I trust you understand that?'

Mills smiled. 'I'm sure it won't be a problem, Professor Green, but it's with the Academic Tutor now.'

His lips twisted in a look of disgust. 'I'll be in contact with her first thing tomorrow.' He turned without another word and disappeared, leaving Mills standing alone holding her empty glass.

Anna Rycroft and her friend, Jodie, had shared accommodation at university, trained together and graduated at the same time. Miraculously they'd stayed in touch even though they now lived over a hundred miles apart. Anna had carefully arranged for them to meet up in town so they could travel to the event together. There was a line of people making their way across the lawn and into the huge marquee; the same marquee used every year for the events held in freshers' week. She remembered how nervous the other new students had seemed six years ago at the start of term, leaving home for the first time, missing their families. She'd felt only immense relief to get away from the suffocating environment she'd experienced ever since she'd reached adolescence.

They collected their complimentary glasses of wine and wandered amidst the chattering groups of students. Looking round for familiar faces, Anna only recognised one or two members of staff. Her friend shrugged her shoulders.

'I'm glad we came together; I don't know anyone,' she

said.

'Green is over there.' Anna nodded in his direction and Jodie pulled a face.

'I hope he doesn't see us,' she said. 'He's creepy.'

Anna nodded and sipped her wine. She'd told no-one about Professor Sydney Green, and probably never would, but he was the reason she'd changed courses midway and become a PE teacher instead of a forensic scientist. When people asked why, she always said the same thing: I want to do something worthwhile, something that will make a difference.

'So tell me, what have you been up to since I saw you last year?' Jodie asked, looking round as she spoke.

'Same old, same old,' Anna replied. 'To be honest I'm getting bored.'

'Not with Luke, I hope. He's such a nice guy.'

'I don't see a lot of him now I'm in training.'

'Still doing the cycling then?'

'More than ever. Mainly triathlons. It's what keeps me sane. It's all right for you, with your own place. Can you imagine what it's like still living with Mum and Dad?'

'Your dad's OK.'

'Yes, but Mum. She's on my case the entire time. Fuss, fuss, fuss. She treats me as if I'm fifteen again. What time am I getting home? What do I want for tea? Will I go shopping with her? Can you imagine me trailing round Leeds with her looking for a hat?'

'You didn't!'

'No, I didn't but she wanted me to. She's been sulking all week.'

'No!' She was scanning the room as she listened.

'When I said that I was thinking of jacking in the job,

they nearly went ballistic.'

'You're not… not really?'

'I'm seriously considering it – resigning and going abroad.'

'What… to teach?'

'Maybe, maybe not. I don't know. Let's get another drink.'

Anna followed her friend in the direction of where the wine was being served. She was soon left behind as she tried to push past excitable groups and then someone stepped in front of her.

'Anna! I'm so glad you could make it!'

She looked up at the tall man who had planted himself in her path.

'Will!'

She hoped her voice hadn't betrayed the mixture of emotions she was experiencing. Here was the guy she'd been infatuated with almost throughout her student days. He was the reason she'd joined UNYCYCLE in the first year. It wasn't a love of cycling but her interest in the trainer. By her second year they had become an item – a turbulent affair that she knew wouldn't last. Her time with him had been a roller coaster ride but she'd never regretted it, even when he dumped her for a first-year student just before her final exams.

'Let me get you another drink.' He pointed at the empty glass she was clutching and took it from her. 'Come with me.'

She followed, waiting as he collected two glasses of red wine. He headed outside and in the direction of a bench, indicating for her to sit then lowered himself down beside her and handed her a glass.

'So, tell me all about you. What are you doing now? Still racing?'

She told him about her job and how bored she was but avoided mentioning that she still lived at home or Luke, reliable old Luke. Will had been so very different. 'At least I've got two weeks off now for half-term.'

'But you've still got the bike?'

'Oh yes, I do triathlons mainly. I don't race for a team but I keep up the training when I can. I want to go to France next year to do the L'Etape du Tour,' she said, knowing he'd be impressed.

Will whistled. 'Awesome! That's some event. How far?'

'One hundred and forty-eight kilometres of the Pyrenean route with two climbs of seven point something percent.'

'That is amazing. Are you doing it on your own?'

'Yep. It's for charity, breast cancer. My aunt Brenda's been in and out of hospital. She's still being treated for it.'

'Well put me down for a donation. That's so cool.' He looked genuinely impressed and Anna felt foolish to be so pleased by his admiration.

'*I'm* off to France next week. I'm doing La Velodyssey!' he announced triumphantly.

Now it was Anna's turn to be impressed. She'd heard of this 750-mile coastal route from Brittany to Spain.

Will leaned back, looking pleased. 'Yes. It will be two weeks of sun and sand with a bit of cycling in-between.'

'It sounds fantastic. I would so love to live in France. I saw this job as a tennis coach out there and almost applied.'

'You should.' Then Will turned to look at her. 'Come with *me* then,' he said, putting his hand on her arm.

Anna was stunned. Perhaps it was the wine on an empty stomach but she was so tempted. The two weeks of half-term loomed ahead. She wondered if he really meant it. He was always so impetuous; tomorrow he might regret it.

'So, what about you?' Anna asked, changing the subject. 'Still doing the same job?'

'Yes, a bit of lecturing, a bit of coaching and research. There's a good cycling bunch this year, some stars in the making, particularly in the road race team. With the Tour de France starting over here next year we've got to put on a good show, haven't we?'

'It's going to be great. I'm doing part of the route on Sunday as a test for next year. It's not exactly the Pyrenees but I can build up for the distance and the Buttertubs ascent is pretty steep.'

'So who do you have as back-up?'

'What d'you mean?'

'Who's assisting with maintenance? Who is going to help with tyres and nutrition? Is there someone to look after you?'

Anna frowned. 'No, I look after myself.'

'I see. So when are you doing Buttertubs?'

'On Sunday. I should get there around lunch-time if things go according to plan.'

They were sitting side by side. Will was twisting his glass round and round as he looked into the distance.

'You know, I can help with the stamina if you want me to,' he offered.

'What d'you mean?' Anna asked, thinking he was offering her private training of some sort.

'Something to improve your performance.'

She hesitated. 'You mean *give* me something to improve my performance?'

'Well, yes.'

'A performance enhancing… something.'

'Shush, not so loud.'

'Will Humphreys! Are you saying that you dabble with performance enhancing drugs?'

'Be quiet, for goodness sake woman! It's not for public consumption.'

'I don't believe it. Are you telling me that you're… No, you're not giving the team… Tell me you're not, Will!'

'Look, everyone is doing it,' he whispered, holding her arm. 'How do you think the bigger universities beat us?'

'Because they have better teams, they always have had.'

'I can't believe that. No. I have to use everything at my disposal, Anna. It's the only way to succeed.'

'Well, I think it's wrong. If you can't win through your own efforts, you shouldn't be competing.'

'What if everyone else is doing it?'

'Then I would get out.'

She stood up to leave but Will remained seated.

'At least think about it, Anna. It could be your passport to a new life.'

As she made her way back into the marquee, she considered whether he meant the offer of drugs or the trip to France for two weeks of sun and sea… and who knew what else.

'Has he gone?' Jake asked when he reappeared carrying two glasses.

'Yes, thank goodness. He just wanted to be sure that his star pupil, Jack Bassett, is not suspended in case it interferes with his forensic work.'

'Why? What does he do?'

'Soil analysis; comparing soil from the crime scene with

material found on the defendant. He works for the prosecution.'

'If Jack's as good at that as he is at cycling, he will be a star, although I suspect he'll be more interested in racing than research.'

'Well I hope my third-years are not going to be too distracted from their course work,' said Mills.

'I heard he's beaten all the uni road race records and they expect him to be the fastest uni racer this year. He'll be representing us in the Etape du Dales next year unless Matthew Watson makes the same miraculous improvement before then.'

'They could both do with a miraculous improvement in their coursework,' she commented.

Nige had re-joined them. 'Still discussing the big fight?' he asked with a grin.

'Jake has been telling me about their aptitude in the cycling arena.'

'It's been a source of much speculation, the records that Jack Bassett has been breaking. Something else you might want to ask Will Humphreys about.' Nige was attempting to look enigmatic.

Chapter 2

Nina was waiting nervously for her turn in the role play. It was day two of Family Liaison Officer training and although she'd been badgering her boss to allow her to attend the course, she was finding it hard going. The other participants seemed so much more mature than her. Maybe they were right – she'd gone for it too soon.

'So… Nina, isn't it? Would you like to take the role of the mother first of all? Duncan, I want you to find out as much as you can from her but Nina, please follow the instructions on this sheet.'

She read the large type on the half page the facilitator handed her. *Say as little as possible about your son – you know he was a gang member but so is your other son, who you want to protect. The police want to speak to him but you won't say where he is hiding.*

'Now, for the rest of the class: the scenario is that a young man has been shot in a gang-related incident. Nina is the boy's mother and Duncan is the FLO appointed to the family. His job is to assist the enquiry, particularly because we suspect the lad was shot by a member of his own gang. I'd like you to begin by making the mother feel comfortable but remember you are not there as a counsellor. It's important to express your sympathy but you are there to gain information which will hopefully lead to her identifying son's killer.'

It was easy for Nina to imagine how the mother would be feeling. If she lost Owen or Tomos she would be devastated but she would be even more defensive of her remaining son. She'd want the killer found but if he was, her other son would be placed in danger. It was easy for her to play the part, much to the annoyance of Duncan, an old copper with many years under his belt. He became harassed by her lack of co-operation and she suspected that he found it even more difficult because of her ethnicity.

'I'm only trying to help you find out who did it, love. You're not helping us, are you?' he finished, as he leaned back in exasperation.

'Then leave us alone,' she shouted, ignoring his use of "love" which really rankled.

'I think we'll stop there,' the facilitator called.

A discussion followed where the group agreed that communication had broken down early in the role play.

'Let's break for lunch and Nina can have a go when we come back.'

They went as a group to the canteen, where a table for eight had been reserved. Several of the participants grilled the trainer about how they were being assessed and whether the role play was being marked. She disclosed that her report on all aspects of the course contributed to the final decision on whether they were suitable to be FLOs. The only other young woman on the course suggested that after what they'd been doing that day, she wasn't sure she wanted to do family liaison anyway.

'It is a very particular role,' their teacher said. 'You have to want to do it and you have to feel mentally robust enough to take it on. It's not something for the faint-hearted but remember, it's only additional to your other duties so it won't be a full-time job. How do the rest of you feel about it, now that you've done a bit of training?'

Nina was relieved to hear that they all had their reservations. She was anxious to do well and could eat very little of her lunch in anticipation of the role play in the afternoon. To her surprise she was involved in the same scenario but this time she played the Family Liaison Officer. Duncan took the part of the boy's father and she hoped he would appreciate how that would affect his emotions.

'I am very sorry about your oldest son, Duncan. I am a mother myself and I can understand how you must be feeling.'

'You can't possibly know what I'm feeling,' Duncan replied angrily.

'I can understand that you must be angry and hurt, which is why we want to find who did this to your son.'

'It won't bring him back.'

'No, but it may help prevent it happening to another young man. You have another son…'

No response.

'We must ensure your other son is kept safe. We can help if you tell us where he is, so we can speak to him.'

Duncan remained silent as Nina cajoled and coaxed him to talk about his surviving offspring. Eventually the facilitator stopped them as Nina appeared to be getting nowhere. However, she was pleased with the way it had gone and when she asked Duncan for his thoughts, he admitted that he probably would have opened up if it was a real situation because Nina was so persuasive. He sounded quite emotional.

They spent the rest of the afternoon giving each of the participants the chance to act as a family member and the FLO. Other scenarios were equally challenging: a missing child, the rape of a teenager and a violent burglary. The seriousness of the situations brought home the gravity of the decision Nina had made when she put in her application. When Nige had asked her whether she really needed to do this, she'd replied that it was important work that someone had to do and not everyone was suited to the task. 'But why are you so special?' he'd asked and she'd just smiled. Then he'd nodded to show he'd understood. 'So it's the race card again is it, Mrs Featherstone?'

If it had been raining, her mother would have said it was too wet to ride but today it was bright sunshine and she was telling Anna that the heat would be dangerous. They'd spent the week arguing about the ride because Isobel Rycroft wanted her daughter to accompany her to see Aunt Brenda in hospital. Anna could be very obstinate, her mother would vouch for that, particularly when it involved training. Given the opportunity she would be cycling seven days a week but often was unable to do so because of her mother's demands. However, her ride on the Etape du Dales route had been planned for months and she was already starting off late.

She let out a deep breath of relief as she left the house and headed towards Ribblehead. It was early and the roads were empty, even for a Sunday. She could feel the sun on her back and the whirring of the wheels soon settled her into a relaxed mood. This was what she really wanted to do, not living at home and travelling to school every day, dealing with awkward colleagues, irritating children and abusive parents. Seeing Will again had made her realise that what she had with Luke was nothing in comparison; in fact she'd been thinking about Will quite a lot since the alumnus event. It was typical of him to be mixed up with drugs but at least he was *alive*. She felt as if she'd been lying dormant like an old tortoise since university.

Will's offer of two weeks in France sounded increasingly attractive as half-term approached. If she went it would be her decision and no-one, not her mother, not Luke, could stop her. She pedalled harder as she reached the brow of a hill then sped down the other side. Perhaps she'd stay in France. The thought had occurred to her when she looked out her passport. Maybe the only way to guarantee a job abroad was to go there for a while. She began pedalling faster. So what if her mother didn't approve? It was time she did what *she* wanted for a change. She concentrated as a white van sped past her too close on a bend. *Road hog*. She lifted herself onto the pedals as she struggled on a particularly steep stretch.

Looking at her watch she reckoned she'd been going for an hour. The sun was getting hotter – really unusual weather for October. The traffic was heavier now she was on the main road again but it was still a pleasant ride. Timing was important today and she pushed herself on, trying not to slow as she became absorbed in her thoughts. When she got back she would tell her family about her plans. She was going to be sensible about it and just go to France for the two weeks to begin with because she'd have to give the school some notice. She wouldn't be able to go before Christmas. She'd tell Luke it was over; he was so absorbed in his football he probably wouldn't even notice. A car hooted as it went by and she waved two fingers. *Road hog.*

At Grassington she stopped to drink water and nibble a biscuit. She didn't like eating when she was out but it would be a long day and she'd brought some snacks, fruit and nuts as well as the packet of biscuits her mother had insisted on. She set off ready for the long climb to the top before she dropped down into Hawes, where she planned a short rest. She told herself she wouldn't have such a luxury when she tackled the Etape du Tour next year and it would be much hotter at the beginning of July in France. However, there was time to build up to that.

Now she was concentrating on her breathing and legwork to get her to the top. At times she wanted to stop but the aim was to build up her stamina and she forced herself to keep going… just a bit further… just round this bend… up to that next bend. Every so often she checked her watch, timing herself for future reference. It was the long climbs like this one that she was worried about; they would make or break her.

It was tempting to rest at the summit but she pressed on, happy to let gravity take over for a short spell before getting her legs going again. She felt pleased with her progress and returned to her reverie, picking up on her previous decision to hand in her notice the moment she got into school on Monday. Having resolved to leave and try her luck in France, she felt relieved. This is what she wanted to be doing. But did she want to be going with Will? She still had the issue of his use of performance enhancing drugs to deal with.

She was surprised how quickly she reached the final run

into Hawes. Swerving to avoid a wagon leaving the creamery, she sped into the main street and pulled over in front of a pub. The pavements were packed with people ambling along, stopping to gaze absently into shop windows. It was tempting to pop in for a sandwich or block of chocolate but there would be no opportunities in the Pyrenees for such purchases and she confined herself to what she had packed. She stepped back into the shade of the building and closed her eyes, relishing the cool breeze.

'Anna!'

Luke Drummond had been sitting outside "The Old Board Inn" with a pint of Theakston for nearly an hour. Anna had told him she was stopping for a few minutes in Hawes and her mother suggested he might meet her and even gave him some cereal bars to give her, in case she'd run out of food. Bored with waiting, he'd gone inside to get another pint and a pie to go with it. As he re-emerged into the sunlight he caught sight of his girlfriend but she wasn't alone, a tall man had his hand on her shoulder and they were deep in discussion. He was fixing her helmet strap under her chin.

Luke stood in the doorway, moving aside to let customers in and out as he watched the couple. It wasn't a long conversation, just a few minutes, and it finished abruptly with the man handing over a bottle then turning to walk away. Anna remained motionless, watching him leave. Only then did he come out from his hiding place and wave to attract her attention before going over.

'Luke! What are you doing here?' Her face was flushed.

'Thought I'd make sure you're OK,' he said offering the

cereal bars. 'Have you got enough to drink?' he added pointedly, indicating the bottle she was carrying.

'I'm fine, you needn't have bothered.'

'Why? Because someone else is looking after you? Who *was* that, anyway?'

'Who? Oh, you mean him?' She shrugged. 'He's just someone from uni.'

'You've kept quiet about him!'

'He's just an old friend.' She was staring at the ground. 'In fact... I might be going on a cycle trip with him at half-term.'

She looked up at him as if judging his response.

'If that's what you want.'

'I think it would be fun.'

He felt as if she'd hit him in the guts. 'Fun?'

'I think I need a break, away from England, from my mother and...'

'And from me?'

'I don't know. I just want to get away.'

'With this... bloke.'

'I knew you wouldn't understand.'

She was packing her stuff and climbing back on her bike. Without another word she rode off.

As soon as she'd left Hawes, Anna stopped. She'd not had a drink and the next stage was going to be critical. The bottle had felt cool when Will gave it to her and she craved something refreshing. She wasn't disappointed. Soon she was off again, beginning the ascent to Buttertubs Pass.

She was surprised what hard work it was, despite having had a break and something to eat. How was she going to manage without stopping on the actual ride? Her legs were beginning to go to jelly and she desperately wanted to step off at the side of the road and sit down. She forced herself to keep going but her head was getting fuzzy and she was having difficulty focussing on the road ahead. She struggled on for what seemed like an eternity before the road levelled out and it became easier to pedal. At last she was going downhill and she had to concentrate hard to stay on the road as it bent to the right, then the left. Something appeared at the side of her and there was a flash of white as the bike came to a sudden halt and she was floating…

Chapter 3

Muriel tapped gently on her neighbour's front door and waited. She knew Mills was in because she'd seen her car arrive back a few minutes before. After a short wait she heard footsteps and the door opened to reveal her neighbour still wearing her outdoor clothes.

'I'm sorry, Mills dear, I just wondered if I could borrow some milk? I'm a bit short and I've got people...'

'Come in – I'll have a look.'

Muriel followed her into the tiny kitchen and watched her half-fill the small jug.

'Is that any good?' Mills asked as she offered it to her. 'I can't really spare more.'

'That's lovely, dear.' It would have to do, Muriel thought as she carried it back home.

She had half an hour before they were due to start and she still had to finish making sandwiches. Having a meeting at seven o'clock she didn't know if they'd already eaten, so she decided to offer snacks. She was still putting the finishing touches to the dining table when the first of her guests arrived.

'Colin! And Arthur. Is it raining again? Come in and leave your coats in the hall,' she instructed her neighbours as she went through, removing her apron and patting her hair down. Arthur was as scruffy as ever but Colin was respectably dressed in smart slacks and a nice hand-knitted jumper that Muriel presumed was his wife's handiwork, God rest her soul. Like Arthur, he was another widower but this one obviously knew how to look after himself.

Soon their leader, as Arthur had called him, arrived bringing a woman with him. Muriel had to fetch another of her dining chairs so they could all sit down and there was barely room for the five of them.

'Muriel, how nice to meet you! I don't suppose you know Catriona?' Stephen asked, indicating the middle-aged woman who had accompanied him. 'She has a strong environmental interest in our little campaign and I took the liberty of inviting her to our inaugural meeting tonight, I hope you don't mind?'

Muriel shook her head, wondering whether she would have enough milk.

'Catriona,' Stephen went on, 'this is Arthur.'

The old man struggled up from his seat and offered the woman a grubby hand before dropping back rather suddenly onto the sofa.

'How do you do.' The woman had a very posh voice and clearly came from the south.

'And this must be Colin Norton,' he added, indicating the man squashed on the sofa beside Arthur.

The man raised a hand in acknowledgement but remained in his seat. Catriona smoothed her camel-coloured skirt under her and perched on one of the dining chairs. Stephen took the armchair at the centre of the rough semi-circle they had formed.

Muriel asked Stephen if she should serve refreshments

but he proposed they start their meeting straightaway, perhaps breaking at a suitable point once they'd covered the agenda items.

'Do we have an agenda?' Arthur asked, turning to Colin. 'Have you seen one? I haven't seen one.'

Stephen cleared his throat. 'I have drafted an agenda, just so we keep to the points that are necessary to address. I always like to work to an agenda.'

He pulled a folded paper from his pocket and smoothed it out across his knee.

'I'd like to welcome everyone to our first meeting of C.A.T.,' he began, looking round the group with a smile. 'Our Campaign Against the Tour.'

Arthur nodded with approval and grinned at Colin, who remained non-committal. Muriel looked at Catriona and wondered how Stephen had met her and whether he was "soft" on her. She wondered idly if Catriona ever shortened her name to Cat.

'... do you agree, Muriel?' Everyone was looking at her.

'Sorry, what was that?' she asked.

'Do you accept the name of the campaign – we need unanimous approval.'

She nodded her assent and looked round at the others, who had their hands held up. She quickly raised her hand.

Stephen nodded. 'Good. Now our aim is simple so I haven't written a long constitution. It is short and to the point: members of C.A.T. agree to do everything in their power to prevent the Tour de France Grand Départ from happening in the Yorkshire Dales. What do you think?'

There was silence.

'Arthur?' he asked. 'Colin?'

'Should that be everything *legal* in our power?' Catriona

was looking quizzically at Stephen.

Stephen looked down at his paper. 'I don't want to get too bogged down in semantics,' he said. 'Much of this will be taken as read.'

'But we wouldn't do anything illegal, would we?' Muriel said, looking round, but everyone was watching Stephen.

'We can discuss details later on. For now I'd like to go through my agenda.' He coughed. 'Next we need to clarify our roles. I assume you will vote me in as chair of the group?'

No-one objected so he declared that his proposal was acceptable to the group. The next item was information about ACRE, the anti-closed roads pressure group that takes action against the regular Etape Caledonia in Scotland.

'In the past they have got over five hundred signatures on a petition to stop the road closure and they've made representations to the Scottish Government. They said that Perth Council acted illegally and failed to comply with legislation for closure orders.' He paused while he referred to his notes. 'They also threatened to take retrospective legal action and seek redress for inconvenience and financial loss caused to local people.'

'Can they do that?' Muriel asked. 'Surely they're within their rights – legally, I mean?'

'Why do they have more rights than local people?' demanded Arthur. 'We have the right to go about our business, don't we?'

'What about when Buttertubs was closed to resurface the road?' complained Colin. 'I had to make all sorts of detours on my egg rounds. I didn't have any rights then.'

Arthur nodded. 'Imagine how much all this road repair

is costing not to mention the inconvenience.'

'Exactly,' agreed Stephen. 'These people in Scotland have got the right idea. We need to challenge the powers that be and make our feelings heard. Which brings me to the next item – publicity. We need to contact the local papers.'

Catriona raised her hand. 'I'm not sure we are only against the road closure while the race is on. My concern is the effect the race will have on levels of traffic and pollution in this beautiful countryside of ours. And what about the effect on the grouse moors with so many people tramping about. Think of the pollution from all the vehicles going through. I would prefer to see it stopped altogether.'

Muriel had agreed to host the meeting because Arthur was an old friend. He'd explained they would be meeting to complain about the cycle race taking place next year. She'd gone along with it but didn't feel as strongly about it as some of them seemed to. She sat listening to ideas being bandied about, including demonstrations, sit-ins and poster campaigns. In the end she slipped into the kitchen to put the kettle on and stayed there, catching odd phrases as the discussion became more heated. When there was a pause, she went in to announce there were sandwiches in the dining room if they'd like to help themselves and asked who would like tea, hoping some would be taking it black.

It was difficult to carry on business in a formal manner with members of the group hopping in and out to replenish their plates, so the discussion drifted with topics ranging from ways of preventing the race to the prices being charged for bed and breakfast over the race weekend.

'I reckon you'll be making a killing,' Arthur suggested to Catriona, his mouth full of food.

The woman blushed and placed the rest of her sandwich on the plate. 'I wouldn't dream of charging my regular visitors any more than usual for that time of year,' she announced. 'In my opinion it would be unethical to do otherwise.' She smiled as she looked round the room before popping the crust in her mouth. 'Muriel, the food is delicious – I won't need any supper after this spread.'

The others agreed and Stephen offered a vote of thanks to Muriel for hosting the gathering. She made a little curtsy, overlooking the fact that it was Arthur who had "volunteered" her house for the meeting despite her reservations. He'd assured her there was no harm in it but she was beginning to think otherwise.

'If everyone has finished, I'd like to get on,' said Stephen, looking at his watch.

The clock on the mantelpiece said eight-thirty but Muriel knew it was a few minutes fast.

'The penultimate item on the agenda is future tactics. We've had some general discussion but now I'd like to list some proposals so we can vote on them.'

Everyone resumed their allotted seats and waited for the vote.

'Number one: leafleting in Hawes and Leyburn next Saturday.'

Arthur put his hand up, nudging Colin, who raised his arm reluctantly, saying, 'If we can get through to Leyburn without going round the lanes.'

Catriona pointed out it was "change-over day" and she would be too busy.

'Me too,' lied Muriel.

Stephen made some notes. 'Two: we should get some posters made. I've already asked Catriona if she would design something, as she is the creative one amongst us.'

They mumbled in agreement while Muriel wondered what the woman did that was so creative.

'Three: we need to start a petition against the road closure as soon as possible. I'll draw up the wording and get copies made but I'll need everyone working hard to get signatures. I can drop them round next week. And finally, we must begin to think about tactics; what lengths are we prepared to go to in order to stop the race all together.'

'I think we should contact the National Park to make the point about the environmental issues too,' said Catriona. 'I think that's most important.'

'Good, would you like to do that?' Stephen made another note then looked up. 'We need someone to take minutes. I can't do all of this.'

After a brief silence, Catriona raised her hand. 'I don't mind taking on the role of secretary – if everyone agrees?'

They did so with enthusiasm. Stephen brought the meeting to a close after suggesting they meet again in a month's time, although he would keep in touch with them by email. Muriel raised a tentative hand, admitting she didn't do emails.

'Don't worry, I'll keep you posted. I'm only down the road,' Arthur explained to the others.

Muriel fetched Catriona's jacket from the spare bedroom, where she'd carefully hung it on a padded hanger – it was beautifully soft wool and such a lovely colour.

'Aubergine, they called it,' the woman offered as she buttoned it up and arranged a silk scarf at her neck, before following Stephen into the darkness.

'We must help you with the clearing up,' Colin offered, when only he and Arthur were left. Despite Muriel's protestations he carried the plates through to the kitchen, piling them on the draining board. Arthur had settled himself on the sofa again and waited until all the washing-up was done. Colin dried the dishes and tidied them away as if he had always done so and Muriel only wished she'd had sufficient milk to offer him a coffee before they left.

'Arthur,' Muriel began as they were putting their jackets on in the tiny hall. 'You don't think that anything that Stephen suggested is against the law, do you?'

'Don't you worry old girl. He wouldn't suggest anything that wasn't legitimate, would he? He's been in charge of the Rotary and summat else. No, he's above board all right.'

Mills drove straight over to Nige and Nina's house after the last lecture in the afternoon. It was a routine she'd been happy to adopt while Nige was taking his sabbatical to look after the children. Nina was back from her course and Mills was interested to hear all about it.

'I found it quite draining to tell the truth,' she admitted. 'It's really a very challenging role if you take it seriously.'

'I think you'll be brilliant at it,' interrupted Nige with his usual enthusiasm for his wife's policing.

Rosie was busy at the table with her colouring book while the boys were on the floor tugging at each other's clothes. One of them, Mills identified Tomos by his black straight hair, clambered to his feet, padded over to his mother and climbed on her lap. The twins were using words now, although Mills found it difficult to interpret what they were saying. Nige, on the other hand, knew exactly what he wanted and told him it wasn't time for tea yet. Owen was up now, tugging at Nina's skirt, calling his own name and pleading with her to let him sit on her lap as well. Peace was restored when Nige went down on all fours and gave him a ride on his back. Inevitably his brother wanted a go and pandemonium broke out again until Nina restored order.

'Rosie, why don't we go and make the tea. Mills will help us. We'll leave the boys to play together.'

Mills followed and buttered bread while Nina made marmite sandwiches for the children.

'So, will you be doing proper family liaison work from now on?' Mills asked.

'If there's a requirement,' Nina replied. 'It depends if there are any issues where it's needed. They said it wouldn't be anything too serious to start with; they try to break you in gently.'

She explained the types of crimes where she might be called, although some of the descriptions she gave were coded in the presence of her five-year-old.

They finished off their tea with a Victoria sponge made by Nige. He proudly produced it from the tin with a flourish, admitting it was the first time he'd attempted it. Everyone was impressed by the result and Nina declared she need never bake a cake again.

'Well, I have to fill in my time somehow,' he declared. 'And Rosie helped me put the jam filling in, didn't you, love?'

She nodded shyly, pushed the last piece of cake into her mouth and wiped her hands on her jeans. Nina smiled and shook her head in mock despair.

'I hear you had some excitement in your lecture last

week,' she commented as she cleaned the boys' hands and let them down from their chairs.

'Fisticuffs,' Nige said.

Mills laughed. 'Yes, it was a bit distracting.'

'What's the outcome? Have they been suspended?' asked Nige.

'No. They each had a warning, that's all. They didn't get to the bottom of who had started it and why. Six of one and half a dozen of the other, the Tutor said.'

'I reckon Jake was right when he said it was over the cycle team,' said Nige. 'Have you asked Will Humphreys yet?'

'No. Why d'you think he would know?'

'He's their coach and Jake says there's been a lot of rivalry between those two lads over the past year. One of them has taken over as team captain and he outrides them all. You need to ask him how the boy can move so fast.'

'Are you suggesting the coach is helping them increase their performance in some way?' Nina asked.

'I couldn't possibly comment,' Nige replied with a grin.

'Why should you have to sort out these squabbles anyway?' asked Nina. 'Surely they have personal tutors to sort out problems between students.'

'They do, but I had to write the report because it happened in my class. The College Tutor called a meeting with their personal tutors.'

'Old Sydney Green I suppose.' Nige said.

'Exactly. He wasn't any help, of course, because all he was worried about was getting Jack back in the lab to carry on doing his work for him. He needs his students to analyse his forensic samples,' Mills explained to Nina.

'You're kidding!' she exclaimed. 'Students doing important work like that?'

Nige sniggered. 'Probably better than he would be. The poor old man can hardly see what he's doing and he's usually asleep in the common room in the afternoons.'

They all laughed but Nina was still looking shocked and asked what forensic work he did.

'He's a soil scientist,' explained Mills. 'He started doing soil forensics about twenty years ago but at that time he just looked at the mineralogy. Since then the analytical side has really improved and he's taken advantage of the new analytical facilities in the department. He can get the samples analysed but it's what you do with the results.'

'They say he reads far too much into the results he gets,' Nige chipped in. 'But no-one can prove it. He does a lot of work for the prosecution.'

'And do they win the cases?' asked Nina.

'Yes – that's the problem apparently. I don't understand the issues,' admitted Nige. 'But that's what I've heard.'

Mills felt they were both waiting for her opinion and she wasn't keen to voice it. In her view the man shouldn't be working in forensics at all. She'd seen a report he'd written for Yardley Forensics and had been appalled. The case had involved a murder where mud from the clothing of a defendant had been analysed. She'd never seen such sloppy work and had sent it back to be edited before she was even able to understand the contents. Normally any analyses of that nature would be accompanied by proof that the laboratory could obtain the correct results from known samples. There was nothing in the report to show that they were capable of getting the right results.

'I have found his work lacking in robustness.'

'What do you mean?' Nige looked puzzled.

'Things to back it up; supporting evidence.'

'I thought forensic work always had to have that,' said Nina.

'It should,' began Mills, 'but when the court is presented with numbers coming from sophisticated instrumentation, delivered by an eminent professor, they may just accept it, particularly if there's no-one to oppose his view.'

Nina announced it was time for the boys' bath and Nige offered to take them up, one at a time. Owen went first, objecting strongly that his brother was remaining downstairs. His shrieks could be heard in the distance until little Rosie went up to help her father placate the boy.

'So,' began Nina, 'how is it with you and Alex?'

'Fine, thank you. He's coming over this weekend – we're going to do some serious walking.'

'Has your lab manager warmed to him yet?'

'Glyn? No, he still behaves as if Alex is going to take his job away from him.'

'And how is Brenda?'

'She's having another course of treatment. It's been such a long time since she's been well enough to come in. I don't know when she'll be back.'

'How awful for her.'

They sat in silence contemplating the treatment she was undergoing for breast cancer then both began speaking at once to change the subject.

'Sorry, Mills, I was just going to say that surely if you distrust the evidence this man Green is producing, you really should tell someone.'

'It's not as simple as that, Nina. I think he feels pressurised to give the prosecution what they want. The only way I could legitimately demonstrate his massaging of the truth would be to appear for the defence. Then I would be able to scrutinise his data and highlight the flaws in it. Until that happens he will continue to mislead the jury and possibly help put innocent people behind bars.'

Chapter 4

Ian Watson often dropped Matthew off at university in the morning, if he was at home. He liked to think that they had a good relationship now that his son had elected to live with him. It hadn't always been so. When the divorce came through, Matthew had sided with his mother, refusing to speak to him, but once he had a place at university it was cheaper and easier for Matthew to commute from Ian's flat in Darlington. The first few weeks had been tricky, with Matthew arriving home drunk or not at all, sending Ian frantic with worry. Eventually they agreed a few ground rules and things improved a little.

Everything changed when Matthew joined the cycling team. No more heavy drinking and late nights; he even began criticising their diet and buying healthier food. Team practice was the key thing, several times a week, although he never neglected his study. Ian was proud of his son, seeing much of himself at that age. He'd been a keen cyclist, although not at his level. Next year Matthew had the chance to represent his university in a prestigious event. It was something that made him feel quite emotional.

'Heard any more about the Etape du Dales race?' he

asked as they waited at traffic lights.

'No. I'm not sure I'll be doing it now.'

'What?' Ian turned to look at his son, but Matthew was staring out of the side window. 'I thought they'd agreed you would be representing the university.'

'Well, it's different now that Jack Bassett is faster than me.'

The lights changed and they set off in a stream of fast-moving traffic.

They'd had this discussion before and got nowhere but Ian was damned if he was going to see his son cheated out of a place on the biggest race of the year.

'You need to speak to that coach of yours, son.'

'I can't. He's not here.'

Matthew could be exasperating. 'When he gets back… or better still, speak to someone in authority. If this Jack Bassett is using something to improve his performance, the university authorities need to know. After all, who would be providing it? Who is the usual suspect? The coach, of course. Do you think it's him?'

'Will?' His son muttered. 'I don't know. There's nothing I can do.'

Matthew stuck his headphones on and the conversation was at an end. It always finished the same way when Ian was trying to be a good father, guiding his son in the ways of the world. He sighed as he concentrated on overtaking the wagon that had been slowing them down and turned onto the campus.

'See you later son!' he called as Matthew dragged his kit bag out and slammed the boot. 'Careful now – and out on the road. We don't want any more bruises!' He'd been concerned when Matthew developed a black eye overnight but apparently they were risks you took when road racing in competition.

'Matthew!' Mills was surprised to find the student standing outside her office when she arrived. His eye was improving but he still looked depressed. 'Come in.'

She unlocked the door and ushered him inside, moving a pile of papers from Jake's chair and wheeling it round beside her desk.

'Sit,' she commanded.

He obeyed. 'I wanted to apologise for... what happened.'

'Thank you, Matthew. It was rather out of character.'

No response.

'In fact I was quite surprised by both of you and I was going to ask you why. However, it's not my business.'

The poor lad looked as though he was going to cry.

'Did you want to talk about it?' she asked, wondering if she was going to have to offer him a tissue.

'Not really.' He was biting his lip and looking at the floor.

'Well, if you need to, you know, in confidence.'

'You wouldn't tell anyone?'

'No.' She immediately regretted what she'd said. 'I mean...'

'It's just that there's no-one to... You can't report someone...'

'Report them? That sounds serious. Do you have a complaint against someone?' She thought of the memo that had recently been circulated on bullying.

'It's not exactly a complaint; more of a suspicion.'

He sat chewing his lip again.

'Matthew. Why don't you tell me what's bothering you?'

She was aware that Jake would come barging in at any moment and she had a lecture in ten minutes.

He took a deep breath and then it all came out. How he had been the fastest road racer on the team, always beating Jack Bassett in the first year. Then the coach, Will Humphreys, started taking a special interest in Jack and suddenly his times were faster and Jack was the star of the team.

Mills started to tell him that it was how sport went, wasn't it. Sometimes a good year was followed by a bad one and perhaps Jack had simply reached a peak. But no, Matthew was adamant. He was sure there was more to it than that. He'd told Jack Bassett so and that was why they had ended up on the floor of the lecture theatre, thrashing about in such an undignified manner. Mills was about to ask Matthew what he thought he was going to do now when the door burst open and Jake appeared. He offered to go away again but Matthew was up and out of the door before he finished his sentence.

'Sorry, did I interrupt something important?' he asked.

'I don't know,' Mills replied. 'I really don't know but I'm going to find out. Where does Will Humphreys hang out?'

The Sports Science Department was the newest building on campus. It had been resourced ahead of the London Olympics in the hope that an international team would make use of its facilities. Mills wasn't sure whether that had come to fruition but there were rumours that it had not fulfilled expectations. However, she had to admit the glass fronted building was impressive and the board in the entrance hall boasted a wide range of sports related disciplines in addition to signs to the sports facilities themselves.

The girl on the desk directed her down the long, wide corridor lined on both sides with eye-catching posters highlighting the work of the department. There was no sign of Will Humphreys name on any of them and Mills wondered what his discipline actually was. There were three names on his office door but only one occupant.

'Will? He's not around, I'm afraid.' The young man was dressed in a track suit bearing the college crest. His feet, propped up on the desk, sported a pair of expensive designer trainers.

'Do you know when he'll be back?' She was standing beside a desk covered in papers and had spotted an envelope addressed to Mr Humphreys. 'Can I leave a message?'

'You can…' The man lowered his legs lazily and stood up. 'But he's in France.'

'When is he coming back?'

'He said it would be two weeks.'

'But surely… in term time…'

'Tell me about it – I'm lecturing back-to-back from eleven.'

Mills sensed he was no friend of Mr Humphreys.

'Is it about Jack and Matthew?' he asked. 'You're from their department, aren't you? I'm Spence.'

'Mills. You know about their fight then?'

'Too right. Caused a lot of waves over here. Will thought he'd lost his best road racers.'

'Did he tell you why they were fighting?'

'No, but I can guess. They're a competitive pair and Matthew doesn't like being beaten.'

'Apparently he used to be the fastest,' Mills prompted.

'Yes. I suppose you've heard the rumours too.'

Mills wasn't sure whether Spence was referring to the drugs so she waited.

'It's all over the department. There's been a request to attend a formal interview from the board organising the university cycle races for BUCS.'

'BUCS?'

'British Universities and Colleges Sport. It wasn't addressed to Will but he's our representative. He was supposed to go next week.'

'Is he back then?'

Spence shrugged his muscular shoulders. 'Hope so. No-one's sure. Jack might know when he's coaching next; he's the team captain still, I assume.'

Mills thanked him and wandered back to the department, where she stopped off in the analytical lab to find Jack Bassett. He was perched on a stool at the bench marking plastic tubes with a pen.

'Hi.' She hoped she sounded friendly.

He put down the pen and pulled his earphones off. 'Did you want to see me?' He looked worried.

'I wondered if you could help me, Jack.' She hoped her smile was reassuring. 'I've been trying to find Will Humphreys but they say he's away.'

'Yeah, he's doing this cool ride in France.'

'Do you know when he's due back?'

He shrugged. 'Next week I guess, or the one after that.'

'You don't have a fixed schedule for training? I thought maybe…'

Jack laughed. 'No, it doesn't work like that with Will. It's all a bit last minute.'

Mills surveyed the bench, where a pile of plastic bags

spilled out of a cardboard box. 'Forensic work?' she asked, already knowing the answer.

He nodded.

'What are you looking for?' Mills asked, curious to find out what Sydney was up to now.

'The usual… Prof Green wants everything; although I guess he'll stick to the usual suite of elements in the matching process.'

'What are you comparing them to?'

He pointed at the dilapidated box. 'These are from the scene of a rape.' He stretched across the bench to retrieve a small bottle of soil. 'And this is from the suspect's trousers.' He handed it to her. 'That's all I know.'

'There must be more details than that.' Mills knew Sydney would have to have details of how the samples were collected, and where from, in order to interpret the results. Presumably he hadn't passed the information on to Jack.

'So, are you doing all the analysis for Professor Green now?' she asked.

'Yes. I work about two days a week for him. It helps with the rent.' He smiled and carried on with his work.

'Quite a responsibility with such important samples.'

'I guess.'

'I suppose Professor Green does all the interpretation?'

'Oh yes. I just get the numbers for him.'

'I suppose you have to do test samples, with known values?'

He shook his head and looked up. 'No, he doesn't. I thought I'd have to try something, you know, to show I get the right results, like you taught us in class, but he said it wasn't necessary. He said he trusts me to get it right.'

'And do you?' Mills asked, half-joking, not expecting his answer.

'How do I know? If I'm not given a test sample, how can I tell?'

Mills should not have been surprised by his mature attitude to forensic work. After all, he was her student.

'Actually,' he went on. 'I'm pleased you asked because I wanted to speak to you about the last piece of work I did for him. It was a murder trial.'

'Go on.'

He swivelled round to face her then looked about him, as if to check in case anyone would hear their conversation.

'It was all done in a bit of a rush. The samples came in on a Friday and I had to spend the weekend getting them ready.'

'You were working in here on your own?'

'Yes, Prof Green said it was OK if I didn't use strong acid. Anyway, I had some problems preparing the samples so I rang him to ask his advice but he was away, so I just went ahead and did them anyway.'

Mills was alarmed that Jack had been flouting the rules and working unsupervised in the laboratory and wanted to say so but she didn't want to interrupt his story.

'So what happened when he came in?'

'I told him what I'd done; it was all recorded in my lab notebook. First he went ballistic and said the samples were useless but then he told me to just give him the data. I offered to reanalyse, I had plenty of soil, but he told me to just give him the results.'

'Has he reported back to the customer?'

'Yes. He appeared in court last month.'

'So he was happy with what you'd done?'

'Yes but I wasn't, so I did them again and came to rather a different conclusion.'

'Are you saying that your results didn't agree with his report?'

'Yes,' he said. 'But he wasn't interested. The case had begun by then.'

Mills left Jack labelling his bottles and walked slowly back to the office. As she passed Sydney Green's room she stopped and without thinking about what she would say, knocked on the door.

'Come!'

He was sitting behind his desk, dressed in his ridiculous bow tie, framed certificates adorning the wall. Immediately Mills felt intimidated. She barely knew the man but all their interactions had been unpleasant. He looked up from his desk and stared, as if trying to place who she was. It was difficult for her to know how to start.

'I saw Jack Bassett just now, in the laboratory.'

He sighed and put down his pen. 'Not more nonsense over this spat with Watson.'

'No, I didn't mean… I was just chatting about his work.'

'Look, I'm not really concerned with his course work…'

'No, I was interested in the forensic investigations he's involved in.'

He picked up his pen again. 'Not really any of your business I would think Dr… Dr…'

'Sanderson, Mills Sanderson.' She was irritated by him and knew she should leave. 'I just wanted to say that if his methodology is questionable, it could leave you open to criticism in court.' Now she'd said it. She waited for his reaction.

'Dr Mills Sanderson.' He had risen from his chair and

was edging round his desk. 'I was working for the prosecution in murder cases when you were in nappies.' He opened the door and indicated for her to go. 'I don't want your opinions, thank you madam.'

'Who's that girl with the Amy Winehouse hairstyle?' whispered Nina, as a young woman came into the cafeteria. She was wearing skinny jeans and an equally tight-fitting top. Her bleached hair was piled up in a beehive style.

'Her? That's Ruby. She's our new researcher,' explained Hazel.

'We have a researcher? Since when?'

'Since the Grand Départ is going through North Yorkshire.'

'So what's she supposed to be researching?'

'Keeping tabs on what's happening in the run up to the event; it's less than a year away now.' She stopped speaking as the girl caught sight of them and came over.

'Hi. Can I sit with you?' she asked.

Hazel beamed at her. 'Yes, that's cool.' Nina threw her a questioning look but Hazel ignored her and went on. 'This is Nina, she's a DS like me, only I've been one longer.'

The girl put her mug on the table and sat down. She offered her hand to Nina. 'Hi, I'm Ruby. It's great to meet you.'

Nina couldn't help but warm to her. She seemed too young to be working but must have some qualifications to be in the role. 'Is this your first post as a researcher?' she asked.

The girl blushed. 'Is it obvious?' she asked. 'I was so lucky to get the job, even though it's only for nine months.'

'Ruby did a psychology degree, didn't you?'

'Yes, well, yes I did. After that I tried so hard to find a job but in the end Dad got me a placement in his office. They didn't pay or anything but it meant they got used to my face, that's what Dad said it was. So when this job came up, I tried for it.' She sipped her drink.

'Nina was on a course when you started,' explained Hazel, 'And you've been on your induction until now, haven't you?'

'Yeah, it was really interesting but there's so much I've got to learn. I can't get my head round the computing stuff.'

'You'll get used to it,' said Nina. 'Sorry, I really ought to get back to the office.'

Hazel didn't attempt to move so Nina left her friend with Ruby, who clearly had found a mentor.

Back at her desk, Nina scrolled through her emails, stopping at an urgent message from her DI.

He answered her call almost immediately. 'Nina, I know you've only just qualified and you can say no if you want to but I'd really appreciate it if…'

'What is it Mitch?'

'We need a Family Liaison Officer and you're the only one available.'

'No problem. That's why I asked for the training, remember?' She could feel the excitement growing with the realisation that *this was it*. She'd been waiting a month for something to happen following the course.

'It's just that usually they like to break the FLO in gently…'

'What's the case?' She was impatient to get on with it.

'A missing person. Her family has only just reported her missing although she's been gone a couple of weeks. For various reasons they thought she might be abroad. Anyway she hasn't returned to her teaching job after the half-term so now there is genuine fear for her safety. We need you to go and see them as soon as possible.'

'OK.'

'Good. The report is on the computer – all the details are there.'

Nina spent just an hour familiarising herself with the case. Anna Rycroft's parents, Frank and Isobel, had reported their daughter missing after she failed to return from a cycle trip through Wensleydale and Swaledale. She lived at home so they expected her to return that evening but they didn't report her missing until the school where she worked started asking where she was. That seemed to wake the family from a sort of inertia and now they were in need of a Family Liaison Officer. Nina reminded herself that her role was not one of a counsellor but of an investigating officer. She would leave the psychology to little Ruby.

Chapter 5

Nina's heart was racing as she walked up the gravel path to the front door of the Rycroft's house. It was important they started out on the right foot and she'd been rehearsing her sympathetic opening remarks. The door was opened by a grey-haired woman, smartly dressed in a white blouse and pink cardigan that matched perfectly the roses on her flowery skirt. Behind her, Nina could see a tidy hallway stretching back to the kitchen, where Mr Rycroft was hovering.

They invited her in warmly and offered tea, which Nina accepted with a smile. They ushered her into a spotless sitting room and she took a seat on the sofa while Isobel Rycroft busied herself in the kitchen. Her husband stood awkwardly so Nina tried to put him at his ease by explaining what her role would be, emphasising that she would be helping her colleagues find any intelligence that might help locate his daughter.

'My wife…' He had lowered his voice so Nina could hardly hear. '…but I think she's gone abroad. She wanted…'

The sound of china rattling stopped him in his tracks and he withdrew to a chair in the corner while his wife arranged cups and saucers on the low coffee table in the centre of the room. The net curtains wafted occasionally with the breeze and the sound of a lawn mower drifted through the open window. Nina repeated what she'd said to Mr Rycroft, to put the woman at her ease, but it did just the opposite.

'Where did you say you'd come from?' she asked. 'I thought there'd be two of you. Do you have a partner, a male officer?'

Nina patiently explained that she was supporting the officers back at base as they carried out their investigations. She told them that DI Turner would be in charge, which seemed to provide some comfort to her. There was a pause in their conversation while Mrs Rycroft poured the tea and handed out biscuits. Her husband seemed sensitive to the awkward atmosphere and asked about Nina's journey down to see them. They were able to engage in light conversation until Nina finally returned her empty cup and saucer to the tray and reached for her notebook.

'Perhaps we should start by you telling me about Anna,' she prompted.

'We gave the policeman that came round our recent photos. We gave him a full description.'

'Yes, and that's very helpful with identification.'

'They haven't found… anyone… you know…' Mr Rycroft looked nervously at his wife as he spoke.

'They would have found her if she'd had an accident,' Mrs Rycroft said sharply. 'I told them, she's gone to France, like Luke said. She told him.' She sounded angry with her daughter.

Her husband looked forlorn.

'Is that what *you* think, Mr Rycroft?'

'Frank. Please call me Frank.' He rubbed his forehead. 'She would have told us if she was going away.'

'You think so?' his wife said. 'I don't think you know her as well as I do. She'll do whatever takes her fancy, that's what she'll do. You'll see. She'll come swanning back in a few weeks as if nothing has happened. Well you wait, I'll show her…'

'Isobel! Please.' The man begged.

She shot him a glance and sat with her hands in her lap.

'I'd like to gain an impression of Anna by talking to you and to her friends. I guess she's quite independent if she cycles long distances by herself.'

'She does triathlons as well.' The girl's father was clearly proud of her achievements. 'She's won trophies.'

'Not recently, Frank, only when she was at university.'

'Which university was that?' Nina asked.

'North Yorkshire, of course,' Mrs Rycroft chipped in. 'We couldn't afford for her not to live at home.'

When Nina enquired about Anna's degree, her mother began another tirade about her wasting her life by becoming a PE teacher instead of studying science.

'And she's a teacher now?' asked Nina, hoping to change the subject.

'Yes, in the big secondary school in town.' Frank looked nervously from Nina to his wife.

'She's not even satisfied with that,' Mrs Rycroft began. 'She's been talking about looking for another job, would you believe.'

'She isn't happy there,' Frank added.

'What d'you know about it?' his wife asked indignantly.

'Just something she said in passing, that's all.'

The afternoon wasn't going at all how Nina had

imagined it but she was gaining a good impression of the relationships between the Rycroft family. She would have liked to have chatted with Frank on his own but suspected it would be difficult to arrange.

'Mrs Rycroft.' She was hoping that she would be invited to call her Isobel but that was something else that wasn't going to happen. 'Mrs Rycroft, do you have any idea where your daughter would be right now?'

'Luke said France. I don't know where. You'll have to ask him.'

When Frank asked her if there was any news from her side she was unable to provide any further information. Ports and airports had been checked but there was nothing. No missing persons meeting her description or unidentified hospital cases. Disappointed by her performance, Nina decided to keep her visit short. She arranged to return on the evening of the following day when Frank said he would ask Luke to be there to speak to her. On her way back to Newby Wiske she pondered on where she'd gone wrong and as soon as she arrived she went to find her friend.

'It was a disaster,' she sighed as she slumped at her desk.

'Here get this down you.' Hazel gave her a mug of tea and sat down opposite her. 'So what happened?'

Nina described her visit.

'It sounds all right to me. You got a good impression, didn't you?'

'Yes, but I don't think they did. *She* definitely didn't like me and he's too scared of her to be honest with me.' She sipped the hot tea. 'Anyway I'm going to meet the boyfriend tomorrow – perhaps that'll go better.'

Their conversation was interrupted by Ruby asking for

their help in accessing a computer record.

'What's she doing?' Nina asked when Ruby had left the room.

'Apparently she's found a cat.'

'What?'

Hazel laughed. 'C.A.T. it stands for Campaign Against Le Tour or the Tour. Something like that. A group of OAP militants out to sabotage the cycle race next year.'

'Seriously?'

'Apparently. She's only just come across them, so she's making initial enquiries about the members.'

'Is it a big group?'

'About half a dozen!' Hazel grinned.

'We shouldn't laugh,' said Nina. 'By next year it could be a significant threat.'

They both giggled helplessly.

Nina's meeting with the missing girl's boyfriend was even more difficult than she'd imagined. It was clear from the body language that Mrs Rycroft didn't like the lad and she could sympathise to some extent. He lounged on the sofa in his work clothes, apparently uninterested in what had happened to Anna.

'She's gone off with this bloke from college,' he said. 'Good riddance, I say.'

'What makes you think that, Luke?' Nina asked.

'She told me when I met her in Hawes.'

'You saw her there?' This was news to Nina. 'Was she all right then?'

'Oh she was all right. Chatting to her college friend,' he sneered.

'That must have been the person who phoned.' Frank

Rycroft spoke for the first time. 'There was a call in the week before; someone asking about her route. I told him I didn't know exactly, but I was sure she'd be going over Buttertubs Pass so she would have to go through Hawes some time.'

'You didn't tell me about that,' his wife said sharply.

'I'd forgotten until you mentioned it. I assumed it was part of some team she was cycling with.'

'She isn't in one,' Luke said. 'Not since university.' He sat with his arms folded, appearing to enjoy the situation.

Nina, who didn't know whether there had been any attempt to locate the mysterious "friend from university", told Luke he might be required to look at some CCTV if they located the man Anna had been speaking to. It sounded, on the face of it, as if he would be the key to Anna's disappearance. If they had gone off together, it ought to be quite straightforward to find them.

Mills was sitting in the office, going through the report that Jack Bassett had given her. She'd asked him if she could have a look through the data he'd described as being of poor quality and he'd suggested a copy of the final report given to Professor Green for the prosecution. Mills was appalled at the sloppiness of the document but could hardly criticise the student; it was up to Sydney to supervise the work and ensure it was of a high enough standard to stand up to scrutiny.

She made copious notes in the margins on every page and scribbled comments on the last one, planning to go through it with Jack in detail, so he understood the robustness with which forensic evidence had to be prepared. When she'd finished she pinned all the pages together again and placed them to one side, planning to catch Jack at the end of the afternoon. She had just begun preparing for the next day's lecture when there was a call from Nina.

'Hi Mills. Sorry to bother you but Nige isn't picking up and I need a favour.'

'Go ahead.'

'I've got CCTV of someone who probably comes from the university. If I send you a photo, can you tell me if you recognise him?'

Mills watched her inbox until the message appeared, pulling up the file so it filled the screen. The man was standing outside a pub that looked familiar but she couldn't place it. The image wasn't good but the height and build reminded her of someone she'd seen before. When she showed it to Jake he immediately recognised the man.

'Will Humphreys, team coach and general waster,' he said. 'What's he done now?'

'No idea.'

She emailed Nina with the news and received a big "thank you" by return, asking if he was around if she came over. Mills tried his phone but there was no reply so she made her way over to the sports department, planning to drop the report back on the way.

'Jack!'

The student was in the laboratory, as usual, but this time he was at the balance, weighing samples.

'Dr Sanderson.'

'I've gone through the report you gave me and made some comments – well, quite a lot of comments actually.'

He looked worried.

'I hope they're useful.'

'Thank you. Prof Green was a bit… he got a bit… when he heard that I'd given it to you. He said it was evidence and should be treated as confidential.'

'Ah.' Mills hadn't thought it through.

'Has he seen you?'

'No.'

'I think he wants to speak to you about it.'

Mills placed the document on the bench. 'Thanks for the warning.'

She was about to leave then had a thought. 'D'you know if Will Humphreys is around today, Jack?'

'Will? Hell, no! Don't you know? He's not come back yet.'

'That's odd.'

'Odd? It's a frigging disaster! We've had no coaching for weeks now. I'm in the Etape du Dales in May next year and there are loads of minor races before that. He was supposed to be giving me extra coaching in the next few months. What if he never comes back?'

'Why wouldn't he?'

'No reason. It's just a pain.' His face changed to a smile and he stood up. 'I've got a sponsorship form in my bag, for the Etape du Tour next year. Will you sponsor me?'

'Another time, Jack.'

Mills went back to her office to let Nina know the situation. Jake was there when she made the call.

'I knew the BUCS was after him,' he said. 'Have they involved the police now?'

'I'm sorry I don't know, Jake. I really don't have a clue.'

Mills left the university early to avoid the Friday traffic. Alex would be there by seven and she wanted to tidy the cottage before he arrived. They'd agreed to eat out but she wondered how busy the "Farmers Arms" would be on such a beautiful evening. She was so engrossed in her thoughts that she hadn't noticed Muriel until she shouted a cheery "hello" at her across the hedge dividing their gardens.

'Are you busy, dear?' she called, waving a sheet of paper.

'No,' Mills lied. Thinking she was carrying a sponsorship form, she added. 'Doing a marathon, Muriel?'

Her neighbour looked puzzled.

'The form…'

'Oh, no dear. It's the petition.'

'What petition?'

'The one to stop those bicycles going through next year.'

'The Grand Départ?'

'Yes, that French one.'

Muriel had made her way into the garden and handed Mills the paper.

'So who's organising it?' asked Mills, looking at the heading. 'Campaign Against the Tour. Who are they?'

'C.A.T., it's a group of like-minded people living in the dale.'

'Do you belong to it, Muriel?'

'Yes. And so has Arthur from down the road. His neighbour, Colin Norton, has joined as well. But it's mainly Stephen Grainger and his posh friend.'

Mills was reading the typed paragraph at the top of the sheet which stated that the undersigned wanted to ban the Grand Départ from taking place through Wensleydale and Swaledale.'

'But why, Muriel? It'll be great fun and bring loads of visitors. Think of all the B&B owners with fully booked accommodation and how busy the shops will be.'

She reddened. 'We feel that the environmental impact of so many visitors will be detrimental to the countryside.'

'Really?'

'Look, I only agreed to join because Arthur asked me to and I felt awkward,' she pleaded. 'You know how it is. They needed somewhere to meet and my house is more suitable. It's just a signature, Mills.'

'I'm sorry, Muriel. I don't think I can. It's nothing personal.'

Muriel smiled wanly. 'I know, dear. To be honest I'm a bit unsure about it all myself, especially the more drastic ideas that Stephen and Catriona have.' She patted Mills' arm. 'Don't worry; I won't stop thinking of you when I'm baking.' She went out of the gate and up her own garden path.

'Thanks Muriel. I'd miss your parkin!' Mills went to go inside then stopped. 'What d'you mean "drastic ideas"?'

'Sabotage, I think that's what they call it, isn't it? That's what *they* want to do next year – sabotage the race.'

Chapter 6

'Want a coffee Nina? Hazel?'

Ruby was struggling through the office door with a mug in each hand.

'I don't know how we ever managed without you,' Nina said, jumping up to take it from her. 'We're going to miss you when you go.'

'Don't say that, she's got a few months yet.'

'Ten weeks exactly. I was only taken on until the Grand Départ is over,' Ruby said, handing Hazel the other mug, before she disappeared back into the kitchen.

'That has gone so quickly,' Hazel said. 'D'you remember when she first arrived – hardly said boo to a goose – and look at her now: competent...' She stopped as the door opened and Ruby re-appeared.

'I wasn't here when Ruby arrived last year,' Nina said. She was reliving the awful time she'd had with her first family liaison case. Since then there'd been another three but none like the first. 'I was doing my FLO training.'

'Oh my God, so you were. That awful missing girl case... what was her name?'

'Anna Rycroft.' Nina would always remember it. There had never been closure for the family or for her.

'They didn't find her, did they?' Ruby stood sipping her coffee, one of the team now.

'No… no, they didn't. They felt she must have gone to France with the university coach and decided to stay, since neither of them has been found.' She sat down at her desk. 'But her father was devastated. He never believed she would go without letting him know she was safe.'

There was a short pause before Hazel broke the silence.

'Well, Ruby, how did you get on with Stephen Grainger?'

The girl pulled a face. 'Not very well.'

'He's in charge of the Campaign Against the Tour,' Hazel explained to Nina.

'I know,' she said. 'He was on the telly the other day, ranting on about the road closures.'

'He says he wants the roads to remain open but really he wants to stop the race totally. He is such a pompous twit.' Ruby had put her mug on the desk and was standing with her hands on her hips. 'Do you know what he said? He asked me to send someone with authority if the police wanted to ask him questions.'

'We should have sent you in as a member of the group,' suggested Hazel. 'Embed you in the gang.' She was laughing.

'I know someone who lives next door to one of them,' said Nina.

They both looked at her.

'Really?' asked Hazel.

'You know my friend Mills,' Nina told Hazel. 'They hold their meetings at her neighbour's house. She tried to persuade her to sign their petition and go on demonstrations with them.'

'Did she?' Ruby looked interested.

'No.'

'But she could,' Hazel said.

'I don't know about that. It would be…'

'What? Underhand? Deceitful? As far as I remember, Mills is as devious as you are, Nina Featherstone.'

Ruby picked up where Hazel left off. 'Would you ask her, Nina? Just see if she'd be up for it? It would be brilliant to have someone on the inside.'

'You are joking, aren't you? There is no way…'

Hazel interrupted. 'There's no harm in asking, Nina. It would only be to keep tabs on what they're up to. Thanks to Ruby we know they're more than a bunch of do-gooders. They may be planning illegal activities and if they are, we should know about it. Mitch is liaising closely with his French counterpart and so far there's been little for Ruby to report.'

'It would have to be totally unofficial,' Nina warned.

Hazel insisted she called Mills right away. Reluctantly she punched in the number while the other two stood over her, listening to her end of the conversation. She dispensed with any chit-chat and launched straight in.

'Mills, I've been asked to ring you to ask a favour. It's about your neighbour, Muriel. She's a member of C.A.T. Yes, we know they are organising protests. No, she's not in any trouble, yet. But we want to make sure it stays that way.'

Nina looked up at her colleagues with a smile. 'Yes, we want to ensure they don't get themselves into any difficulties… you know, with the authorities. That's why we were wondering whether you might get involved with her a bit.'

Nina pulled a face and shook her head. 'No, there's no

problem. I just wanted you to perhaps… maybe go along to a meeting… see what they are planning? Just to check that they aren't into anything, you know, serious.'

She sat while her friend expressed the view that they were a group of harmless nutters – except for Muriel, who had wandered into it without understanding what they were doing. 'So will you do it, Mills? As a favour?'

Eventually Nina replaced the receiver. 'She says she'll ask Muriel if she can attend the next meeting.'

'Yes!' shouted Ruby and gave Hazel a high five.

Nina sighed and shook her head slowly. 'The things you get me into, Hazel. You should be setting a better example to our young friend.'

Mills was mystified by Nina's phone call. Alex had laughed when she'd told him that their next-door-neighbour was a member of the Campaign Against the Tour. He'd met her three months ago when he'd moved into Laurel Cottage and Muriel had made a huge chocolate cake, just because he'd said it was his favourite. At the time they'd discussed what C.A.T. stood for and agreed they were against its principles entirely. Mills would have to explain to Alex why she suddenly wanted to join the group or he'd think she'd gone mad.

She deliberately left work early to catch Muriel before Alex arrived home. It was sometimes difficult to get away from her neighbour once she started chatting but this time Muriel seemed to be in a hurry.

'Sorry, love, but I can't stop,' she said when Mills knocked. 'Come in and talk while I finish these scones.'

She was cutting out thick rounds of dough and placing them carefully on baking trays. The kitchen was overpoweringly hot although the back door was wide open.

'I've got to get these done before I go out or there'll be nothing to give them tomorrow.'

'Are you having another meeting of your group?'

Muriel wiped her forehead with a floury hand, leaving a white residue. 'We meet twice a week now it's getting close to the time.' She was bending over, feeding the trays into the open oven. 'Stephen says we need to step up our game.' She closed the oven door and straightened up, wiping her hands on her apron. 'Did you want a cuppa?' Her offer was unconvincing.

'No, it's OK. I can see you're busy. I just wanted to ask about the group. I wondered whether you needed any help.'

'Help?' Muriel looked puzzled.

'Do you need another pair of hands in the group? I couldn't do *twice* a week but I could come along sometimes.'

Muriel looked flustered. 'You'd better ask Stephen – he's in charge. Are you sure? You didn't seem... I mean you said...'

'Yes. But I've been thinking about it and, you know, as it gets nearer... Anyway, I'll ask him. Will he be around tomorrow?'

'Yes. Seven o' clock. Best come round beforehand, so you can see him before we start.'

Mills left Muriel to her baking and went next door to prepare the evening meal. She was beginning to tire of having to plan something to eat every day. When she was single she could snack on some cheese or a bowl of cereal, but not now. Alex couldn't be fobbed off with beans on toast. Fair enough, they shared the cooking but it still meant being so organised!

She was taking the mince out of the fridge, and was rooting through the onions to avoid those that had sprouted, when the front door slammed.

'Hi!' she called.

She heard his backpack thump to the floor in the tiny hallway and stopped herself from shouting to him to move it out of the way. She knew he was late because he'd been doing the monthly invoices at the lab for her. She couldn't complain.

'Give us a lager,' he called from the sitting room.

She bit the inside of her mouth and said nothing. Just let me finish this, she muttered as she opened the window wider. She carried on with the meal until he came to get the cold lager himself.

'Don't bother to ask,' she called, as he disappeared again.

'What?'

'Nothing.' She looked in the 'fridge but he'd taken the last can.

She could hear the television – some useless game show. 'What are you watching?' she called. But there was no answer.

It couldn't have been more than ten minutes later when she'd finished the bolognaise sauce and left it to simmer. She went into the next room to find Alex sprawled across the sofa, fast asleep. She was tempted to wake him with an accidental-on-purpose knock to the leg. Instead she sighed and went out into the tiny garden to cool down. There was no breeze. The humid air seemed to press on her, making her even more irritable. There was nothing for it but to get the pasta on and eat.

Alex wandered into the kitchen as she was draining the spaghetti.

'Can I do anything?' He yawned loudly.

'No.'

As they ate, Alex described his day in minute detail. Glyn had been a complete – well… He'd been obstructive and bad-tempered. He'd called Alex an idiot.

'Why?' asked Mills.

'I was explaining to him why we had to use timesheets. It's the only way we can get on top of the finance.'

'But we said we would hold off on that until I'd had a chance to talk to Brenda.'

'I don't think we should wait. She's not well. It could be weeks. The sooner we get a system in place the better.'

Mills was tired of the same old arguments about money. Brenda's way of running the business was rather unusual; she didn't seem to have a particularly robust system for invoicing. In fact, there didn't seem to be a system at all. Mills had rationalised the pricing so it was consistent but it had been based on historical costs not any concrete reasoning. *Reasoning* was Alex's forte. Alex was the most rational man she knew. He had decided that everyone should complete timesheets so they could calculate exactly how much time was spent on every piece of work. He always had to allocate his own time in his last job, he argued.

'I told you Glyn wouldn't agree,' Mills said after a while.

'That's putting it mildly.' Alex was concentrating on winding spaghetti round his fork. 'He effectively called me a young upstart!'

'Well you are.' Mills meant it but he thought she was joking.

'The man's living in the twentieth century.'

'Yes, he probably is. I expect he liked it then.' Mills knew she sounded sulky but Alex would never be drawn. He'd moved in with her perfectly happily, treated the place as his own and seemed oblivious to the fact that sometimes, just sometimes, he could be unbearable. Aware that they spent far too much time talking about work, she changed the subject.

'Nina asked me to go along to one of Muriel's anti-Tour meetings.'

That got his attention. 'Why?'

'To see what they're up to, what they're planning.'

'Are you going?'

'Yes.'

He went back to scraping the last of the sauce from his bowl. 'It's not dangerous I suppose?'

'Why would it be dangerous?'

'I don't know. Perhaps they're planning to bomb Hawes or something.'

'Don't be daft.' She cleared the table and Alex went back to the sofa. 'Fancy a walk or something?' she asked. Anything to escape the cottage.

'Not fussed. I'm pretty knackered actually.' He was on his iPad.

She changed her shoes and went onto the moor above the village, reaching her usual flat rock that made a relatively comfortable seat. She needed time to think about what was happening to her – to them. Before he moved in it had been fine but now they were together every day it was becoming so confining. It was the first time she'd been in this position and she wasn't sure it was what she really wanted. To make it worse her father and Fiona kept on about meeting Alex. Introducing him to her family would make an even bigger thing of their relationship – and she wasn't sure she really wanted that.

'We're so lucky with the weather,' Tamsin called to her friend Jade as they followed their instructor across the rough moorland.

'I told you it would be fine,' the woman leading the photography course called back. 'It's not far now. I just wanted you to get a chance to photograph Buttertubs Pass. It will be in the news next month in the run up to the cycle race. It could be useful practice if you want to take some shots of the race in July.'

'As if,' muttered Jade.

There was a breeze on the top but it was warm and there were sufficient clouds to make their photographs interesting. Tamsin was pleased she'd persuaded Jade to join her because otherwise she would have been the only single woman in the party. The other five members of the group consisted of two couples and a man in his forties or fifties. That would have been creepy, she thought. The old man kept asking the leader technical questions about stop numbers or focus lengths that meant nothing to her – and Jade, who wasn't interested in the technical stuff, was making faces at her and muttering "loser" under her breath.

The woman in charge ushered the group to a grassy hill and pointed at the slope opposite. 'Buttertubs,' she said.

'Weird name,' said Jade.

The woman ignored her and began to give directions and advice on how to optimise the features in the sky above the hill.

Tamsin watched a car appear from the left, pass the Buttertubs and then disappear again. There was a drop below the road and only low wire fencing stretching on the edge. A sheep could fall down there if it slipped, she told Jade.

The single man had set up a tripod and was waving a light meter around unnecessarily. The couples were advising each other or arguing, she couldn't tell exactly. Jade had plonked herself on the ground and was lighting up a cigarette. Tamsin prepared to take some shots in the direction of Buttertubs Pass. It looked rather a boring scene, she thought, and decided to focus on the sheep nibbling at the edge of the tarmac. She unpacked the massive telephoto lens, attached it to the SLR and pointed. At first she couldn't find the sheep and it was difficult to keep the camera steady. Perhaps the old man wasn't so daft after all, she thought. She captured a few shots of sheep then rested before having another go. This time someone had parked on the road directly opposite where she was photographing, spoiling the view.

She continued to focus, hoping it would go away until there was a hand on her shoulder and the leader was asking her about her composition, suggesting politely that she took longer views of the scenery – since this was supposed to be a landscape course.

When she'd gone, Tamsin made one last attempt to find those sheep. The vehicle was still there and, damn, a bike. The next few seconds went slowly as she clicked the shutter once… twice… three times. The bicycle was curving over the railing… the rider was sailing through the air… She let out a cry as she dropped the camera to peer down into the valley below. Everyone was staring at her.

'The cyclist – did you see?' she cried.

Only the old man nodded. 'I saw something fly past. Probably a seagull.'

'But it was red and white.'

The cyclist was red and white; how could it be a bird? She couldn't get them to believe her and it became embarrassing. 'Didn't you see it, Jade?' she asked her friend on the way back to the car.

'I was nearly asleep with boredom. It's the last time I let you talk me into one of your daft ideas.'

'Well I'm going to ring the police when we get a signal because I know what I saw.'

'I'm sorry but we'll miss the rest of the course now,' Tamsin told Jade as they drove back from Newby Wiske.

'No problem. It wasn't much fun with them old people anyway. Can we do a course with some young blokes on it next time, eh?'

Tamsin ignored her friend, she was always on about pulling a good-looking lad.

'So what did the police say?' her friend asked.

'They wanted to know exactly what I'd seen.'

'Didn't they do that yesterday?'

'Yes but then they didn't know if it really was someone going over the edge.'

'And was it?'

'Yes. They sent a rescue team to have a look and they found him, the cyclist, last night. He was badly injured but he's in hospital.' She started crying again.

'What's the matter?'

'I just keep thinking that he could've died.'

'If you hadn't reported it.'

'No thanks to you.'

'Look, I didn't know what you were on about. The others didn't think you were right.'

'Well, anyway, he's in hospital in a coma. I do hope he recovers.'

'Happen they'll give you a medal,' Jade said, laughing.

'Yeah, right.' Tamsin put her foot on the brake and stopped the car.

'What's up?' asked her friend, looking alarmed.

'The photos – I've got photos, haven't I? I should have given them to the police when I was there.'

She turned in her seat and backed the car onto a track into a field before setting off back in the direction they'd just come. At the police HQ she ran back through the building to the office where she'd spoken to a uniformed officer. It was empty. Back in the corridor she bumped into a woman who asked if she could help.

'I wanted to hand in my photos,' she explained.

Once the woman understood why she wanted to submit photographs, she offered to download them using her computer and led her upstairs to an office occupied by an Asian woman and a young white girl.

'Ruby, Tamsin here would like to give us her photos of an accident on Buttertubs yesterday. Can you help her with that?'

'Sure,' the girl said and indicated for her to hand over the camera.

It took just a few minutes. She gave them the best two photographs, showing the cyclist just before he left the road and on his way down. Both women thanked her, promising to pass the information on to the uniformed officer dealing with the case. She left with a sense of relief

– she could drive home having done her duty.

Nina and Ruby were still looking at Tamsin's photographs when Hazel came in.

'What is it supposed to be?' she asked.

'It's the road accident on Buttertubs Pass,' said Nina.

'Strange, all I can see is a white blur and a bicycle.'

'A cyclist came off at the corner by Buttertubs – that's why they told me about it. It's on the Grand Départ route,' Ruby said, turning her head to one side. 'You can see the bicycle on this one,'

Hazel studied it from various angles. 'Has it left the road?'

'I think so.'

'What's in the other one?'

'Just a red and white blur,' said Ruby. 'Oh shit – look it's the rider. She's caught him just as he left the road.'

'Was he killed?'

'No, he's in a coma apparently. There will be questions about the road surface, that's for sure. I reckon this will be big on the local news once they get hold of it.'

'Well, it's not our problem,' said Hazel, settling down at her desk.

Mills felt uncomfortable from the minute she entered Muriel's cottage. The anti-Tour group was seated round the edge of her neighbour's sitting room with cups and saucers and tea plates balanced on their knees. Everyone looked up to see who had come in and Muriel attempted to introduce her. They nodded in turn then resumed their conversations, leaving her standing by the door as her neighbour disappeared into the kitchen, returning with a teacup and plate. To her relief, two old gentlemen made a space for her between them on the sofa.

'There, Colin and Arthur will look after you, won't you dears? Help yourself to a snack.'

Mills muttered that she'd eaten but accepted the tea just as a middle-aged man dressed in orange corduroy trousers knocked a spoon against his cup to call the meeting to order. He embarrassed her by welcoming her to the meeting, explaining to the group that she came from next door.

'I expect you've been wondering what we've been getting up to?' he asked.

She smiled politely.

'We have a lot to get through tonight so I'll crack on,' he said.

There followed a list of actions taken by members over the past couple of weeks They mainly consisted of putting posters up in local shops and pubs and tying placards to telegraph poles. He proudly unrolled a proof copy of the latest poster, fresh from the printer.

'It's time we moved up a gear,' he said. 'The big day is only a couple of months away and we need to show our teeth.' He smiled and looked round the group.

The poster was a garish representation of a wolf's head, blood dripping from its fangs. It read "STOP THE RACE". Mills was puzzled and the silence that followed suggested others were too.

'What happened to the idea of keeping the roads open?' asked the man sitting next to Mills. 'I thought it was going to say "Keep the roads open".'

A smart middle-aged woman straightened up in her chair. 'We need to stop the race completely if we are to save the environment, Colin.'

Colin leaned across to speak to the other old gentleman. 'I thought we agreed "Keep the roads open". Didn't we, Arthur?'

Their chairman was turning pink. 'We can't afford to send out mixed messages. We can't ask the roads to be kept open for the race *and* say the race should be stopped. Catriona is right, the only answer is to stop the race completely.'

'That'll never happen,' muttered Arthur under his breath.

Before anyone could argue Stephen rolled up the poster. 'So we'll put these up around the villages as before. Now, I want to talk about the petition.'

'I got a few more names,' offered Muriel.

'Unfortunately we haven't enough to make the necessary impact,' reported Catriona. 'I believe we need at least a thousand signatures before we claim reasonable support. What do you think, Stephen?'

'Yes, Catriona and I discussed this earlier and we agree that we might have to abandon the idea of delivering it to Downing Street.'

'Bit of a lost cause then, isn't it,' remarked Arthur, resting back with his arms folded.

'That's where you are wrong, my friend.' Stephen was leaning forward in his chair with a strange grin.

Mills felt he looked slightly manic. She caught his eye as she watched him and looked away quickly. Was he suspicious of her presence, she wondered.

'This is in strict confidence,' he went on. 'So I hope our new friend here understands that.'

He was talking about her. She blushed as they all stared.

'What I am going to suggest is controversial and radical

but I ran it past Catriona and she agrees that we have no choice.'

There was complete silence as they waited.

'The Etape du Dales will be held next week. We are going to spread tacks on the route. I suggest Buttertubs Pass, since it is high profile.' He laughed. 'Literally!'

There was a stunned silence. Mills glanced over to Catriona, who was looking down at her lap.

'Isn't that dangerous?' asked Muriel.

'No but it will cause quite a bit of chaos,' Stephen was looking pleased with himself.

Catriona smiled. 'It's clever because the disruption of that race will cause the organisers of the Grand Départ to think again. After all they can't afford any hiccups, can they?'

Stephen obviously felt confident because he asked if anyone else had any questions. Colin muttered to Arthur that the man was getting beyond a joke but nothing was said openly. Mills noticed that Muriel had kept quiet throughout the evening and was busying herself by clearing the plates away. The meeting soon ran out of steam and Stephen left with Catriona. Colin and Arthur went off to the pub together, leaving Mills to help Muriel tidy up.

'He's quite a character, Stephen,' said Mills as she dried the dishes.

'Hmm.' Muriel was concentrating on the contents of the washing up bowl.

'What about putting tacks on the road?'

'I don't know really. What do you think?'

'Sounds a bit drastic.'

'Yes. That's what I thought but he's in charge, isn't he?'

'So will you be out there spreading tacks?'

'Oh no, I leave that up to the others. I'm not, you know, up for doing those what d'you call it – guerrilla tactics.'

Mills smiled, pleased her neighbour wouldn't be around when the group was arrested. Because she would be ringing Nina as soon as she got back next door to warn her of the plan.

Chapter 7

'Sit down, son. I'll get you a drink.'

Ian opened the cupboard, found the whisky bottle and poured them both a large one. Matthew hadn't made much sense on the way home but Ian gathered that Jack Bassett had been in an accident.

'So he's in hospital?'

Matthew was taking large gulps of whisky. 'He's in a coma.'

'That bad?' Ian sat down next to him. 'Could be the break you need, son.'

Matthew leaned forward. 'He's really bad. What if he never comes round? What if he dies?'

The boy was distraught. 'None of it makes sense. It's a complete farce!'

'What d'you mean?'

His lad drained the glass and slammed it down on the table beside him. 'He was on the Etape du Dales route, going down Buttertubs when – bang! – he's over the edge.'

'A puncture?'

'Don't know! They brought the bike into uni today to have a look at it. They say it's a mess.' He shook his head then hunched his shoulders. 'I didn't want to see it. I kept thinking it could've been me. He would still be down there now if someone hadn't seen it happen by sheer chance. What if it was me and I was lying there with no-one knowing where I was.'

'Well, I still think it's a blessing in disguise,' said Ian. 'The Etape du Dales is only ten days away and he won't be fit for it. It's your chance, Matthew, don't you see?'

'It was thoughtful of you to come, Matthew. I'm sorry you can't go in to see him.'

They were seated in the cramped family room outside the intensive care unit. He hadn't realised that only close relatives could visit and arrived expecting to see his friend. Jack's mother was the only other person waiting to go in and she seemed grateful for someone to talk to. There were bags under her eyes and she kept drawing her cardigan round her even though Matthew was sweating.

'How is he?' he asked.

'Still in a coma. They're doing tests, you know, like MRI scans and so on. It's such a shame you can't go in. I sit and talk to him but it seems rather odd. I wondered if we should play music when we're not here. They say that, don't they? My husband says leave the radio on but what do *you* think?'

Matthew had no idea what would be appropriate but when she asked him if he could provide the sort of music Jack would prefer, he agreed to make up a compilation of his own favourite bands and bring it in next day. When they were mates they'd been to a few gigs together in the local pubs and seemed to have similar tastes after all.

Suddenly she whimpered. 'It was so unexpected,' she said, rifling through her handbag until she pulled out a tissue. 'I couldn't take it in when the police rang. Of course I knew he was out training but even Ray didn't know he was going over there.'

Now that Jack lived in halls, his parents wouldn't know where he was from day to day, thought Matthew. He'd moved out when Will took over as coach; before that, Jack's dad had been training him. That's when it all changed and Jack's performance suddenly improved. Of course, Will had been gone for over six months now but Jack continued to ride like a pro.

'He was training on the route of the Etape du Dales,' he said. 'The race is in less than two weeks. He was expected to do well.'

She was still crying quietly. 'Ray, my husband, he went to fetch his bike. They'd taken it to the university but he wanted to get it home; it was very expensive. I didn't want to see it so he put it in the garage.' She shuddered. 'But now he says it isn't Jack's bike. Do you think he might have borrowed one from someone else? Is it a university bicycle?'

'I don't think so. We have to provide our own, unless he was trying one out. It might have been a demo I suppose.'

'Could you find out where *his* bike is, Matthew? Ray's getting all hot under the collar about it and he'll be at the university next, and I don't want him upsetting them again.' She looked up quickly as if anxious she'd spoken out of turn.

Matthew waited.

'I expect you heard about the fuss he made last year, when that new coach took over? Ray was very upset that Jack wanted someone else to train him but I could understand. It's difficult, isn't it, when you're so… close…'

Matthew could sympathise. His own father had taught him to drive and that was horrendous.

Once Mrs Bassett started talking it seemed impossible to stop her. She was relating how her husband had accused Will Humphreys of doping Jack to improve his performance.

'He has improved a lot in the past year,' Matthew commented.

She looked him straight in the eye. 'You don't think… do you?'

'No, of course not.' He looked away from her gaze as the door opened and a young couple came in.

They sat together, whispering; the man with his arm round her, comforting her. Jack's mother went silent and Matthew wanted to leave but didn't know how. Eventually a cheery man in scrubs put his head round the door to inform Mrs Bassett that they'd finished with her son and she could go in. Matthew explained he was leaving and promised her he would bring some music in the next day.

'Don't forget to ask about Jack's bike,' she called.

He went straight back to the university to find out what had happened to it. Matthew knew Jack's dad had bought it for when he was training him and it was worth a fortune. Nothing was too good for his son. Matthew had done evening and weekend jobs to save for his own but it wasn't half as good. But if Jack had wrecked a demo bike, he guessed he'd be in for a big bill.

Mates in the team wanted to hear how Jack was and he couldn't tell them much. He asked around but no-one had any reason to believe Jack wasn't on his own bike. He was looking for Spence, who'd taken over in Will's absence, and found him in his office with his feet on the desk reading a magazine.

'Just doing a bit of research,' he grinned, opening his desk drawer and shoving it away.

'Jack Bassett,' Matthew said.

'Bad business. Really bad luck. He'll miss the big race. I suppose you want to know if you'll…'

'He's in a coma. He might die!'

'Are you sure?'

'It's serious. What was he doing? How did it happen?'

'The police reckon the road might have been slippery on that bend. It's been dry for a long time, a sprinkling of rain overnight and bingo!'

'Bingo?'

'Well, you know…'

'He's a very experienced rider. He should be able to handle the road conditions.' He knew he was whining and stopped talking.

'Gee, I know it's hard when a mate gets hurt but I didn't think you two were friendly.'

'We're not. Quite the opposite but something isn't right. What about the fact he wasn't riding his own bike? Did you know that?'

Spence lowered his feet to the floor and swung round in his chair. Now he had the man's attention.

'No-one seemed to notice when it was sent here but Jack's dad says it's not his bike,' Matthew continued. 'Was he on a demo or did he borrow it from someone here?'

'I have no idea,' Spence replied slowly.

'So you don't know where his bike is. Was it stolen?'

'Matthew, he would have told me if he'd lost it. That was his last chance to do the route of the Etape du Dales. He wouldn't have done it on a bike other than his own; have you seen that beauty?'

Matthew nodded. 'Ring Jack's dad and tell him. Otherwise he'll be in here to find out for himself.'

Spence looked worried. 'OK, right away. Thanks Matthew.'

It was so hot that Nina had decided to wear her sleeveless sundress to work and was surprised when her boss, Mitch, asked if she had anything more suitable.

'What d'you mean "suitable"?' she demanded.

Hazel looked up from her desk, ready to wade in.

'I mean more suitable for visiting a family to tell them that their missing daughter's cycle has turned up.'

Nina stared. Hazel went back to her work. Mitch handed her a sheet of paper.

'It's the identification report on the bike found at the bottom of Buttertubs with the injured lad. Turns out the ID belongs to your Anna Rycroft.'

Hazel exchanged a glance with her.

'You mean the boy was riding her bike?' Nina asked.

'Not clear what was going on, to be honest. I need you to go and see the family. Find out if there's any connection between her and this...' he referred to the sheet. 'Jack Bassett.'

Nina rang Anna's mother and arranged a visit, allowing sufficient time to go home and change into a sombre outfit. She timed it so the twins would be having their nap and she was able to slip in and out of the house with only a brief "hello" and a kiss for Nige.

Mrs Rycroft looked flushed when she opened the door and led Nina into the lounge. She was relieved to find they were alone.

'They told you about Anna's bike?' she began.

'Yes. We couldn't take it in, not after all this time, I mean. Frank says it can't be right. He says it must be a mistake. He would've been here but he can't just leave work at a moment's notice.' She sat down opposite Nina.

'There's an identification mark on the frame, in case it's stolen. It's registered on a database that the police can access. We are sure it is Anna's bike.'

'So this lad stole it? Where did he find it?'

'We don't know. He's in hospital and we can't talk to him yet. He's very poorly.'

Mrs Rycroft did not look sympathetic. 'If he took it, he'll know where she is, won't he?'

Nina had the same thought but she'd been taught not to give hope to relatives unless there was a good basis for it. 'We really can't say anything yet. Obviously we'll talk to him as soon as he's conscious but meanwhile… she may have known him. He's a student at the university.'

'She left six years ago. I don't see how she'd know a student there now.'

'He's in the cycle racing team, just like Anna was when she was there. UNYCYCLE, have you heard of it?'

'I left all that to her father. Frank might know of him. What's his name?'

'Jack Bassett.'

She shook her head. 'I'll tell him. And Luke might've heard of him.'

Nina waited, giving the woman the space to talk – something she'd learnt on the course.

'Six months it's been,' Anna's mother began. Then her demeanour changed and she continued angrily. 'Nothing.

You'd think she'd at least tell her own mother that she's safe. We've had nothing from her since she left, not even a postcard.'

Nina was shocked at the outburst and surprised that the woman was so confident that her daughter was alive and simply not making contact. If Rosie had disappeared like that, she would have been distraught – convinced that she must be dead or she would have been in touch.

'Is there anything else you want to know?' Nina asked.

'Such as?' Her tone was defensive and cold.

Nina shrugged. 'I don't know exactly. Maybe you could tell your husband and Luke what I've said and let me know if anything occurs to them.'

'I doubt Luke will be interested. We haven't seen him since she went off. They weren't close. Best speak to him yourself.'

There was no offer of a cup of tea. No tears. No self-blame or guilt trips. The course she'd attended had prepared her for anguish but not for this indifference. She could feel that she was being watched from behind the net curtains as she unlocked the car and made her escape. The visit had shaken her: the lack of concern, the coldness.

Back at HQ she reported her visit to Mitch.

'I wonder why she's so sure that her daughter just went off,' he said, scratching his head.

'She didn't say but we know that the coach at the university was the last person seen with her and he's never reappeared either.'

'You think they went off together?'

'Don't know. No-one's seen them, although they're supposed to have gone to France. If they did, they've not come back or we would've been alerted. There's a notification out for them.'

'And we have no connection between the girl and this lad in hospital?' Mitch asked.

'Only that they both raced for their university team.'

The DI was sitting on the edge of the desk swinging his leg absently. Suddenly he jumped up.

'I'm going along the corridor to ask for another search of the area below Buttertubs,' he said. 'Why would a bloke want to borrow a girl's bike? His must still be out there!' He slammed the door behind him.

'Depends.' Ruby was looking up from her desk.

'Meaning?' Nina asked.

'Bikes designed specifically for women have a step over and no bloke would be seen dead on a bike like that. But she's a road racer and her bike won't look much different to a bloke's. I prefer a man's bike anyway; what about you?'

Nina looked at her in surprise. 'I have no idea, Ruby. I wasn't allowed to ride one when I was growing up; it wasn't considered ladylike.'

Ruby laughed. 'Seriously?'

Nina nodded. 'So basically you're saying that he may have been riding Anna Rycroft's bike?'

'Only if they were the same height.' She stood up. 'I think DI Turner is right,' she said, making for the door. 'I'm going to ask him if I can observe the search for Jack Bassett's bike,' she declared.

The vehicle took them up the track from Muker as far as it could go, stopping by the gate that opened onto the rough moorland. Ruby could feel her heart beating fast as she jumped down onto the uneven track and followed the constables. It was early and although the sun was low, she could feel it was going to be hot. A couple of the lads had been teasing her on the way up and she was determined not to get left behind or do anything they could use to make fun of her.

They were walking over rough ground but they reached the area below Buttertubs surprisingly quickly. There they stopped to drink water and listen to instructions from the officer in charge. It was a lighthearted affair since all they were required to do was to look for Jack Bassett's bicycle. Soon Ruby was following a line of policemen as they moved slowly over the ground. She'd received specific instructions to keep well back so she didn't tread on anything before it had been cleared by the search team.

Half an hour went by and nothing. An hour and still nothing. The sun was beating down now and they stopped to drink from the bottles of water they'd been supplied with. Men wandered off to relieve themselves. Ruby looked about her, wondering where she could find a secluded spot. There was no shelter close by so she waited until the search resumed and kept back, letting the line move further ahead until she could slip unnoticed to one side; the last thing she needed was to draw attention to herself. She edged away slowly, walking backwards to increase the distance between them, watching the line all the time. Once or twice her foot caught in the vegetation and she almost stumbled. Eventually there was a hundred metres between her and the group. A few steps more and she could crouch down to hide sufficiently.

Suddenly she was reeling backwards into the heather and lying flat on her back with the sun blinding her, giggling at her own antics. She rolled over gingerly with the strong smell of putrefaction in her nostrils. Thinking she'd fallen over a dead sheep, she picked herself up onto all fours and peered round. At first she couldn't comprehend what she was seeing. Flashes of red and white, black hair, brown flesh. Then she let out a scream that attracted every single one of the police constables and she went on screaming until they were by her side, where she remained paralysed on all fours. A distorted jumble of limbs – barely any tissue covering the bones. The red and white university team outfit lying like a deflated balloon. The face was gone but Ruby knew that she had found Anna Rycroft.

Chapter 8

'Will the family have to identify the body?' Ruby asked.

Hazel had been sitting with the girl ever since she'd been brought back from Swaledale. She'd been in a terrible state and they thought it best that she remained in the office to calm down for a while. She would be offered counselling if she wanted, of course, but meanwhile she just needed reassurance and mugs of tea.

Nina could tell something was wrong the moment she came in and saw her. Hazel gave her one of her looks, indicating that there was a problem.

'Come and get some tea, Nina,' she said with forced cheerfulness, ushering her friend out of the door and down the corridor.

'What's going on?' Nina asked.

'Ruby was at the search for the lad's bike at Buttertubs. She tripped over a body.'

'What body?'

'It's not official but it looks like your girl.'

'Anna?'

'Well, they found her bike, didn't they? Wearing a university team jersey, red and white. Long dark hair…'

'But she'd been missing for months!'

'That's why Ruby's in such a state. It wasn't very pleasant apparently.'

'She saw it?'

'Worse than that – she found it.'

They went back to the office where Ruby was staring into space holding her mug in both hands.

'Another one?' Hazel asked.

'Yes please.'

Ruby looked pale and Nina asked whether they should take her home.

'No, it's all right. It's just been a bit of a shock, you know. I haven't seen a dead body before, not even…'

'It must have been very badly…'

'Yes.' She gulped. 'They said she'd been there for six months and the animals… they'd…'

'Yes. It must've been horrible.'

'Will they make her family identify her because… well…'

'If they can confirm it's her without the family having to, they will.' Nina was thinking that she would have to visit the family as soon as possible and when Hazel returned, she went to see Mitch.

'You've heard that we've found your missing girl?' he asked.

'Yes. Poor Ruby. I guess I should go to see the Rycrofts?'

'Yes, they were going to send a couple of constables round but I said you'd inform the family yourself.'

It hadn't occurred to her. It wouldn't be the first time she'd had to break such bad news but never to a family she'd got to know beforehand. That was going to be hard.

'OK. Is there anything you particularly want me to discuss with them?'

'Such as?'

'How she died?'

'I think it's pretty obvious, Nina. She came off the road at a dangerous bend. It'll cause waves locally. I've already been asked whether it's safe to go ahead with the Etape du Dales on Buttertubs Pass.'

Nina ignored the remark. 'What if the family ask whether she died when she fell… or was lying there for days, suffering.' The thought filled her with horror.

'Until we get a coroner's report we won't know. The body was apparently fairly well decomposed so I don't know how precise they can be.'

Nina left his office feeling anxious. It would be another trip home to change into something "suitable" before she could set off to the Rycroft's. She went back to her desk to collect her bag and found Ruby busy on her keyboard.

'I told Ruby she should go home,' Nina said to Hazel.

'So did I, but she wants to get on.'

'They haven't found Jack Bassett's bike,' Ruby said, without looking up. 'That's what they were looking for and they haven't found it.'

'Well, they probably stopped when they… when you…' Hazel suggested.

'No, they carried on searching for several hours, because it was a crime scene. I've just texted one of the guys and he says there's no sign of a bike.'

'That doesn't make sense.' Nina said, and Hazel agreed.

Ruby was concentrating on the monitor in front of her. 'So I'm just going to check whether anyone else has found it. I'll access the register for a search. It will tell us if it has been found anywhere and if it was registered as stolen by Jack.' They waited. 'No, nothing. Oh well, I'll flag it up now anyway.'

'I don't know when I'll get back, Nige. I can't rush off when I've just broken such awful news to the family.'

Nina transferred the contents of her handbag into her old black one and checked the mirror.

'No problem. I knew it wouldn't be easy.' Her husband was pulling a mock sad face. 'It's shepherd's pie for tea. If you're late we'll eat it all up, won't we Tomos?'

She gave him a quick kiss on the lips and left him wiping away the lipstick.

During the journey she rehearsed what she would say. On the course they were told not to say "Sorry for your loss", it was too much of a cliché. Whatever you say, it won't be enough, so don't beat yourself up over it. Do what comes naturally but do think about what you want to say before you open your mouth, they'd been told.

The family car was parked outside the house, so at least they were at home. She sat for a moment to gather her thoughts before heading for the front door. It was a relief when Mr Rycroft opened it.

'Nina, this is a surprise. Although I told Isobel you might be back if you'd found out where that lad found the bike.'

'May I come in, Frank?'

He opened the door wide and ushered her inside. She waited to follow him into their front room and took a seat. He remained standing in front of the window, making it difficult to see his face against the sunlight pouring in despite the net curtains.

'It's about Anna,' she began. 'Not the bike. The thing is… I mean…'

'They've found her, haven't they?' His voice was level, calm even. 'Dead?'

Nina nodded.

'Below Buttertubs?'

She nodded again. There was a lump in her throat.

'I've been thinking about it,' he continued, 'and it was obvious really. If her cycle was found below the road then that was the most likely spot.'

He moved across to the chair by the fireplace and slowly sank into it. 'Poor Annie. And Isobel thinking she'd run away from us.'

Nina remained quiet, letting him take in the news.

'That lad, the one in a coma...' he stopped as if weighing up the situation. Then his demeanour changed from puzzlement to concern. 'Isobel won't be back until later.'

'I can stay if you like.'

'Would you? Would you do that?' He stood up, leaning on the arm of the chair for support. 'I'll make us a cup of tea, then. There might be some biscuits.'

Nina let him go, wondering if she should offer to help. She quickly wrote a text to Nige, telling him she'd be staying. As she pressed "send" there was a crash followed by a low moan. She ran into the kitchen to find Frank kneeling on the floor picking up pieces of china.

He looked up when she went in. 'That was her best teapot, the one she keeps for visitors.' His shoulders started shaking and she found herself crouching beside him with her arm round his shoulder.

'You go and sit down, Frank. I'll make the tea.'

'The biscuits are in there,' he muttered, indicating a large round tin on the table. 'The one with the birds on.'

Nina finally reached home just before nine.

'Your dinner's in the dog!'

Nige was messing about as usual but stopped when he saw how shattered she was. He made her sit down and fetched a glass of wine.

'Was it awful?'

'Pretty much.'

'Want to talk about it?'

She shrugged. What was there to say? Two people had lost their only child at the age of twenty-seven. A father was crying for his daughter – a mother expressing such heart-felt anger.

Mrs Rycroft had not come back from visiting her friend by five so her husband rang the house to tell her there was some news. No, he couldn't tell her over the phone, just pass the message on to Isobel. Unfortunately his wife's friend had somehow convinced her that it would be good news, so she came rushing in with a look of expectation. Her reaction, when Frank told her that their Annie's body had been found, shocked Nina. The woman screamed, calling her daughter all sorts of horrible names, accusing her of doing it to spite her mother and saying it served her right for trying to get away from her. Her husband tried to pacify her but she lashed out at him.

Eventually Nina suggested they rang a friend or relative. By the time her sister arrived, Isobel had exhausted herself and was in the kitchen, having slammed the door in their faces. Nina was worried that the woman might do herself some harm but Frank convinced her she would not. The sister seemed a sensible sort who spoke to Isobel through the door and soon she was being escorted to bed with something to help her "relax". Nina was unsure that it was the best way to deal with grief but it seemed the only way for Frank to get some peace that night.

She finally left when all seemed calm again and she'd convinced Frank to persuade his sister-in-law to be there in the morning. As she left, he asked if someone would be required to identify the body. Did he want to see his daughter again, bearing in mind she had been in her resting place for six months? Nina cringed as she said it but how else to put it? Frank understood immediately and said he'd come if need be but not otherwise. She squeezed his arm and let herself out, pulling the door behind her. In the car she started crying gently but was howling as she joined the A1.

'Another glass of wine, love?' Nige asked.

'No, I think I'll have a bath and go to bed. Can you manage?'

Without waiting for an answer, she dragged herself upstairs and went into the bathroom. She watched the water pouring into the bath then she undressed and stepped in, washing away the unpleasantness of the day – aware that Anna's family were not so lucky.

She was sitting in her bathrobe on Rosie's bed, watching her daughter as she slept. She would never be able to express in words how thankful she was that her little girl was safe with them that night. She was disturbed by the light changing slightly as the door was opened onto the landing.

'It's Mills,' Nige whispered. 'Shall I tell her you're asleep?'

Nina shook her head. She kissed Rosie lightly on her forehead and crept downstairs.

'Mills.'

'Bad day?'

'You could say that.'

'I won't keep you. I just wanted to let you know what

happened at the C.A.T. meeting.'

It was a couple of seconds before Nina grasped what she meant.

'They're planning to sabotage the Etape du Dales on Sunday.'

'What?'

Mills explained it was a cycle race over a route not dissimilar to the first leg of the Grand Départ. 'They're going to put tacks out to puncture the tyres.'

'When?'

'Not sure. I assume it will be Saturday night or early on Sunday. I thought I should let you know.'

Nina was confused. 'Surely the aim of this group is to keep the roads open for the Tour de France. Why are they interfering with this race?'

'They don't just want to keep the road open, they want to stop the race altogether.'

'OK. I'll let our researcher know. She may want to speak to you directly though.'

'That's all right, I'll be at the lab all day if she wants me.'

Nina thanked her friend and Nige took the phone back. He disappeared into the kitchen returning with another glass of wine.

'No really… I should…'

'Drink it. It will do you good. The kids are asleep and I haven't told you about my exciting day visiting the supermarket and mending the puncture in the paddling pool.'

The post-mortem report came back two days later. Nina was dreading it because she would have to visit the family again. She'd kept in touch by phone and the conversations had been difficult, with Mrs Rycroft cutting her calls short with a terse thank you.

The result of the PM was that the girl had died of her head injuries resulting from the fall. Nina looked through the report for any indication that she'd been wearing a cycle helmet. Towards the end there was a statement that injuries would have been less severe if she'd had a hat on.

'Ruby, it says here that Anna didn't have a helmet on when she fell. Is that right?'

'She wasn't wearing one when she was found. I assumed it had come off; she would've been wearing one on the road.'

Nina knew she could check with the family but there would also be CCTV somewhere along the route – a local webcam if necessary – to confirm it. And then she remembered how the boyfriend, Luke Drummond, had actually seen Anna in Hawes on the day they assumed she met her accident, literally minutes before it happened. He'd seen her talking to someone. He would know if she was wearing a helmet.

She re-read the report to see if the girl would have suffered but it wasn't clear. Spinal injury, broken limbs, head trauma and exposure, all contributing to her final demise. If there was an inquest it would all be spelled out for them and, since it appeared to be a road accident, it would be necessary. She would tell the family that they would hear more at the inquest and leave it at that. The last paragraph suggested that the smoothness of the tarmac surface, following the repairs made the previous year, may have caused the cyclist to veer off the road if she was going too fast and braked on the bend by the Buttertubs. Nina thought about the anti-Tour group: they would make a big deal out of a remark like that if it became public.

'Nina?' Ruby was looking across the desk at her. 'Can I ask about C.A.T.? I spoke to your friend, Dr Sanderson, and I passed on the information about "plan tack attack".' She giggled then apologised.

Nina did her best to supress a smile. 'I heard.'

'I wondered what was happening about it.'

'I guess they'll send a couple of patrol men out to check the road before the race.'

Ruby looked disappointed.

'We can't do anything until they do something we can prosecute them on, Ruby.'

'S'pose so. But when a group in Scotland did it, they tested the tacks for DNA.'

'If they find some I'm sure they'll follow it up. We'll have to wait until Sunday to find out.'

'Well, I'll be up there watching the race and if I see anything…'

Nina smiled at her and shook her head. They would miss young Ruby when her secondment finished in July.

The meeting with the Rycrofts went as badly as she'd imagined. Anna's mother asked her abruptly if she wanted tea when she arrived and sat down quickly when Nina told her not to worry. She explained the outcome of the PM to them but they had no questions for her. Then she explained that an inquest would be held.

'Do they suspect that it wasn't an accident?' Mr Rycroft asked anxiously.

Nina reassured them that it was simply to establish whether there were any reasons for the accident to occur. She was going to say "such as road conditions" but decided not to. Frank Rycroft reassured his wife, pointing out that the coroner wouldn't have released the body for the funeral if he wasn't satisfied by the postmortem.

Now for the other reason she was there. She waited with Mrs Rycroft in silence while her husband found contact details for Anna's old boyfriend. Nina rose awkwardly to receive the scrap of paper with Luke's phone number and asked when the funeral would be.

'It will be a private affair,' Mrs Rycroft said, pointedly. 'Just family.'

'Oh, I thought… I…'

'Just family,' she repeated as Frank led Nina into the hall and out onto the street.

'She's not happy with the way it was handled,' he confided apologetically. 'It's no reflection on you, Nina. She's more affected than she seems, if you know what I mean.'

'I understand.' Nina unlocked the car. 'I am so sorry.'

'I know, dear. I know.' He was looking anxiously up and down the road. 'I just hope she didn't feel anything. I can't bear to think of her lying there.'

'And don't worry about the inquest, Frank.'

'The inquest,' he repeated. 'Well, I suppose they have to get to the bottom of it all. At the present time we just want to see her put to rest.'

Nina drove to the main road before ringing Luke Drummond on his mobile. Nina hadn't spoken to him since Anna's body had been found and she wondered about his reaction to the news. It took him a little while to register who she was but when she asked him whether Anna had a helmet the day he saw her in Hawes, he was very sure of himself.

'Oh yes, she was wearing it all right. That coach guy was all over her, doing the straps up under her chin before he left. It was on her head while I was talking to her; before she rode off. Why are you asking?'

Nina explained that Anna was not wearing a cycle helmet when she was found.

There was a pause.

'Do they know what caused the accident?' he asked finally.

'No, we're waiting for the inquest.'

'I guess she took the bend too fast… or had to swerve for a sheep – you get sheep wandering along the road up there.'

Nina waited to see if he had anything more to say but he fell silent. So she thanked him for his help and hung up. Gratefully she pressed the "home" icon on the satnav and started the engine.

'Any news of how Jack is getting on in hospital?' Ian asked his son.

'He's still in a coma.'

'Are you going to visit him again?'

'There doesn't seem to be much point.'

'Why not? I thought his mum was glad you made that compilation of music for him.'

'Yeah but… it's hard, you know…'

Ian concentrated on the winding road towards Hawes. It had been his idea to drive his son around the route of the Etape du Dales on the weekend before the big day. He thought it would give him an impression of the challenges and help him pace himself. So far it had not been a success.

'Now up here the route becomes steeper until we reach

the main road in Wensleydale.' There was no response from Matthew so he shut up until they reached Hawes and turned towards Buttertubs.

'Can we stop at the top?' his son asked. 'I want to see where Jack came off.'

Ian drove steadily up the steep incline, imagining his son pedalling hard at the front of the pelaton. It was years since he'd led the group himself but the feeling never left him. He would be there, cheering Matthew on with pride. He changed up a gear as they reached the top and began the gradual descent to the lay-by by the swallow holes known as the Buttertubs. As he indicated to pull in, he saw there was already a car parked although there was sufficient space for them both, just.

Matthew jumped out and walked across the road to peer over the edge before examining the tarmac. Ian emerged more carefully and shut the car doors. Turning to look back he spotted the owner of the car on the other side of the road, apparently hammering a notice into the ground beside the entrance to the Buttertubs. Ian could just make out the words "Death" and "Cyclists". He crossed over to inspect the notice as the driver pulled away. It wasn't, as he'd expected, a sign warning motorist to be aware of cyclists. No, it was threatening cyclists and condemning the closure of the road during the Grand Départ in July. In summary, it warned cyclists that they were a target unless the road stayed open.

Matthew laughed when he read it. 'Some idiot,' he commented.

'D'you think it might affect the Etape du Dales?' Ian asked.

'Nah, they don't close the road for that.'

'I wish I'd got the registration of that car,' muttered Ian. 'Perhaps we should report it anyway. I can give them a description.'

'Don't fuss,' replied Matthew. 'He's probably just a crank.'

He uprooted the placard and flung it over the edge of the road. He watched, fascinated, as it fell; aware that Jack Bassett must have dropped in much the same way.

Chapter 9

Fridays were always hectic at Yardley Forensics with customers anxious to receive results before the weekend. For that reason, Mills ensured she had no commitments at the university and was always there in good time. This morning Alex had driven them in and they'd spent the entire journey arguing. He was installing a new software system that would track the samples as they came in, monitor their progress through the laboratory and produce customer reports ready to be sent out. Mills could see it would be a huge improvement but certain members of staff, particularly Glyn, were not impressed.

'I'm not saying it won't help our efficiency, Alex. I just think you could have handled it more diplomatically.'

'Do you?'

'Yes. I would have…'

'*You* weren't around, if you remember.'

'It was Easter, we have exams to set and mark!'

'I'm not complaining, Mills. I'm just saying that you aren't in charge of it and I am.'

'And I'm saying I would have discussed it with Glyn first.'

Alex let out a loud sigh. 'You always have to have the last

word, don't you?'

'Yes,' said Mills.

But he didn't laugh.

As soon as he'd parked the car, Mills jumped out and went straight in. She threw her bag on the desk and walked briskly down the corridor to find the lab manager.

'Glyn.'

'Mills.' He didn't look up from his paperwork. 'I need you to check this load of work. Your boyfriend is too busy with his so-called LIMS system,' he said pointedly.

'It must be such a nuisance with the change of software, Glyn. If there's anything I can do…'

'You can get these checked,' he said, waving at a pile of folders. 'They're already overdue.'

She carried the folders back to the office and set to work without even stopping for coffee. She didn't see Alex until lunchtime in the tea room.

'Where have you been hiding?' he asked as he made two mugs of tea.

'I've been busy finalising customers' results; urgent, overdue results.'

He didn't notice that she was irritated.

'Well, I'm ready to change over to the new LIMS software this afternoon.' He looked pleased with himself.

'Does Glyn know? Have you spoken to him?'

'Not yet. I will.'

'You better had, Alex. You better had.'

She took her tea back to the office and carried on with the paperwork. The pile of folders was diminishing and she hoped to get all the results out by the end of the day. But she hadn't catered for "LIMSgate" as Donna called it when she came running in, red in the face and panting.

'You better come quick. Glyn's going mental.'

Mills spent the rest of the afternoon acting as intermediary in a stand-off over installation of Alex's new toy. The laboratory manager refused to allow his computer to be updated despite Alex's protestations that the new system wouldn't work without his involvement. Alex stomped back to the office while Mills tried to reason with Glyn who was ready to hand in his notice. He would not be reasoned with until Mills admitted she would let Alex go before she would see Glyn leave his post as laboratory manager.

In the end Mills obtained Glyn's agreement that they would discuss the situation on Monday after he'd had the weekend to think about it. Mills promised to talk to Brenda, although she was unsure how fit her boss was to have such conversations. She wouldn't put it past Glyn to approach Brenda himself anyway. Meanwhile, for the rest of the day, they would continue to issue results to customers using email and paper copies.

Mills would have preferred to work late and travel home alone but without her own car she was forced to leave with Alex. He turned on the radio and neither spoke for the first half of the journey.

Eventually he turned to her with a smile and said, 'I thought we could go out somewhere tomorrow. What about a trip to the sea or for a long hike?'

'I'm busy tomorrow,' Mills replied. 'There's another meeting of C.A.T.'

'You can miss it for once – it's pointless, anyway.'

'I told Nina I'd go.'

It was a miserable evening and, not for the first time, Mills regretted asking Alex to move in with her.

Stephen Grainger had called a special meeting of the group because it was the morning of the day before the Etape du Dales. Muriel was fluttering around when Mills arrived, panicking about what to serve her guests.

'I'm making coffee,' she confided, 'but some may prefer tea.'

Mills shrugged and was relieved to see Arthur and Colin coming up the path. She'd grown quite fond of the old gentlemen and wondered why they'd become involved in the protest when they seemed so quiet and unassuming. Before long the group was assembled and as usual Stephen took command.

'I thought it apposite to get together before the big day tomorrow. As you know Catriona and I have planned a day of action to include a sit-down protest across the route.'

'Where exactly?' asked Mills, immediately regretting such a direct question. Everyone was looking at her.

'On the road to Buttertubs of course,' Stephen responded. 'At the very top, before the descent.' He looked around the room. 'Volunteers?'

He waited. And waited.

'What if it's raining?' Muriel asked.

'We'll get wet,' Catriona replied. 'We have to be willing to make sacrifices for the bigger cause. I'm behind you Stephen – all the way.'

Colin grinned across at Arthur.

'Arthur? Colin? I'm waiting.' Stephen sounded like an old-fashioned schoolteacher and Mills wondered what his occupation had been.

'Yes, we'll be there,' Arthur agreed.

Muriel made an excuse about having to go into town and

Mills remained non-committal. She was interested to see this protest but unsure whether she should be involved.

Stephen went on to outline another activity for the day. 'I know some of you don't approve...' He was looking at Muriel. 'But I will be using tacks as a means of slowing down the cycles as they descend Buttertubs.' He looked up to see their reaction. 'It will be a warning to those who are still insisting on closing the roads for the Grand Départ.'

Muriel opened her mouth then closed it again, giving Mills a pleading look. She remained silent. Arthur and Colin exchanged glances but said nothing.

Catriona straightened her posture and made supportive noises. 'I think Stephen is right to take a firm stand,' she finally remarked.

As soon as the meeting was over, Mills went back home to let Ruby know what was planned.

'Thanks Mills, that's great. 'I'll tell the local team to keep a look out and collect them up. If there are any tacks out on the road, we'll find them and get DNA evidence.'

Ruby arranged to meet two uniformed officers early on the morning of the Etape du Dales to drive with them to Buttertubs Pass. She wanted to be around if they found any tacks on the road – it was important they didn't destroy valuable evidence. It was only the second time she'd been so far north in the Dales and she was struck by how remote it seemed. As they drove, the chatty policeman called Alan informed her that there would be hundreds of entries to the race that day and it would be quite a sight to see when the pelaton arrived. He was a keen cyclist himself so was full of information about the race. His mate was less vocal but the two men were clearly amused by the task and made endless jokes about the job until she felt compelled to join in.

'Hopefully we'll be able to *pin it* on someone,' she said as she climbed out of the car.

It was a bright day but a strong breeze blew the clouds in front of the sun, forming shadows that moved quickly across the road. It was still early, the place was deserted and they were able to wander about on the road without interruption from traffic. At first it looked as though it had been a wild goose chase but once they applied a systematic approach to the search, Ruby let out a scream.

'Here's one!'

The officers were sceptical, suggesting that just one could be a coincidence. But once she had her eye in, Ruby spotted another. The black tacks, which were easily lost on the tarmac surface of the road, had rounded heads, like those used in upholstery. The quiet officer was holding one between his fingers for her to examine until she reminded him that she was going to try to get DNA evidence from them. He produced an evidence bag and the rest of the tacks, twenty in all, were sealed in the bag for forensics.

While they were packing up, a car had stopped.

'Can I help you?' the constable asked as the occupant wound down her window.

It was a woman in her thirties or forties. She looked nervously at him. 'Is it about the accident?' she asked.

'Accident?'

'The lad knocked off his bicycle. I saw it, yesterday.'

'Yesterday?'

'I was coming the other way, from Hawes, and as I turned down, I saw him falling off. The car just kept going. I told him to report it but at the time he said he was all right. I offered to act as a witness if he needed me to. I think there was some damage to his bike.'

'But the lad was OK?'

'Yes, he didn't seem hurt, just shaken.'

The officer stepped back as if to let the woman drive off but Ruby ran forward.

'May I take your name and a contact number?' she asked.

After the woman had driven off, Ruby told her colleagues how there had been a similar accident on the bend. This near miss might be relevant, she explained. They went down to Hawes for a late breakfast then took up position back at Buttertubs to watch the race. The two officers had been ordered to split up when the race was passing through: one monitoring the ascent while the other watched the descent. Ruby chose to go down to Buttertubs and the afternoon passed off without incident. She wished she'd made a better choice when she found out later that Alan had single-handedly prevented a pair of protesters from blocking the road.

'They suddenly sprang out from the crowd, just after the leaders had gone through,' he explained. 'An unlikely pair. He was in baggy shorts and she was dolled up as if she were going to church.'

'What did they do? Lie in the road?' asked his partner.

'No. They just stood there waving their arms about. Nearly knocked one bloke off his bike.'

'How did you sort them out?'

'With the help of some irate spectators who dragged them physically back onto the grass verge and held them down until they'd all gone through. I was more worried about *their* safety.'

'They'll be members of C.A.T. and they're the people

responsible for the tacks,' she informed them.

As soon as she was back in the office, she rang the woman driver who had witnessed the "near miss". She asked her for a few details, including a description of the car that had knocked the bike over and of the cyclist. The details were not terribly helpful: the vehicle was a white car or van, the cyclist was a male of average height and average everything else. He was dressed like most cyclists in leggings and a jersey that was red and white.

Ruby sat staring into space. The office was empty. It was Sunday, no-one else was about and she wasn't on duty. Three accidents involving cyclists, all occurring at the same place within a few months. Was it really a coincidence? If it wasn't, then her job was to make the connections. She took out her A4 lined notepad and began a list of what she knew – her "intel". There wasn't much but she now knew that accident number three involved a white vehicle. The page below "accident two" remained blank for a while. If only the lad could remember anything about how he came to fall over the edge, now he was out of his coma. Then she remembered that there had been witnesses to his fall: the photography group. And the girl, Tamsin, had left them two pictures of the accident.

Ruby pulled both pictures on the screen and peered at them. They were blurred but it was possible to make out the cyclist and an indistinct smear of white that was presumably the car. *Another white car.* If only she had a clearer picture of it. Was it possible that the vehicle might be in another photograph taken before the impact?

Her call was answered by the young woman called Tamsin. She was puzzled at first but soon agreed to send Ruby the rest of her photos.

'I did give you the best ones,' she offered when Ruby told her she was looking for more evidence of the accident taking place. 'Like the really good action shot with the bike up in the air and the lad…' She giggled nervously. 'I was going to enter it into a competition but I saw in the paper that he's in a coma so it didn't seem right to use it.'

'Thanks, anything else you have on the road before or after the accident would also be good.'

'Have you asked the others?'

'Others?'

'The other people in the group. There were seven of us all together, although my friend was having a ciggy at the time so she won't be any use.'

'Do you know how to contact them?' Ruby asked, her heart beating faster.

'I can give you the leader's number – she'll be able to tell you.'

Mills was dreading Monday morning. She was terrified that Glyn would stick to his guns and demand that Alex leave the lab. Brenda was still in hospital and so she'd been unable to tell her about the situation. In some respects that had been a relief. The atmosphere over the weekend was almost unbearable and she only relaxed when Alex announced he was going to watch the bike race on Sunday. He didn't get back until late and she assumed he'd stayed out deliberately. It was a mutual decision to travel to work in separate cars that morning.

Donna reported that Glyn hadn't arrived for work by nine, which was unheard of. Either he was making a point of being late or had decided not to come in at all. Mills waited for a phone call or email by way of explanation but nothing happened. Alex kept demanding to know if he should go ahead but Mills continued to stall him.

'You can't fiddle with his computer without him being here.'

'I can,' he replied.

'I know you can but you mustn't,' she ordered. 'I don't want you to do anything until I've spoken to Glyn.'

She sent her lab manager an email, begging him to get in touch and tried his number again. It was all she could do. Unopened mail delivered by courier lay on her desk so she pushed "LIMSgate" to the back of her mind and concentrated on the packages. They contained a variety of samples, all destined for forensic analysis. She could hardly pass them on with no lab manager to sign the chain of custody, so she went through them to see if she could initiate any of the jobs.

Most were routine DNA analyses that could be given directly to Donna in Glyn's absence. One or two were more complicated and she pushed those to one side. The last one was from a firm of forensic consultants for soil analysis, a job for Timothy and his mass spectrometer. He'll be pleased, she thought, as she flicked through the paperwork and made a few notes. The samples had been assessed by the prosecution but it didn't say where the work was done. Curious, she turned back to the start of the report and read it thoroughly. It was a serious rape case where soil from the defendant's trousers had been compared to a sample from the crime scene and the conclusion was that they were a match. However, the defence was now asking Yardley Forensics to repeat the analysis using their more sensitive instrumentation as a check on the work.

Her heart was pounding as she finished the final page of the document. She felt there was a strong possibility that Sydney Green had been the prosecution's analyst and she knew he could get things wrong. Jack had confirmed that. It was even possible that these samples were the very ones she'd discussed with Jack last year. She had not only been sent the original material from the crime scene and the defendant's trousers but also examples of material from the locations where he worked as a gardener at weekends. There were four soils in individual bags. How she wished she could discuss it all with Alex. Instead she prepared a long and detailed set of instructions for Timothy that would ensure nothing was left undone in the analyses of these very important samples. Time was of the essence, with the trial beginning in the following month.

When the message finally came back from Glyn later that day it was short and to the point. He wasn't going to show his face in the lab again until Alex had apologised. Then, and only then, would he discuss implementation of the new system. Mills forwarded the message to Alex's email with firm instructions to send an apology immediately. She was expecting Alex to object and was willing to suffer a public argument with him if necessary but she would win, she was determined. The mood she was in, if she had to choose…

To her surprise, Alex sent Glyn a grovelling email and was rewarded with a grudging acceptance. Their lab manager would be back in post tomorrow.

'Thank you for that,' Mills offered.

'No problem,' Alex replied. 'The man's a prick but we need to install the system.' He grinned and walked off.

Chapter 10

'They said it was OK to visit; now you're out of intensive care.'

Matthew was standing awkwardly at the end of Jack's bed, clutching a box of sweets.

'They've got you up,' he added unnecessarily.

'Yep. They told me I've got to get moving.' He pointed to his legs. 'If you can find a wheelchair we can go down to the café.'

Matthew was gone for several minutes. He reappeared with a small upright wheelchair – the sort that had to be pushed, Jack noticed as he shuffled himself into it. The corridors were long and he wished they could go faster. It was embarrassing to be so completely under his friend's control and he was pleased to be parked at a table, finally, waiting for coffee and something to eat.

'You look so much better,' Matthew remarked when he returned. Neither had much to say.

'Well, I *was* in a coma.'

'I know. It must've been… well, really…'

'I'm fine.' Jack finished his doughnut and took a sip of coffee. It was still too hot to drink. 'Tell me about the race. Mum said you'd replaced me.'

Matthew was biting his lip. 'It was all right.'

'So where did you come?'

'Somewhere in the hundreds, I'm not sure until they publish the times.'

'Respectable then.'

'Yes… but *you* would've been faster.'

'No doubt.'

'Still, at least you're OK now.'

'Yes.'

Jack concentrated on his drink, looking around, watching an old man in a dressing gown moving slowly past with a Zimmer frame.

'Thanks for the music, by the way. Mum said you'd done it for me.'

'That's all right. They said it might help. Did it?'

'Don't know. I can't remember much, not even the accident.'

'Not how you came off?'

'No.'

'Was it the road surface? It hadn't rained for a while; I thought it might have been slippery on the bend.'

'I've no idea.'

'You heard about the mix-up with the bikes?'

'Mum told me. She says they haven't found mine. I'm gutted.'

'At least you're OK. You can always get a new bike.'

'Oh yes?'

'Sure. UNYCYCLE won't see you without something to ride, will they?' Matthew sounded faintly contemptuous.

'Why are you so sure?' Jack wondered if he'd heard something.

'Well, you're their blue-eyed boy, aren't you? At least you

were Will's.'

'Well he's not around anymore, is he?'

'That's true. Maybe you'll be slowing down now.'

'What's that supposed to mean?'

'Nothing.'

'No, go on. Get it off your chest.'

People were turning to stare.

'Nothing, I'm sorry. I didn't mean anything. The important thing is you're OK.'

He stood up, went to the wheelchair and pulled it from the table. Soon they were making their way back to the ward along the endless corridors. Matthew pushed Jack to his bed and watched him struggle onto the chair before returning the wheelchair to the corridor before he left.

Mills spotted Matthew in the main entrance to the hospital. She concluded he was probably visiting Jack Bassett now news he was out of the coma was spreading through the university. Wondering whether it was appropriate for her to drop in while she was there, she first made for the information desk to seek out the Oncology Centre. She was directed to the Mowbray Suite, where Brenda was seated quietly staring out of the window. Mills gently tapped her shoulder. Brenda's face transformed into a smile that strangely accentuated her pale skin.

'What d'you think of the scarf?' she asked, patting the brightly coloured silk that was knotted at the back of her head. 'Not really me, is it?'

It wouldn't have suited Brenda's previous dishevelled and chubby appearance but now it gave her an artistic look.

'It's different,' was all Mills could muster.

The room was bright and cheery but there was no hiding

why Brenda was there.

'I've finished the chemo for today,' she said. 'D'you want something to drink? I'm parched.'

'I'll get them,' Mills offered.

Once they were seated together in comfortable chairs at a low table with their coffee, Brenda explained that she liked to rest for a while before leaving. Mills offered her a lift but she had a taxi arranged in a couple of hours. So they sat and chatted, Mills avoiding any discussion of work until Brenda insisted she tell her how things were going.

'How's that Alex of yours getting on?' she asked as she raised the mug with an unsteady hand.

'Fine.' She wanted to keep upbeat. 'He's putting in the new software we discussed – to manage the work better.'

'Good. Good. And it's all going well?'

'Yes, fine.' Mills sipped her coffee slowly.

'Everyone else OK?'

'Yes, fine.'

'I don't suppose Glyn was too impressed with changes to the computer system. It took him ages to get used to the old one.'

'He's fine with it, really.'

Brenda bent to replace her mug on the table, positioned it carefully with both hands then straightened up again slowly. 'That's not what he told me.'

Brenda was looking directly at Mills. 'He sent me an email at the weekend offering his resignation.' She was waiting for a response but Mills couldn't answer. 'I didn't see it until Monday – wasn't feeling too good. I told him not to be so daft and to get back to work immediately.' She was looking at Mills throughout. 'I understand Alex apologised and now they're the best of friends?'

'I'd hardly say that... but it is back to normal again.' Which was more than *her* relationship with Alex was, she thought.

'You must talk to me, Mills. I'm not incapable, just incapacitated but it's here...' she indicated her chest, 'not there.' She tapped her forehead.

'I'm sorry, Brenda. I didn't want to worry you.'

'I know. But it's more worrying when the first you hear is a message from your lab manager threatening to leave!'

She smiled wanly as she leaned back in her chair. Her headscarf was slipping, exposing the few fine hairs that remained on her scalp. Mills gently repositioned it and Brenda took her hand.

'You know I rely totally on your good judgement, Mills. I know what a good scientist you are.'

'But not a good manager?'

'All in good time.'

They sat together chatting until Mills felt she should let Brenda rest.

'I thought I'd pop in to see one of my students. He was in intensive care for several weeks but he's on the neurological ward now. I might just say hello.'

'Was that the lad that came off his bike?'

'Yes, Jack Bassett. Did you read about it?'

'It was a peculiar thing – a strange coincidence. I heard that my niece's body was found when they were searching for his bike. She'd been missing for months. She was a cycling enthusiast too.'

'I'm sorry. Were you close?'

'Not really. I've never bothered with family. But I was touched when Anna said she was doing a cancer charity race. She was going to do a race in the Pyrenees this year.

It was for me, if you see my meaning.'

'Wow.'

'I was cross I couldn't make the funeral but I wasn't allowed to miss one of my sessions here.' She smiled at Mills. 'You tell your student he is lucky to be alive.'

She said goodbye to her boss and promised to visit soon.

'And next time, come to the house. I don't like you seeing me in here,' she complained.

'But it's so conveniently close to the university, Brenda,' Mills joked as she left.

There was just time to drop in to see Jack Bassett before the end of visiting time. She was given directions at the front desk and soon located the ward. She spotted him sitting alone beside his bed, reading a magazine. There would be no harm in wishing him a speedy recovery.

'Hi, I just wondered how you are doing.'

He appeared quite surprised to see her and stared for a few seconds before responding.

'Dr Sanderson! Hi!' He smoothed his fringe down and pulled his dressing gown tightly round him.

She stood awkwardly, wishing she'd brought something for him. 'I heard you were getting better... out of the coma...'

'Yes.'

'Do you know when you might be out of here?'

'No. They don't tell you much. They've operated on my leg but it isn't right and they've threatened another op before I leave.'

'I guess you won't be back in lectures soon then.' Mills hoped she sounded upbeat.

'No, I doubt it'll be before the end of term.'

'That's a shame.'

'It's the cycling that gets me. I'm not sure how the leg will affect it, you know.'

Mills thought of Brenda's words. He was lucky to be alive. Not something she felt she could say directly. 'Still, at least you're still in one piece.'

'Yeah.'

There was an awkward silence. It was now or never, thought Mills. 'D'you remember helping Professor Green with some soil samples last year,' she began. 'You were preparing them in the lab when I spoke to you.'

'I did some work with the microprobe but he never used it. It didn't matter – I was still able to write it up for my project in the summer.'

'Why didn't he use your results?'

'Don't know.'

'Did anything ever come to trial?'

'He wouldn't have told me.'

'So you don't know what happened?'

'No.'

She waited but he was looking down at the cycling magazine beside him on the bed.

'Well, I'd better be going Jack. Glad you're on the mend.'

Then as she left, she thought of something else. 'I guess Matthew was here to see you today?'

'Yes… he was.'

That's good, thought Mills as she left. At least one disagreement has been resolved.

'Stephen Grainger is waiting downstairs,' announced Hazel.

Nina and Ruby looked up simultaneously.

Nina jumped up and made for the door. 'It's OK, it's for

me.'

'What's she seeing him for?' Ruby asked as the door slammed. 'He's the guy from C.A.T.'

'Is he?' Hazel didn't seem interested.

'Is it about the demonstration on Sunday?'

Hazel was busy on her keyboard. 'Nope.'

Ruby knew not to push it with Hazel but realised she was being teased when her colleague looked up and grinned across the desk.

'If you must know, he pushed a reporter off the pavement into the road when she was trying to get a story from him about his protest. She's charging him with assault, or at least she wants to.'

'What's he like?'

'Pompous, arrogant, thinks he's better than everyone else.'

'He's been a local councillor…'

'And involved in a load of good causes, no doubt.'

'So what will Nina do?'

'Persuade the reporter that it was all a misunderstanding and ask them to shake hands and make up.'

The phone on Nina's desk interrupted their discussion and Hazel resumed her work while Ruby, who was nearest, lifted the receiver and began searching for a pen.

'Could you repeat the name… how do you spell that… thanks… what? Righto. See you later.' She put the phone down. 'Wow!'

'What now?' Hazel asked. 'Have they found the Ripper at last?'

'No, they've found Jack Bassett's bike!'

'Oh, well I suppose Jack will be pleased, whoever he is.'

'No, you don't understand. His bike was stolen. That's

why they couldn't find it!'

'Is this the one they were looking for when you... you know...'

'Found Anna Rycroft's body? Yes, it was. And now it's turned up in Bishop Auckland.'

'Don't tell me – one of the light-fingered lads from thereabout.'

'Apparently he came across it when he was travelling back from a day out in the Dales. He saw it lying by the side of the road at Buttertubs Pass and popped it into his white van meaning to hand it in but forgot all about it.'

'Yeah, right.'

'Until he was stopped by the traffic police for having no insurance.'

When Nina reappeared, Hazel insisted on Ruby retelling the story of the stolen bicycle. 'And what was the lad's name?' Hazel was laughing so much she could hardly speak.

'Jo Richie,' replied Ruby. 'I don't see why that's so funny.'

'Well he won't get rich doing such daft things, will he?' she commented. 'So what's happening to him?'

'They've taken a statement. He won't change his story. He says he found it at the weekend although we all know it must've been weeks ago. He's got previous for joy riding but unless we can disprove his story they can't charge him.'

'Any thoughts?' Nina asked her.

'Nope.'

'Did he definitely say it was Sunday?'

'Yes. Adamant.'

'But you were up there most of the day, weren't you.'

'I suppose.'

'What time did he say he found it?' asked Hazel.

'Not sure,' Ruby replied. 'But I bet he doesn't realise what was happening up there on Sunday.' She had picked up the phone and was ringing the number on the paper she'd used to make notes. 'Hi… Yes… Is he still there? Good. Ask him what time it was when he found the bike. No… I'll tell you later. Let me know what he says then I'll explain.' She sat listening for a while. 'OK… Oh, by the way – was there much damage to the bike? Was it punctured? And the back one?' She made a few notes, thanked them and said she would expect their call. Then she put the phone down and scribbled on her notepad.

'Why did you ask about the damage?' Nina asked idly.

'Just wondered. I thought it might explain how the rider came off and over the edge.'

'And did it?'

'Not really. Apparently the front wheel was bent sideways – to the right. I would have expected the opposite.' She showed them the sketch she'd made. 'If he was coming into the bend and flew off there, the bike must've been stopped like that.' She pointed to a rough drawing of a bike with the front wheel turned to the left.

Neither Hazel nor Nina made any comment. Ruby shrugged and put her notepad away.

Hazel was asking Nina about her interview with Stephen Grainger when the phone finally rang. Ruby was ecstatic. 'Lunch time? What does he call lunch time? That's not very specific… Never mind. There is no way he could have taken it then. Why? Because I was there watching the cycle race. There were over nine hundred competitors going past over that time. I think we would have noticed if a van had stopped and picked up a bike.'

She grinned at the others while listening to the response then put the phone down. 'They think he may change his story when he hears that.'

Hazel waited until Nina had left the room before asking Ruby how she was getting on with her work on the anti-cycling group. 'After all, that's what you were seconded to us for,' she said, pointedly. 'You seem to be too preoccupied with your phone calls about a bicycle to discuss the leader of C.A.T. with Nina, despite the fact she has just been talking to him.'

Ruby sat biting her lip, not looking up from her desk.

'You've only got another month with us, Ruby. You need to focus.' She stopped because the girl looked as if she was going to cry. 'How far have you got with your report?' she asked more gently.

'I've made a list of the members – I was going to ask Nina if I should include her friend, Dr Sanderson.'

'I wouldn't think so.'

'OK. Well I've given a note of each of the meetings she attended and what was planned. There's the protest on Sunday too… and the tacks. The tacks are being analysed for DNA.'

'Are they? And what are you hoping to glean from that?'

'I'm pretty certain it'll show that Stephen Grainger put them on the road.'

'We'll need his DNA but if it does match, he'll be brought in to tell us why he was sprinkling the road with tacks that could cause a serious road accident.'

'That's why I was interested in the bicycle, Hazel. I wondered if Jack Bassett's accident was caused by a puncture.'

'And was it?'

'No. Both tyres were still inflated.'

'Concentrate on your job, Ruby. If you'd told us you wanted DNA from Stephen Grainger, Nina could have politely requested a sample when he was here. You're going to have to be pretty sure of your facts before we can invite him in again.'

Hazel walked out of the office without another word, leaving Ruby to reflect. She had been going to tell Hazel about the photographs that had come through from the group who saw Jack Bassett's fall but it didn't seem a good time. Most of the shots were out of focus or out of sight of the road but several were quite interesting. The best were still the photos Tamsin had taken. All that could be seen in the one where Jack had come off the road, was a white blur but the photo taken prior to that showed Jack still on his bike and a small white something to the left. Even better, although the previous shot showed only the back of the bike, there was more of the white thing although it was still out of focus. However she expanded the picture, nothing made it any clearer.

Normally she would have immediately asked Nina or Hazel for help but after the lecture she'd been given about keeping to her own work, there was little she could do about it. She closed down the files and returned to her report on C.A.T. Finally the call came through telling her that Jo Richie was now admitting that he picked the bike up on the day Jack Bassett had his accident. Ruby thanked the caller and carried on with what she was doing. It was none of her business, she told herself bitterly.

Chapter 11

It was a beautiful evening so Mills suggested a walk. She hoped it would be a chance to discuss their situation and clear the air. Alex had hardly spoken all week. There had been plenty of opportunities but the atmosphere had been difficult at work and at home.

'I'm thinking of going to visit my parents this weekend,' Alex announced as they arrived at the river.

They stood side by side on the bridge, watching the water moving slowly.

'That's nice,' said Mills.

Alex was always asking her to come with him to Gloucester to meet his parents. She'd found excuses on several occasions but this time it didn't sound as though she was invited.

'Yes. I thought I'd take Friday off, if that's OK?'

He knew she always went into the lab on a Friday, so he definitely didn't want her to go with him.

'Yes, that's fine.'

'I'll be back Sunday night.'

As they walked back up the hill, Mills was not unhappy with the arrangement. It would relieve the pressure to remain polite when she wanted to shout at him for being so… so… difficult. She looked forward to having the place to herself for a few days and she had already planned to spend some time at the weekend working on the data from the rape case – if Timothy had produced some results for her by then.

As they arrived back, Alex shot inside before she had noticed Muriel waving from her window. Mills obediently went to her neighbour's gate as the front door was flung open.

'Have you got a minute, dear?' Muriel asked.

'What's the matter?' Mills went into the hallway.

'It's about Stephen,' confided Muriel. 'Do you think he's getting a bit… you know… over the top?'

Mills considered him far more than "a bit" over the top but replied, 'Perhaps.'

'I've heard he was asked to talk to the police.' She looked at Mills, waiting for a response.

'Why?'

'I don't know but I expect it was after the protest on Sunday. Did you go?'

'No.'

'Nor did I; nor did Arthur and Colin. We thought it a bit extreme. I don't mind the petitions and stuff but demonstrations? That's certainly not my style.'

'I was rather concerned about the tacks,' offered Mills.

'So were we! I said to Arthur it could cause a nasty accident. We didn't think that was a good idea at all!'

'So did Stephen go ahead anyway?'

'We don't know, dear. There will be another meeting on Saturday but to be honest, I wish I hadn't agreed for them to meet in my house.'

'I know,' Mills said sympathetically.

'You will come on Saturday, won't you?' begged Muriel.

Relationships at Yardley Forensics were now on an even keel again. Glyn appeared to have enjoyed his stand against progress, albeit a short one, and was beginning to get to grips with the new system as Alex introduced it to the laboratory. The rest of the team members were happy to learn and there was a definite buzz around the place as they helped each other with the new formats. Mills left them to it and went to the mass spectrometry lab.

Timothy had worked really hard to analyse the soil samples as quickly as possible and offered her a set of preliminary results, if she wanted to take a look. She let him explain to her what he'd done to achieve what she wanted, thanked him and went back to her office with the file. Timothy had done an excellent job. The results were neatly collated so she could see the values for individual elements at a glance. Now she had to find some patterns. Fortunately the day stretched before her with no interruptions, except when Donna asked if she wanted a sandwich brought back from town.

Hours later Mills had a pile of paper in front of her, none of the tables showing any patterns. She needed to clear her head and stopped for a hot drink. In the tea room, Glyn was telling Donna about the new LIMS system and how it would save him quite a lot of time.

'Of course, it takes a while to get it set up but once it's in place… well!'

Mills smiled. She chatted to them as she made a mug of tea and told Glyn how she was trying to match the soil samples.

'I'm not having much success with the pattern

recognition system that Alex installed,' she complained. 'Nothing matches anything, although the prosecution's data suggests that two samples are a close match.'

'Sometimes it depends on how much you have of the majors,' Donna said.

Glyn was looking at her in surprise.

'What d'you mean?' Mills asked.

'When I was doing my project at uni, I divided everything by the major elements and it all fell into place. Mind you, I was looking at atmospheric pollution.'

Glyn laughed.

'No. You're right,' said Mills. 'If it's worked before.'

She rushed back to the office with her tea and began again. It had been the answer when she had soil from the North York Moors analysed for iron at the university three years ago. It was past six o'clock when Alex disturbed her concentration.

'I'm off.'

'OK.' She didn't look up until the door had slammed.

'I hope you don't mind me bothering you again,' Mills asked Jack as she placed a paper bag containing a box of chocolates on his locker.

'No, it's kind of you to bother.' He was seated beside his bed, fully dressed.

Jack's appreciation made her feel guilty. She knew she wouldn't have bothered to visit a student in hospital if it wasn't that she was seeking information for herself.

'So, how are you feeling?'

'A bit better, thank you Dr Sanderson. They said I should be going home soon.'

'That's great. I guess you'll need to rest your leg for a

while.'

'Yes, although I've got exercises the physio gave me... and I've got to come back to outpatients to see them each week.'

'Well, it's good news anyway.' She perched on the edge of his bed. 'Jack, when I was here before we spoke about some work you were doing for Professor Green but I wasn't sure about the details. It was a rape case?'

'Yes it was.'

'He did the mineralogical examination?'

'Yes and I did some microprobe work.'

'You said that didn't confirm his findings.'

Mills waited while he seemed to consider his reply. 'Let's say we weren't in perfect agreement.'

'Do you still have your results?'

'Yes, of course. It was my summer project. There'll be an electronic copy in the department.'

'Great.'

'Can I ask *you* something, Dr Sanderson?'

'Sure.'

'When I asked Mum about my accident, she said no-one knew how it happened but now she says they've found my bike so I thought there must be some information. Mum doesn't want to know. But I do.'

'I expect she'd rather forget about it. It must have been pretty worrying when you were unconscious for weeks.'

'How can I find out d'you think?' He knew exactly what he was doing. It was common knowledge she worked with the police on occasions and had friends in the force.

'I'll see if anyone knows if it's being investigated formally,' she offered. 'Although I imagine it won't be if no other vehicle was involved.'

'I keep trying to remember what *did* happen but it's still a complete blank.'

Mills went straight to the university to dig out Jack's project report from the files. It was fifty pages long and took ages to print out but she was going to read it from cover to cover and needed a hard copy. By the time she'd driven back to Harrogate it was nearly the end of the working day and Glyn was beginning to panic.

'I've got three sets of results to report and the computer's frozen. Where's Alex?' he demanded.

'I don't know,' Mills admitted.

'I thought *you* were supposed to be here,' Glyn muttered before storming down the corridor.

'I *am* here,' she replied to herself, but she knew she'd let them down.

With a sigh she went to Timothy's lab.

'Dr Sanderson, did you want me to repeat any of the samples?' he looked at her anxiously.

'No, it's all right, Timothy. I wanted to ask a different sort of favour. I know you're clever with computer software and I wondered if you could help.'

His face lit up. 'Of course.'

'Glyn's computer has frozen. Would you mind taking a look?'

He followed her to Glyn's office and she left them working together on the problem. She had a couple of files to check before the results went out that afternoon and there was no time to start on the rape case. As soon as Timothy came in to inform her that Glyn's computer was working again, the lab manager arrived with more reports to check.

She finally packed up at seven and by the time she

reached Mossy Bank, Alex had eaten and gone out. The next morning he was up early, packing.

'I might as well go straight off from Harrogate this evening,' he said as he was leaving the cottage.

'How long will it take for the lab to do DNA testing?' Ruby asked Nina as soon as she came into the office.

'Let me get in the door, young lady.' Nina laughed as she took off her cardigan and hung it over her chair. 'Now. What DNA tests?'

'The tacks? They went to forensics days ago.'

'Were they marked urgent?'

'I don't know. Uniform sent them off.'

'D'you know where they sent them?'

'No.' Ruby looked sheepish.

Nina laughed again as she picked up the phone, pressed a few digits and waited. 'Hi there!' There was a pause then she said, 'Have you been sent some tacks for DNA analysis? Ruby wants to know.' Nina listened for a while then thanked the person at the other end. 'I don't know, Mills. I think Ruby might know something – she's been in touch with them. You could ask her but I think it's being handled by uniform.'

She put the receiver down. 'That was Mills Sanderson. Yardley Forensics has them, they're looking at them now.'

'When will we know the results?'

'That depends whether they can find any DNA and, if there is, whether there is a match. I assume there won't be – unless Mr Grainger has been in trouble before, which I doubt.'

'So that will be the end of it?'

'Not necessarily. It rather depends on whether you give

us a good reason to check his DNA.'

She switched on her computer and began typing. 'By the way, Mills asked about the bike that was taken from the accident. Apparently the lad is a student of hers. She might ring you.'

Ruby nodded without saying anything that could be construed as taking an interest in something outside her "proper" work. Hazel had made her views quite plain. She clicked on the new photographs that had come in from the group members but none were as clear as Tamsin's. She labelled them all and moved them into a folder she'd named "white car", unsure what further action she could possibly take.

The call from Mills came in the afternoon when Hazel and Nina were in their weekly meeting with DI Turner. It was the news she was expecting: DNA had been found on the tacks but no match.

'It's really kind of you to let me know so quickly,' she said.

'No problem. Nina said you were waiting for them… and to be honest I thought you might be able to help *me*.'

'Really?'

'Yes. It concerns a student of mine who had a cycling accident. He fell and was unconscious for a long time. He's much better now but can't remember how he came off the road.'

'You mean Jack Bassett?'

'That's right! You know about it then?'

'Yes, I joined the search for his bike. Someone took it from the road – it's just been found.'

'Do you know if there's to be any follow up? Jack is keen to know what happened; *he* can't recall anything about it.'

'I honestly don't know. *I* think there should but… well… it's not the first accident… in fact there's been one fatal one, his and a near-miss, all at the same spot.'

'Buttertubs?'

'Yes.'

'What do Nina and Hazel say?'

Ruby wanted to say that they told her to shut up and get on with her job but she knew better than to do so.

'Have you spoken to them about it?' Mills persisted.

'Oh yes. I've told them. I'm concentrating on C.A.T. though'

'OK then, Ruby. I'll keep in touch over that. There's another meeting with Stephen Grainger tomorrow. I'll let you know what he's planning.'

'Please, especially if there's anything that we can use to bring him in for DNA testing.'

'Ah, I get you. You're talking about tacks.'

Mills was up early to continue her calculations, even though she hadn't gone to bed until after two in the morning. Without Alex to distract her, she was finding the work exhilarating and sat with her calculator as she filled a bowl with cornflakes. She was still in her pyjamas when Muriel knocked.

'You *are* coming to the meeting?' she asked.

'Of course.' She looked at the clock. Ten minutes to get ready. 'I'll be round in a tick.'

Stephen had begun lecturing the troops already. They were sitting in a circle, all eyes on their leader. Mills knew for a fact that neither Muriel nor Arthur agreed with anything he proposed and she was pretty sure Colin felt the same. He smiled weakly as she sat down between him and Arthur on the sofa.

Stephen was reporting on progress with the petition, which now carried two hundred and sixteen signatures. He clearly considered it a great success despite the fact it had taken nearly a year to achieve and most of the names were probably friends and relatives of the five other people in the room. No-one enquired what was to be done with it since, with only a few weeks to go it would be unlikely to change anything. There was no way C.A.T. would close the roads or stop the race but no-one had the guts to say it to Stephen's face. Mills was tempted but thought it unwise to draw attention to herself.

Surprisingly Stephen did not seem to register the general lack of motivation that had permeated the group and continued to extoll the value of direct action. Suddenly he became very serious, leaning forward to confide something to them – something they must all agree to treat in absolute confidence. He looked round the circle as they nodded solemnly, one by one. Pausing for dramatic effect, he then confessed to them that he'd got up before dawn on the morning of the Etape du Dales and sprinkled carpet tacks over the short piece of road beside the Buttertubs. Mills hoped he couldn't detect the rosiness she felt in her cheeks. Muriel looked at her, Arthur looked at Colin and Mills looked at her hands.

There was silence. Catriona was the first to speak: she congratulated him on his courageousness. Arthur cleared his throat before asking what effect the tacks had had. *He* hadn't seen anything in the press.

'It was merely a trial,' Stephen replied. 'To see that it could be done. On the day of the Grand Départ we will need to pool our resources and cover a much larger extent of road. We should cover the entire stretch on the ascent to Buttertubs and all the way down the other side.'

He pulled a sheet of paper out of the file on his knee. 'I've calculated that if we cover about half a mile each, we'll have a good chance of bringing the race to a halt.'

He was met with silence.

'I've sourced a good supply of tacks so you'll not need to buy them; best not draw attention to ourselves.'

'Must've told them he was carpeting a mansion,' Colin muttered under his breath.

'We'll need a lot of tacks to cover half a mile,' observed Arthur.

Catriona sprang to Stephen's defence. 'No, no. The idea is to sprinkle them lightly, so they're not easily spotted.'

Colin straightened up in his chair beside Mills. 'You do realise that there will be security in place for the race. They had tacks on the route of the Tour de France last year. I read they're going to ensure it doesn't happen over here.'

It was the first he'd spoken up and he had everyone's attention. 'It will be a serious matter if anyone gets caught.'

'That's why we have to be careful.' Stephen was referring to the paper in his hand. 'Of course there are important things to address. For example, wear a mask so you can't be identified.'

Arthur sniggered. 'That's going to look a bit suspicious isn't it?'

Mills looked across at Muriel whose face was a mixture of horror and disbelief.

'If anyone wants to leave C.A.T. they'd better go now,' boomed Stephen, 'because I only want supporters in my team.'

Muriel looked across at Arthur and Mills but no-one

moved. As she told Mills afterwards, 'It was a bit difficult since I was in my own house. I could hardly walk out and leave you all, could I dear?' Mills was in an equally awkward situation because she wanted to keep in touch with C.A.T.'s activities, so she remained seated. In fact no-one budged and the meeting went on for another hour with Stephen proposing various protest actions in the run up to the event, including wearing garish T-shirts bearing a range of slogans including "The cycle race is a disgrace", "Save the environment, stop Le Tour" and "Cycle races are ruining the Dales".

As the meeting drew to an end and Muriel started collecting the teacups, Stephen raised his hand.

'By the way,' he said. 'I've booked Fremington village hall for a public meeting at the beginning of next month. I thought it was time we got the public on our side. It's on the seventh of June at two o'clock. Don't forget now. I expect everyone to be there with me on the platform.'

Chapter 12

Mills spent Sunday immersed in Jack's report. It was lengthy and much of it was detail of the methodology but there was a large section containing tables of results. He'd used the university microprobe, a sensitive instrument for obtaining precise information on the mineralogy of the soil samples. She made notes as she went along and, by the time she stopped to make a sandwich, she had a good understanding of the work. She was impressed with the way he'd carried out the final analysis and felt confident in the results.

A small section in the introduction referred to previous work using microscopy to evaluate the mineralogy. She guessed this must be Sydney Green's preliminary analysis. Jack had avoided any discussion of these results in his report but when Mills compared the two sets of data, they did not agree. The samples were divided into two groups labelled A and B. Mills assumed this was to avoid identifying them as being from a police investigation. She guessed they were from the crime scene and from the defendant – if they did indeed relate to the rape case. Certainly there was very little soil in group B, suggesting they were the scrapings from the defendant's trousers.

Green's evaluation of the mineralogy had suggested that the two groups had identical mineralogy but Jack's report completely repudiated that conclusion. He stated that there was no indication that the two groups were from the same location.

Mills put the report down and considered her discovery. Since she was providing evidence for the defence, she should be privy to this previous work but she'd only seen what was provided by Professor Green and it contained no mention of Jack Bassett's report. Had his supervisor been so unhappy with the work that he wouldn't consider it valid data? Perhaps it arrived too late? No, it was dated months ago. She was tempted to call Green to confront him with it but she needed all her results before she could do that. Turning on her laptop, she began tabulating Timothy's results and compiling diagrams to demonstrate her findings. To her delight, not only could she show that her results agreed with the microprobe but her chemical values were confirmed by Jack's mineralogical data.

It was five o'clock when she closed the laptop and went to the 'fridge where a pre-packed salad and a bottle of chilled white wine were waiting. Ordinarily she would have told Alex all about her successful day but then he would've been around and they'd have been discussing it together as she worked. But tonight she was happy to sit alone on the sofa munching her way through the layers of lettuce and various salad items straight out of the plastic bowl with no-one to tell. She would've asked Alex whether he thought it a good idea to confront Sydney Green, if he'd arrived back that evening but, contrary to her expectations, he'd not appeared by the time she went to bed.

*

She woke early next morning, her head full of numbers from the rape case. She opened the door into the garden and ate her cereal with her back against the stone wall. She would normally delight in the warmth of the sun but this morning Alex's absence weighed on her. He was obviously making a point in not informing her he'd not be back last night but she wasn't certain what it was. As usual, she avoided the question and turned to her work. As she drank her tea, she decided that she was going to confront Professor Green with Jack's report. It was always quiet in the lab on a Monday morning and they wouldn't miss her for the few hours she would be at the university.

She left so early the roads were still quiet and she was on campus as the cafeteria opened. She studied her paperwork while sipping a cappuccino before searching out Sydney Green. Always one to be punctual, he was seated in his office on the top floor, apparently marking exam papers. He was clearly irritated to be interrupted but made an effort to make her welcome, offering her a seat.

'What can I do for you?' he asked amiably enough.

Typical of him to think he can help *me*, she thought, but smiled back at him.

'I've been reading Jack Bassett's dissertation,' she said.

He looked puzzled.

'The one he did last summer,' she added.

He nodded slightly and sat back in his chair but said nothing.

'Well,' she began, 'I've been studying Jack's findings. It was a good piece of work.'

'Thank you.' Did she detect sarcasm in his tone?

Mills resisted the temptation to respond and continued the speech she'd prepared on the way in. 'I couldn't help noticing that his results didn't confirm your own.' She knew she had to be diplomatic but hoped he'd respond by agreeing with her and making some excuse for his own failure to get it right.

'Jack is a good student, otherwise I wouldn't employ him to help me out, but he's learning and he's no expert in this area.'

'I wondered if the soils were part of a criminal investigation?'

'They might have been. I don't remember.'

He was looking a little agitated and Mills backtracked a little. 'I suppose in those circumstances you would have to present your own conclusions – not Jack's?'

'Naturally.' He looked at her quizzically. 'Is there a reason for all these questions, Dr Sanderson?'

She couldn't say without asking him directly if the samples were from the same rape case that her lab was working on. Instead she shrugged and said she had an interest in forensic investigations.

'Oh yes,' he said pointedly. 'I hear you do a bit at that laboratory in Harrogate. Is that Yardley woman still running it?'

Mills bristled. 'She's actually off sick at present and I'm standing in for her.'

'Oh.' He appeared amused. 'Well, good for you!' he said sardonically.

Mills struggled to remain calm. 'I'd better be going over there now and make sure everything is running smoothly,' she said, making for the door. 'We've got an important rape case that we're working on.' She left before he could say anything.

There was still no message from Alex when she checked her mobile. She drove faster than usual with the radio blaring and swore at anyone who got in her way even though, fortunately, they couldn't hear her. The lab was calm and everyone was fully occupied. When she went down the corridor to find a coffee, she was surprised to meet Alex coming the other way.

'Where have *you* been?' he asked. 'I want your signature on this order for the additional software we need to keep Glyn quiet.'

She looked at him and waited.

'What?' he asked.

'Where have *you* been? You didn't come back last night!'

He was looking round to see who was listening. 'I told you.' He was almost whispering. 'I said I'd come straight in this morning.'

'No you didn't. You said you'd go straight off from here on Friday.' She was sure he'd said he'd come back Sunday night.

'I think you're wrong.'

'I don't think so.' She left him standing in the corridor and went to make a coffee. It wasn't important, she told herself. It didn't matter. Perhaps she had got it wrong. There was no way to prove it, one way or the other.

When she returned to her desk, the requisition form for the software was lying there. She signed it and put it in the internal mail, despite the fact Alex was working only a few tens of metres away and he'd intimated it was urgent. She cleared her desk of all her other pending files and started work on the final report for the rape case. It wasn't the most important or pressing piece of work but she was determined to make a good job of it to show Sydney Green that she was a better forensic scientist than him. He was another one with a big ego.

During the afternoon her concentration was broken by a call from Newby Wiske. She'd been so engrossed in the case and distracted by Alex's absence that she'd completely forgotten to ring Ruby to report on the meeting of C.A.T. on Saturday.

'I don't want to push you but I need to keep my report up to date,' Ruby said.

'No problem. I should be apologising to you.' Mills went on to describe what had happened at the meeting.

'Did everyone agree to distribute the tacks on the day?' Ruby asked.

'Far from it. I don't think many of them, if any, were very keen – except Stephen and Catriona, of course.'

'We should try to dissuade them if we can.'

'Stephen Grainger has organised a public meeting on the seventh of June. I can't imagine the public will approve of such tactics if they're discussed then.'

'Perhaps we can make sure it is, Mills.'

'Will you be coming then?'

'I don't see why not. Hazel says the aim is to keep the public, and the cyclists, safe, so it would be better to prevent them using the tacks in the first place.'

'That's true. I'm sure there will be another meeting before June the seventh. I'll be in touch and we can arrange to meet beforehand if you like.'

'That would be nice. I liked the bit of Swaledale I saw when I came before, even though the first trip was rather scary.'

'Scary?'

'Yes. It was when they were searching for Jack's bike.'

She seemed to hesitate. 'It was me that found the body.'

'The body?' Mills repeated.

'Anna Rycroft. She was the fatality. She'd come off her bike at Buttertubs as well but she didn't survive the fall. They said it was an accident.'

'That's a coincidence.'

'I don't think it is. I've seen Jack's bike and I don't think the damage is explained by an accident. I've got some photographs taken at the time and...' She stopped suddenly. 'I shouldn't be telling you all this, should I?'

'I'm sure Nina won't mind. I know her. She'd want me to know what happened. Go on.' Mills tried to keep the excitement out of her voice.

'I've been given some digital photos taken by a group who were near Buttertubs at the time Jack came off his bike,' Ruby explained. 'I can see another vehicle; it's blurred but it's definitely there.'

Mills thought of Alex. 'Look, we've got someone here that works on digital things. If you can send them, we can have a look to see if we can enhance them.' She had no idea whether what she was saying was correct.

'Would you?' Ruby sounded delighted.

'Of course. Email them over and we'll take a look.'

Her heart was racing when she came off the phone. Perhaps they would be able to see what had caused Jack's accident after all.

Normally Mills would have rushed off to tell Alex but this afternoon she contained her excitement and made the finishing touches to her report for the defence in the rape case. It was after five when she'd finished but the solicitor was still at her desk.

'Hi, Rajani here, how can I help?'

Mills explained that she'd finalised her findings.

'And is it good news?'

Mills took a deep breath before explaining briefly what they had done to test the samples.

'OK. So you've tried to match the major elements and the trace elements?' Rajani asked. 'The prosecution were only looking at the minerals, weren't they?'

Mills was impressed at how quickly the woman had understood the process. 'Yes and that can be very misleading.' She hesitated, unsure how honest to be with the solicitor.

'I found the whole report from the prosecution rather confusing I'm afraid, Mills.'

'To be honest I have concerns about it. The report doesn't say who did the work but...'

'I can find out for you.'

'Thanks. Anyway, our analysis is much more detailed and it fails to indicate any match between the defendant and the crime scene, although there are similarities between the soil on the defendant's trousers and the soil from the gardens where he works.'

'That's very useful, Mills. Can you email me the report and I'll get back to you with what we need for the court presentation.'

'When will that be?' Mills asked, thinking it would be months away.

'The middle of next month. Are you going to be free?'

'Free?'

'We'll need you to appear as our expert witness.' She paused. 'That is all right, isn't it Mills?'

Mills felt a sour taste in her mouth. She'd never appeared in court before, Brenda always dealt with that, or Glyn.

She'd been on the training course but there had never been an opportunity to put what she'd learnt into practise. 'Yes,' she answered without confidence. 'Yes, of course.'

It had been a long day and not a particularly pleasant one. She looked for Glyn to ask about acting as an expert witness but he'd gone and the lab was empty. Even Alex had left for the day although they were usually the last two people in the building. She gathered her belongings and made for the empty car park, half-hoping she would find the cottage empty when she got home. The air was close and humid, the queues out of Harrogate slow and the car was unbearably hot after sitting in the sun all day. She was soaked in sweat, her hair was beginning to frizz and she looked a mess by the time she got home. One word from Alex and she knew she'd let fly at him.

Inside the cottage was always cool, there was even a breeze blowing from the back door, accompanied by the gentle scent of lemons. She threw her bag down in the hall and walked through to the kitchen where Alex was busy at the stove. Through the window, her chequered tablecloth fluttered on the tiny garden table.

'There's time to have a shower before dinner's ready,' he said without turning round. 'I've put some wine in the 'fridge.'

Mills wanted to say she didn't want alcohol but went upstairs without responding. When she returned, Alex was sitting outside with a glass of beer. He came into the kitchen when he saw her and began serving the meal.

'I did my lemon chicken,' he explained. 'I thought it would go with salad. I got some ice-cream for after.'

She carried her plate outside and sat waiting for him to join her. He was busy pouring a glass of wine for her, which she accepted gracefully.

'So, how was your day?' he asked, once he was settled and they'd begun eating.

A morsel of chicken stuck in her throat as she tried to swallow and she took a sip of the wine. It was cold and sharp – it tasted expensive, she thought. There was still a lump, even though her mouth was empty and tears began welling up. She put her knife and fork down, unable to eat.

'Not good, eh?' Alex was grinning. 'The day or the chicken?' he asked.

Mills shook her head, unable to talk. It had been a horrible day from the meeting with Prof Green right through to the news that she was to appear in court as an expert witness. It wasn't Alex's fault. He was obviously doing his best to patch things up.

'Eat your salad before it gets cold,' Alex joked.

They finished their meal without speaking but by the time he brought her favourite ice-cream, she was feeling more like her old self. He poured her another glass of wine and chatted about his visit to his parents. They were pleased to see him but he'd wished that Mills had been there too, he said. They insisted she goes next time. They really wanted to meet her. She smiled at him.

'And I'd like to meet your folks – your dad, I mean – and Fiona, they sound like fun.'

'Fun?'

'Have they said any more about coming up for the Grand Départ?'

'No.' She really didn't want them coming to stay and hadn't actually mentioned it to them a second time.

'You should ask them again.'

When they were washing up Alex told her there had been

a phone message for her. 'Nige rang. He said your Head of Department wants to see you. Tomorrow afternoon at two, he said.'

She went to the phone to find out what it was about.

'Nina? Is Nige there? He says Professor Cole wants to see me?'

'Yes, he told me you'd probably ring to find out. I'm afraid he knows no more than that. D'you think he's going to offer you a full-time post?'

'I don't know. Unlikely but I can't think what it can be.'

'Why don't you pop in for tea afterwards? I'll be around from five.'

'OK. And I want to ask you about appearing in court. You've given evidence lots of times, haven't you?'

'Yes, several times. What's it about?'

'We've been analysing soils in a rape case and I've been asked to appear for the defence.'

'Hmm.'

'What d'you mean, hmm?'

'Nothing. Rather you than me though.'

'Nina!'

'Sorry, let's talk tomorrow. I might be able to give you a few tips.'

When she came off the phone, Alex was there with coffee and a sort of apology. He had originally planned to return on Sunday but had changed his mind and thought he'd told her before he went – if he hadn't, he was very sorry. She forgave him and they seemed to be back in a better place. She wanted to tell him about Sydney Green and the court appearance and the photographs that Ruby wanted enhanced but all that could wait until they were at work.

*

It was such a lovely day and everything had seemed so much better in the morning but Mills was still curious about why the Head of Department wanted to see her. She'd taken the precaution of dressing up a bit for the sake of the meeting. It took longer than usual to find a parking space and by the time she'd walked what seemed miles in her posh, uncomfortable shoes, she was only just on time.

She was shown into the large, carpeted office by Professor Cole's personal assistant. As the door shut behind her, Mills was surprised to see that the Head wasn't alone.

'You know Professor Green?' he asked indicating the figure seated on the low sofa next to the coffee table.

'Yes.' The reason for the summons was becoming clearer.

'Please sit down.'

There was nowhere else to go but next to Sydney Green.

'The reason I invited you in today is because Sydney has come to me with a problem.' He looked from Green to her and back. 'He has a bit of a conundrum, you might say. I'm sure it can all be sorted out amicably.'

Please get on with it, thought Mills, wanting to know what the man had been saying about her.

'Sydney, as you know, is a well-respected forensic analyst and he tells me he's been working on a very high-profile case.'

High-profile? Mills waited for him to come to the point.

'It turns out that his work for the police has proved, without doubt, that they have arrested the right man and he remains on remand until the case comes to court in a few weeks.'

Professor Green could clearly contain himself no longer. His face was turning bright red. 'Yesterday I received a call from my contact on the case to ask me to review a report submitted by the defence.' He glared at Mills. 'You know who wrote that report, Dr Sanderson, don't you?'

'If it is a report issued by Yardley Forensics yesterday and concerns two sets of soils in a rape case, then yes I do. I wrote it.' She was ready for him.

The Head intervened. 'You do realise that this is a very awkward situation for the department. We appear to have two members of staff working on the same material, coming up with opposite views of what the data mean.'

'Yes,' replied Mills.

'When the trial comes to court, only one version will be believed. One piece of work will be discredited.'

'Of course,' Mills hoped she sounded confident.

'Whichever way it falls, the university will be discredited.'

'No. My work does not come from the university,' Mills argued. 'Only Professor Green can discredit the university.'

Green looked at the Head with a horrified expression. 'You're not going to allow her to speak like that?'

Professor Cole looked perplexed and sat for a moment looking at his hands. When he looked up again he appeared to have reached a decision. 'I have no alternative, I'm afraid. Dr Sanderson, I am going to have to suspend your activities at the university until this all blows over.'

Chapter 13

'That's what he said: "until it all blows over". At the time I couldn't think of anything to say that didn't sound like whinging. Green is out to get me and the Head has found a neat way of resolving the conflict within the department.'

Mills had left the university and found Nige at home looking after Tomos and Owen.

'I suppose the press could have a field-day with two academics slogging it out in court,' he said, 'but they might do that yet.'

'Well, thank you, Nige. That makes me feel a lot better.'

'You could be doing us all a favour by exposing how useless old Sydney is.'

'I don't really want my first appearance as an expert witness to be under any kind of spotlight,' admitted Mills. 'I'm really nervous about it.'

'Nina will help you there. She's got all the moves when it comes to court appearances.'

When Nina arrived home, she went through the court procedures and gave Mills a practice run while Nige made a pot of tea and looked after their offspring.

Mills took the opportunity to ask Nina about Anna Rycroft. 'She was the missing girl you began your family liaison work with, wasn't she?'

'Don't remind me. Dreadful, the way it ended.'

'I hear they found her body at Buttertubs.'

'Down below. She'd fallen from the road... with her bike.'

'What caused the accident?'

'They don't really know. The inquest just said accidental death.'

'Is that what they put when it's a road accident?'

'Not necessarily – they can put traffic collision as a cause. Why the interest?'

'Oh, I was just talking to Ruby and she told me how she'd found the... how she'd...' Mills looked across to see if Rosie was listening but she seemed absorbed in her colouring book.

'Yes, she fell over her body.'

'It must have been horrible for her.'

'It was. Anna's body had been lying there for months and had been almost destroyed by animals...'

'Can we change the subject, girls?' Nige interrupted her.

'Of course.' Nina poured Mills another cup of tea. 'So how's Alex?'

'He's fine,' replied Mills. 'He spent the weekend with his parents in Gloucester.'

'You didn't go?' Nina looked surprised.

'No, I had work to do. This rape case, you know.'

'Oh, right. But you are going to meet them eventually?'

'Of course.'

'And he'll meet your dad and the famous Fiona?'

'Yes but I'm too busy at the moment.'

'Don't worry about the court appearance, Mills. I'm sure you'll do fine. Remember, an expert witness is there to help the court – not one side or the other. And remember, always address your answers to the decision makers: the judge and the jury, not the lawyer.'

Ruby had been quick to send Mills the photographs of Jack's accident. They were in her inbox, attached to an email, thanking Mills profusely for offering to look at them and explaining that she'd selected the best two but there were more if she wanted them. The most dramatic shot showed Jack as he flew from his bike, the other was taken prior to that, when he was on the edge of the road. As Ruby had pointed out in her message, there was a white blur that could be another vehicle – possibly the vehicle involved in Jack's accident.

When Mills showed the pictures to Alex and asked if he could do anything with them, he snorted.

'Do you have the originals?'

'What d'you mean?'

'Presumably these have been transferred from a camera onto someone's computer and then sent to you?'

'Yes.' She thought for a second. 'In fact they may have been sent from a computer to Ruby and then on to me.'

'I need the original memory card if you want me to work on the image.'

'What difference will that make?' Mills was thinking it could take a while and the owner may not even have kept the shots as they were rather blurred.

'Then I know I'm working with the uncompressed data. Who knows what changes will have been made by the computer software as the pictures were transferred.'

He waited while Mills replied to Ruby's message, asking if she was able to get the memory card from the camera owner.

'What's it all about anyway?' He perched himself on the edge of her desk.

'Jack Bassett's accident.'

'Who's he?'

Mills explained why she was interested in the white vehicle, if that's what it was.

'You think it caused his accident?'

'Ruby seems to think so. I'm not sure why.'

'Well, I'll see what I can do, although it's not really my area.'

He went to leave but Mills called him back.

'Alex, I've been working on the rape case data; I meant to talk to you about it before but... well, anyway, I've got some good results that I need to plot out so the defence can show them to the jury. They've got to be big enough to be clear.'

Alex looked puzzled.

'I can plot them,' she assured him. 'But I thought you might know the best way to present them... a special software package or something.'

He smiled. 'I'm sure I can produce something that will be a credit to Yardley Forensics,' he said with a wink. 'Just give me the data and tell me what you want.'

After he'd gone, Mills brought Ruby's photos back onto the screen and stared at them. It was fortuitous that there were photographers there when the accident happened but it seemed to her that the best witness was Jack Bassett – if he could only remember what happened.

Mills was late home and it was her turn to cook. She rushed in to find Alex peeling onions. Before she had a chance to say sorry, he gave her a kiss and told her that Muriel had called. She really wanted to talk to Mills.

'You go round, I'll do the bolognese. Knowing her, I'd better hold off the pasta. You could be gone a while.'

Mills knocked gently on Muriel's door, hoping it would be a quick chat. Perhaps she just wanted to give her some scones or show her a new piece of knitting, if she was lucky.

'Mills, love, come in. Did your young man tell you I'd popped round?'

'Alex, yes.'

She stepped inside, hesitating in the hall but Muriel insisted she went through to the tiny sitting room. To her surprise, Arthur was there.

'Hello young lady.' He waved a hand from where he sat.

Muriel indicated to Mills to sit down before she began. 'Arthur and I have been having a serious chat about C.A.T.'

'We're not happy,' he added.

'No.' Muriel went on. 'We're getting a bit anxious about the big day.'

Mills nodded in agreement.

'The thing is,' Arthur said. 'I'm happy to object to something in a peaceful manner. I've written to the paper and encouraged my friends to do the same but I do draw the line at vandalism.'

'The tack business,' explained Muriel.

Mills nodded again, trying to decide what strategy to adopt.

'Muriel suggested we asked you what you thought,' Arthur said, looking at her expectantly.

'Well,' she began slowly. 'I don't think it would be a good

idea to do anything that might cause injury to anyone.'

'Exactly!' said Arthur. 'That is what I told Muriel. We're not vandals. Didn't I say that?'

'You did,' she agreed. 'But is it vandalism if it's in a good cause?'

'I suppose you have to follow your conscience,' said Mills. 'But we can tell Stephen what we all feel.'

'And Catriona; she's with Stephen on everything.' Muriel was looking at her eagerly.

'Which leaves Colin,' Arthur said.

'How does he feel about it?' Mills asked.

'I haven't spoken to him yet but I suspect he'll be with us. He's a very quiet and reserved chap, as you've probably noticed. It was his wife who did all the talking for them both. He hasn't been the same since she passed on, poor soul.'

Mills wasn't clear who was the poor soul, Colin or his dead wife. Colin Norton was certainly unlikely to be spreading tacks in a gung-ho fashion unless forced to do so.

'May I suggest we confront Stephen with our reservations at the next meeting?' Arthur was struggling to his feet. 'I've got to get back to heat up my dinner.'

Mills and he left together. Arthur lived down the lane but as he turned to go he patted her arm and thanked her. 'Muriel gets a bit stressed over these things and I feel guilty because I talked her into joining the group. I wish I hadn't got involved at all now.'

She let herself into the cottage where the smell of cooking drew her to the kitchen. Alex was outside setting the table.

'Eating *al fresco* again tonight?' she called.

He signalled to her to add the spaghetti to the pan of boiling water.

Soon they were enjoying the last of the sunshine as they ate dinner.

'Are you in the lab tomorrow?' Alex asked. 'Or at the university?'

Mills wound the pasta round her fork while she planned what to say.

'I'm not going in for a while.'

'Why not?'

'I'm banned.'

'Banned?'

'Not exactly banned – more suspended, I suppose.'

Alex looked across at her, his fork midway to his mouth. Mills watched a piece of spaghetti sliding slowly back onto his plate.

'What *have* you done?' He sounded quite shocked and Mills wondered what he imagined she might have been suspended for.

'Nothing,' she replied indignantly. She would have to explain because the case could impact on the laboratory. 'The rape case – the one I asked you to help with diagrams – guess who's working for the prosecution?'

Alex shook his head. 'No idea.'

'Sydney Green.'

'And he is?'

'Professor Green – the soil scientist at uni. Jack Bassett does work for him. I saw his report. It's rubbish...'

'Hold on, calm down. I still don't see why you've been suspended. Is it to do with the case?'

'The Head doesn't think I should bring the university into disrepute by challenging Prof Green's results.'

'And are you?'

'Yes.'

'Oh dear.'

'What? You mean I shouldn't appear for the defence?'

'No, but I can see it's awkward for the department.'

They finished their meal in silence, Mills unable to understand how Alex was always willing to see both sides to any argument.

'How long are you suspended for?' Alex finally asked.

'Until the trial is over.'

'Well, that's not so bad, is it?'

'They haven't suspended Green – they obviously don't believe I am right.'

'Are you?'

Mills picked up the dishes and stormed inside without another word.

Without her lecturing to distract her, Mills was able to finish the diagrams for the court case in a couple of days and Alex helped her prepare them on large stiff boards. They looked impressive and Alex told her so.

'Not that I know what it means,' he laughed.

'I can explain…'

'No, please don't worry. I'm sure it's all good stuff but I'll leave the chemistry to you.'

Mills rang Rajani to let her know the boards were ready and was surprised when the solicitor said she would come down to collect them herself.

'It'll be interesting to see where the work is done,' she said.

It was late afternoon before Rajani appeared, dressed in a simple but beautiful sleeveless cotton dress, carrying an expensive-looking handbag the size of a small briefcase. She offered a tiny hand and introduced herself.

Mills felt clumsy and awkward beside her. She offered her tea but she said a glass of water would be fine. Mills rushed down the corridor to fetch the water and bumped into Alex.

'Who's your visitor?' he asked.

'It's the solicitor, she's come to pick up the diagrams.'

'Shall I come and say hello?' he asked.

'Why? What for? No.'

He looked disappointed. Clearly he'd been captivated by her visitor's sophisticated appearance.

Mills gave Rajani a detailed description of what the diagrams showed and, once again, was impressed by how quickly she picked it up. Rajani gave Mills a breakdown of what would happen at the trial but no advice on how to present her evidence.

'Is there anything I need to know about the way to present my analyses?' she asked.

'No, Mills. It is important that you are not influenced in any way by me or any of the defence team. It's your expert opinion that the court want to hear.' She took a few sips of water. 'There is just one thing. You wanted to know who had prepared the report for the prosecution.'

'Oh, I know. Professor Green.'

'How did you…'

'I recognised the data; it was work that a student of mine had done.'

'A student?'

'Well, his work wasn't in the report.'

'I think you'd better explain.' The solicitor looked worried.

Mills described how she'd realised it was Green's work and went on to tell her about the meeting in Professor Cole's office. When she'd finished she could feel her cheeks burning. 'It won't affect the trial, will it?'

'I hope not. Can you put what you've told me in an email please?' Her tone was less friendly now and Mills wondered whether it was all going to be a disaster.

Jack was hoping that the ward round this morning would result in him being discharged. He was bored with hospital and wanted to go home. It took all his effort to get up and dressed, but he was ready by his bed when the consultant arrived with a couple of students, hoping he looked fit enough to be discharged. As usual, he was asked how he was feeling.

'Absolutely fine,' he replied.

'How's the leg?'

'Fine.'

'No pain at all?'

'No.'

'And in yourself? Back to your old self? You're not feeling tired?'

'No,' he lied.

The consultant inspected his notes. 'I've got the results on your latest blood samples. We've got an interesting problem here that we haven't been able to get to the bottom of,' he said. 'When you were admitted we noticed that the viscosity of your blood was higher than normal, that's one reason we put you on the heparin injections to avoid any clotting.' He was addressing the students now, who were looking at him with interest. 'Now we seem to have a different problem: anaemia.' He turned back to

Jack. 'Which is why I asked if you were feeling tired.'

Jack didn't answer. He was busy thinking. Thickening of the blood rang a bell. It was something in connection with the injections Will had given him.

'I'm keeping you in until we can trace the source of the anaemia. We'll get more bloods off you today and I'll book you in for some routine tests as a matter of urgency.'

When the group had gone, Jack went to his iPad and searched for blood viscosity and road racing. The connection was clear; a particular drug called EPO, used by cyclists to enhance their performance, caused thickening of the blood or increased viscosity. The effect of this was the potential to form clots resulting in a heart attack. Jack hadn't asked what Will had put him on; he didn't really want to know at the time, it was simply a "booster" which he had assumed contained banned steroids. It seemed possible that the syringes contained the banned drug EPO.

Jack spent the hours before lunch researching the drug erythropoietin, as EPO was called. He studied the risks, anxious to find out how long it stayed in the body. Not long, apparently, but the effect on the red blood cells lasted a lot longer. There was no way he was going to inject himself with it again but he really didn't want to tell the medical staff what he'd been doing. His last dose must have been over three weeks ago now, so his blood ought to be getting back to normal.

He hardly touched his food when they brought it. His head was buzzing and he felt exhausted. Climbing onto the bed, he curled up, relieved that he could drift off without anyone bothering him.

His mother appeared in the afternoon, clutching a plastic

bag full of the usual assortment of clean clothes and snacks.

'I brought some clean underpants,' she informed him – and the rest of the ward.

'Thanks, Mum.'

'Well, sit up. Did they say when you can come home?'

He shook his head. 'More tests.'

She sighed. 'What tests? I thought the leg was mending well. That's what they told me. I've been getting everything ready for you coming home. Now what's happened?'

'Some blood thing.' His head was muddled and he just wanted to rest back on his pillows.

She stood up and marched out of the ward, saying she would find someone.

Jack dozed until she was back, looking concerned.

'They said there's been a sudden drop in your red cell count and they need to find out the cause. When I asked what it might be they said they didn't know but could be some internal injury!'

There was panic on her face. Now she was worrying him.

'It's probably nothing. The food in here, that's all.'

'Don't be silly Jack.'

She rang her husband on her mobile and told him the news. Jack could tell that he was trying to calm her down but she was in tears when she said goodbye. A nurse came in to find out what was happening and took her outside. Jack could see them in animated conversation. He watched his mother leave and the nurse came back, explaining that she thought it best that he had some rest. Jack thanked her and shut his eyes.

He must have been asleep for only a short while because when he woke there were still visitors in the ward. He spotted Matthew Watson at the nurses' station. He was talking to a male nurse, who shook his head, and Matthew went to turn away. Jack waved and when his friend saw him, he spoke to the nurse again. This time the man nodded and Matthew came in.

'They said you were asleep and shouldn't be disturbed.'

'I was.'

'I can go if you're tired.'

'I'm tired but stay. I want to ask you something.'

Matthew sat down beside the bed.

'It's about Will and the training.' He didn't know how to say what he was going to divulge. 'About how Will was helping me… my performance.'

Matthew looked anxious.

'You were right… about me taking something. Will gave me something. Once a week. An injection of something.'

'What?'

'That's the thing. I don't know exactly. But I have an idea. I thought it was steroids but they've been saying here that my blood was thick when I came in and that started me thinking. I looked it up and I think it was EPO.'

'No!' Matthew looked horrified. 'I knew it. I bloody well knew it.'

Jack thought he was going to leave but he remained seated. His expression was angry but slowly his face relaxed. Perhaps Matthew knew their rivalry no longer mattered, not now his leg was knackered.

'The thing is, Matt, they say I'm anaemic now, which is like the exact opposite of what EPO is supposed to do. D'you think it's like a withdrawal effect?'

'Don't know. Is there anything on the internet?'

'No.'

'Have you told them that you've been on EPO?'

'Of course not.'

'Shouldn't you?'

They were interrupted by a porter arriving with a wheelchair. He'd come to take Jack down for a CT scan. It wasn't a complete surprise to Jack – he'd read that anaemia could be an indication of cancer.

Chapter 14

Mills was surprised to receive an email from Matthew Watson requesting a meeting when she was next at the university. She replied that she wouldn't be around for a while, suggesting instead that he called her mobile. His response indicated that it was personal so perhaps he'd better leave it until she was in. Not wishing to ignore him, particularly after the business with Jack Bassett, she offered to meet him in the cafeteria at the university. Anyway, she knew he visited Jack and thought she might find out if he'd remembered anything about his accident.

Matthew was sitting at a table with other students from his class but when he saw her he jumped up and came over immediately.

'I'm sorry if it's put you out. I know you said you were busy.'

'Not busy, Matthew, just not on campus much at the moment.'

'I heard we've got someone taking over the rest of your course.'

'Yes. I'm sure he'll be fine.'

'But you will be setting the exam questions?'

This took Mills aback. She hadn't thought about how

long the suspension might last.

'Did you want a coffee?' she asked. 'I'm getting myself one.'

'You're OK,' he said.

She fetched her cappuccino and settled down at the table opposite him. 'So, what's the problem?'

'It's not a problem, not really. Just a question. I wondered if you know when Will Humphreys is coming back?'

'Will?' She recalled her conversation with Spence. 'His department should know.'

'No they don't, or they won't tell me.'

'I haven't spoken to his colleague since last year, when Will was in France. Presumably he's been back since then?'

'No.'

'Really? Is he on a sabbatical?'

'I don't know but I need to speak to him. It's about Jack.'

'Does he know about his accident?'

'I don't know but I need to ask him something.'

'I don't suppose I can help?'

'No, not really.'

'You could try emailing; he probably looks at his university messages.'

Matthew nodded.

'How is Jack? Is he out of hospital yet?' Mills asked.

'No. He's got a problem with his blood. Anaemia.'

'I'm sure they'll be able to treat that quite easily.'

'Can they?'

'Of course. A few iron tablets and he'll be back to normal.'

Matthew looked a little happier as he thanked her for the chat and joined his colleagues at the next table again.

Mills was finishing her coffee when she spotted Jake coming over.

'I heard you were not going to be around for a while. What's going on?'

She explained her suspension to him as he sat with his mouth open.

'You're not serious? Old Green has had you suspended?'

'Shush, I don't want the students to know!'

'You won't keep it quiet for long,' he warned.

'Well, please keep it confidential for now at least.' A thought occurred to her. 'Do you know what's happened to Will Humphreys?'

'No, what?'

'I mean do *you* know where he is?'

'No. Is he missing?'

'He went to France last summer and when I spoke to someone in his department, he thought he might be staying away to avoid speaking to the university sports body about suspected doping in his cycle team.'

'Really?'

'And he hasn't been seen since.'

'A bit extreme. Perhaps *he's* been suspended as well!'

He had been joking but Mills wondered whether there might be some truth in it. She planned to email him herself to find out. Her curiosity aroused, she also thought she might visit the hospital again, as she was already "in the area".

Jack's mother had arrived punctually at visiting time, as she always did. She quizzed him about how he felt and what they'd done to him while she tidied the contents of her carrier bag into his locker.

'Green vegetables, that's what they say for anaemia, isn't it? Spinach and all that? I brought some apples and dates. I thought perhaps dates would be good.'

She sounded only slightly stressed but Jack knew she would become increasingly distraught with time.

'They said they'd sort out the right treatment when they find out what's causing it.'

He didn't tell her that the consultant had listed a number of possible causes of his low red cell count, none of which were very pleasant. He'd quizzed him about any illnesses he'd had in the past and treatments he'd received.

'And you've not been on any medication in the past few months – or even years?'

Jack had assured him there had been nothing prescribed, failing to mention that he'd had subcutaneous injections of EPO every week for the past year. The man had scratched his head and declared himself temporarily "flummoxed". The word had amused Jack, even in his weary state. Flummoxed, he'd repeated to himself until he dropped off to sleep.

He was beginning to tire of the investigative tests, resenting the intrusion into his rest. His day now consisted of lying on his bed and sleeping until the porter came to collect him for another tour of the hospital. They were giving him medicine but he didn't feel much better for it yet and the phlebotomist appeared for blood samples increasingly frequently.

'I want to find a doctor to speak to,' his mother was saying. 'Your father said I should find someone in authority and demand to know what is going on. I won't be long.'

Good luck with that, Jack thought. No-one knew what

was going on. Of course he ought to tell them about the EPO but that only explained the thickening of his blood. It had nothing to do with the anaemia.

His thoughts were interrupted by a female voice asking him how he felt, once again. Thinking it was another nurse, he was about to give a blunt response but, opening his eyes, he was confronted by his lecturer, Dr Sanderson.

'Sorry, did I wake you?' she asked.

'No, no.' He struggled to sit up.

'Matthew told me you were still here, so I thought I'd drop in to see how you were.'

'Not bad.'

'He said they were sorting out something before they released you. Did he say anaemia?'

'Yes. It's a pain.'

'You must feel quite faint.'

'Yes.'

'In fact, I wondered if that might have been the cause of your accident. Maybe you became dizzy.'

'No, I can't remember but I'm sure it wasn't that.' His red blood cells would have been higher than normal when he was out on Buttertubs. He'd shot up that hill like Bradley Wiggins.

Then she said something that really made him sit up.

'I've got some photographs of your accident.' She was rummaging in her bag. 'I thought they might jog your memory.'

She produced her iPad and turned it round so he could see the picture displayed on the screen. He stared at the image until he realised that it was of his body flying through the air, his bike apparently above his head.

'Wow!'

'Exactly,' said Dr Sanderson. She turned the tablet back, found the next picture and showed it to him. It was just as he was coming off his bike.

'What's that white thing?' he asked.

'Don't know. Could be a vehicle – a car or a van perhaps.'

He studied the detail but it was impossible to make anything out.

'I might be able to enhance the image,' she offered.

'Really?'

'We're trying. Obviously if someone drove you off the road, we want to find out.'

'We?'

'The police; I help at a forensics lab, as you know.'

He was still examining the photographs when his mother arrived and Dr Sanderson took back her iPad and left after brief introductions.

'I've spoken to a registrar,' Mrs Bassett announced. 'They seem completely…'

'Flummoxed,' Jack finished the sentence for her.

'Exactly.'

'I suppose we have to wait while they do their tests,' she said in a resigned voice.

He didn't tell her about the pictures of his fall, it would only upset her, but he couldn't get them out of his mind. When his mother finally left, he sank back on the bed and drifted off, running the day of his accident in his head. Trying to make himself remember what happened. Trying to visualise the white vehicle.

Matthew tracked Spence Hatt down to the gym. He was talking to a group of students but it didn't seem to be a proper class, they were just chatting as far as he could see. He hovered until he was finally able to catch the lecturer's eye. He wandered over, looking at his watch.

'Hi,' he said. 'Are you here for the time trials? They're not until this afternoon, Matt.'

'No. I wanted to ask you something…'

'Go ahead.' He turned to the group of students and indicated for them to hang around.

'…about Will Humphreys.'

'Oh yes? What's that then?'

'Is he coming back to uni?'

Now he had Spence's full attention. 'Why d'you want to know?'

'There's something I want to ask him.'

'Can't I help? I've been covering your training long enough.'

'It's not about my training.' He hesitated. 'Actually it's more about Jack's training – or his performance, to be more precise.' He hoped it was clear what he was getting at.

Spence moved closer, turning his back on the students. 'What d'you mean exactly?'

Matthew's heart was beating faster. He took a deep breath. 'I want to ask Will what he was giving Jack.'

Spence looked blank.

Matthew tried again. This time he would make it as clear as he could. '*I* think it was EPO.'

The man still appeared confused. 'What's that then?'

Matthew didn't know whether he was bluffing but now he was feeling more confident. 'It's a drug to increase red cell production.' He felt he knew everything there was to know about it now. 'It's used to carry more oxygen in the blood.'

The students had tired of waiting and were gravitating towards the door. Spence didn't even notice.

'Do you have any proof of this?'

'No. That's why I want to find Will. He's the only one who will know for certain.'

'He's hardly likely to admit it, is he? The university authorities wouldn't be very happy, mate.'

'It's not about that.'

'Then what's your problem? You want some too?'

Matthew really disliked his manner. He spoke slowly through gritted teeth. 'I want to know because Jack is in hospital and it might be important that the doctors know what he's been taking.'

'OK.' Spence backed away a little and held up his hands as if to stave him off. 'Easy.'

They stood facing each other for perhaps half a minute.

Then Spence folded his arms. 'Look, I don't know what he's been up to but I know the BUCS wants to talk to him. I think that's why he asked for time out with the university authorities.'

'Are you in touch with him?'

'He sends the odd email and text.'

'His email address bounces back with a message saying he's abroad.'

'I know but he will answer if you ask him to.'

Matthew thanked him and they walked out of the gym together.

'Keep in touch, mate,' Spence said. 'And don't forget to come this afternoon. You're our best hope with Jack out of the picture.'

'Nina?'

She was concentrating on her report and didn't look up. 'Yes, Ruby. What is it?'

'Mills said she'd look at those photos of Jack Bassett's accident.'

'Did she?' She was only half-listening.

'To enhance them, to see what the white thing is.'

'OK.'

'Is it all right to ask for the original memory card from the camera?'

'You'll have to ask the owner, I guess.'

'But what about the official stuff... paperwork.'

'Is it an active investigation?' Nina looked across at her, knowing the answer.

'No.'

'It's not official then, is it? You must make them aware of that.'

The office went quiet again and Nina could hear Ruby busy typing. She assumed she was contacting the photographer.

'Nina?'

'What?'

'I know it's not official... not yet, anyway...'

Nina raised her eyebrows, an expression Hazel had said was a very effective deterrent, but clearly didn't work on young enthusiastic researchers.

'...but I was thinking. This white vehicle could be Jo Richie's van.'

'The lad who took the bike?'

'What if he didn't? What if he drove Jack Bassett off the road and took the bike away to hide it?'

'That's a serious allegation.'

'Couldn't we look at his van to see if there's any damage to it?'

'Not without some justification and even then it would be difficult to prove the damage was caused by the accident.'

'There'd be forensic evidence – like paint from the bike.'

'Ruby, at the moment you've only got a white blur. Get Mills to improve the image and, if it is a white van in the photo, we'll talk about it again. You're lucky Hazel isn't in this afternoon or she'd be tearing you off a strip for even looking at those photos.'

'I wanted to find out because the woman who saw the last near miss at Buttertubs said it was a white car or *van* that nearly hit the cyclist. You must admit it's a coincidence.'

'There are plenty of white vans around.' She went back to her report. 'There are always coincidences. Anna Rycroft and Jack Bassett both cycled for the university but so did lots of other people – every year. You concentrate on the C.A.T. project and keep Hazel happy.'

Ruby wanted to get on with the digital enhancement of the photos immediately but waited until Nina had left the office for the day before ringing Tamsin. She explained that the pictures she'd sent by email were not adequate and could she please borrow the camera's memory card.

'Are they still on the card?' she asked.

'I think so,' Tamsin said. 'Yes, I haven't removed any of those, not yet. What should I do with the card? I don't want to post it.'

In the end Tamsin offered to take it directly to the Harrogate laboratory so they could remove what they needed and return her card immediately. Ruby sent her directions by email and then a message to Mills, letting her know to expect the memory card, by hand. She spent a few minutes updating her meticulous notes, even though, as Nina had pointed out, the investigation was not official. Not yet, she thought. Not yet.

'The diagnosis is pure red cell aplasia, Mrs Bassett. It means he is not able to produce the red cells that are necessary to carry oxygen round his body. That is why we're giving him transfusions.'

She'd been horrified to find her son attached to a bag of blood and ran out immediately to find a doctor. Her hysterics had resulted in a staff nurse promising to locate a consultant for her to speak to.

'Is he losing blood?' she asked. 'Is he hurt inside?'

'No. I can reassure you on that score, Mrs Bassett. Jack has had a whole range of tests and we are now fairly certain that he's just not able to make the red cells at the moment.'

'Why not?'

'That's what we can't understand. It's pretty unusual and we aren't sure what's happening. It seems to have occurred after the accident – perhaps as a result of the trauma of the fall. The immune system is a complicated thing. I'm waiting for the results of a bone marrow biopsy to tell us more.'

She knew that bone marrow was for leukaemia. 'Has he got cancer?' she asked, appalled.

'We've run scans and have ruled out any tumours,' he said. 'We have to wait and see what the results tell us. If it's caused, as I think it may be, by a lack of the hormone that controls the production of red cells, we can give it artificially.' He looked at his watch. 'I really must go. I've got a clinic running.'

He had gone before she could thank him. She could see her son lying motionless with the line attached to his arm. He looked asleep when she arrived and the nurses warned her that he was getting weaker – but the blood would help. She sat by his bed until eventually he opened his eyes. She called his name and stroked his face until after a while he focussed on her.

'Jack, sweetie, it's Mummy.'

'Hi, Mum.' He sounded very weak.

She tried to get him to drink but he wasn't interested. She chattered about what she and her husband had been doing since yesterday. She joked about how his father had been rubbish in his game of golf and there was a weak smile from Jack. Then he said something so softly she couldn't hear above the other noises in the ward.

'I saw a car,' he repeated.

'Where?' she asked.

'Before I fell. I saw a car.'

'Did you?'

'A white car.'

'Before the accident?'

'Yes. Tell someone, Mum. Tell them.'

'Of course I will, sweetie.' She stroked his forehead. 'You get some rest and I'll come in this evening.'

Visiting time was over and everyone had gone. She left the hospital in tears, struggling to wipe them away as she drove home. They thought themselves so lucky that he'd survived the accident and come out of the coma without any brain damage. They were planning a big party for when he came home. She'd been foolish to think it was all over when this red cell aplasia was threatening his life. That's what the doctor had said when she asked him how serious it was: *it could be life threatening if we can't control it.*

Chapter 15

Mills had been waiting on the green in Reeth since one o' clock but there was no sign of Ruby. Finally she gave up, locking the car and making her way down to the hall alone. Fremington village hall, situated on the Grinton road, was often used for social occasions and educational presentations but rarely for a protest meeting. When Mills arrived the place was empty save for the small group of committee members. Stephen was abnormally jovial, laughing and joking with Catriona, who had dressed up in a pink linen suit for the occasion. Arthur and Colin shuffled the furniture around until there were two tables at the front with six chairs. Everything was prepared by half-past and Mills sat at the back of the hall next to Muriel, watching the others congregated at the front.

'Just look at Arthur and Colin. They're like Stephen's bodyguards, standing there either side of him.'

'I don't think they'd provide much protection if he was attacked by anyone,' observed Mills.

Muriel giggled. 'No, you're right there. They wouldn't say boo to a goose, would they?' She folded her arms, leaning back on her chair. 'Funny really – they hardly spoke before Arthur lost his wife but now they're almost inseparable.'

'That's nice.'

'Arthur says Colin wasn't always quiet, though. He was quite sociable in his day. I think their wives were good friends and that's why they became pals when they both found themselves on their own.'

Once Muriel started there was no need to respond and Mills stretched her legs out.

'Arthur has family that comes from time to time. I suppose they might live far way away but Colin... of course he never has anyone come to stay as far as I can tell.'

Stephen was signalling for them to join him. Neither of them had wanted to sit up at the front but as the public began to arrive, Stephen insisted they all took their places.

By two o'clock there were thirteen people sitting in the audience, mainly towards the back of the hall. Mills, recognising no-one, asked Muriel if she could see anyone she knew.

'No, thank goodness,' she replied. 'I wish he'd get on with it.'

At that moment, Stephen called the meeting to order. He began by introducing the organising committee, as he referred to them. Mills shrank back in her seat as he called her Dr Millicent Sanderson. Muriel waved nervously when it was her turn. There followed a long tirade from Stephen about the disgraceful way the Grand Départ had been organised without consultation. He went through the route in great detail, and then invited Catriona to describe the impact on wildlife and the environment. Muriel and Mills exchanged glances. Arthur and Colin looked across at them. No-one had said that she would be participating in the presentation. Mills had to admit that Catriona gave a good performance, even though much of what she said about the environmental impact was totally over the top. When she'd finished, Stephen took the floor again, describing what plans C.A.T. had for the day of the race.

Mills watched Ruby creep into the hall and take a seat at the end of a row near the back. She was just in time to hear Stephen listing the direct action planned for the event. He described the banners and posters that would be on the route and the leaflets they would be distributing.

'…and finally, but most importantly we will be blocking the route and laying tacks across the road surface to disrupt the race as much as we can. I hope you will join us.'

Mills counted. Now there were just ten in the audience, including Ruby. She was waving her hand to attract Stephen's attention.

'Surely any disruption on the day will be illegal?' she asked.

'You can't make an omelette without breaking some eggs,' he replied, looking rather pleased with himself.

'But it would be dangerous,' called a man in a yellow T-shirt with a bicycle logo on the front. 'You can't put tacks on the road!'

The woman beside him shouted in agreement.

'I think you'll find,' Stephen replied, 'we will have to take such action to get our message across.'

'Well who are you trying to get it across to?' the man in the T-shirt shouted, looking round with a grin. 'Not exactly the whole of the dale here.'

Ruby jumped up. 'I agree. If you distribute tacks on the road, tyres will be punctured and accidents will happen. You'll be risking lives.'

Stephen stood to answer but Ruby continued. 'Are all of

you willing to do that?'

There was a brief silence. Mills wasn't sure what Ruby wanted her to do. Should she stand up and say no, she wouldn't risk lives?

'Well? Are you?' Ruby repeated.

Stephen was on his feet. 'I can answer for us all when I say that we are ready to do our bit to prevent the race going ahead.'

'I won't endanger anyone's life!' It was Muriel, red in the face but on her feet and almost shouting. 'I'm willing to protest but I'm not going to hurt anyone!'

Colin pushed himself up from his chair. 'Nor will I.' His voice was so soft it was barely audible.

Arthur stood and Mills followed suit, leaving only Catriona seated.

Stephen, who was still standing, looked round at them.

The ten members of the audience began cheering, their clapping sounding like small arms fire in the almost empty hall. As the applause stopped, Stephen announced that the meeting was at an end and if anyone wanted to sign the petition, it was at the back of the hall. Mills slipped out quickly to catch Ruby who had made for the door as soon as the meeting was over. She was waiting outside.

'I'm not sure whether that went to plan,' she said.

'Oh I think it went exactly the right way,' Mills said. 'Everyone wanted the opportunity to say no.'

'Except the snooty woman in the suit.'

'Catriona? She's a friend of Stephen's.'

'Nobody else seems to be.'

'I think this may be the end of C.A.T.'

'I hope so,' said Ruby. 'That was the aim really.'

They could see the others drifting out of the hall and so

they quickly moved up the road to where Ruby's car was parked.

'Let's go for a cup of tea,' Mills suggested. At home in Mossy Bank, Ruby might be spotted by one of the group. She guessed that on a Saturday afternoon in June no-one local would be sitting in a teashop in Reeth. The café was busy but they found a table away from the window and ordered tea and cake.

'Hey, this is really cool,' Ruby said, excitedly. 'You are so lucky living here.'

Mills nodded. 'The girl brought the camera card to the lab,' she reported. 'Our digital guy took what he wanted and she's got it back now.'

'Thanks for that. I really hope it shows something.'

'Well, it certainly looks like it could be a vehicle.'

'A white van?'

'You think?'

'If it is, we might know who owns it.'

Mills knew better than to ask for details. 'I showed the pictures to Jack when I visited him in hospital. It didn't jog his memory.'

'Shame.'

'Anyway,' said Mills, changing the subject, 'we seem to have reduced the risk of any injuries in July.'

'Thanks to you.'

'Me? I thought *you* started the mutiny.'

Ruby laughed. 'It worked anyway.'

Monday morning traffic in pouring rain wasn't a good start to the week. Alex had offered to drive, so Mills sat patiently trying to ignore his impatience as they hit the outskirts of Harrogate.

'Ruby was asking about the enhancement you're doing on her photos.'

'Oh, does she need them urgently?'

'I don't think so but she's keen to find out if it's a white van for some reason.'

'A white van? Why didn't you say – it might be easier if I know what I'm looking for.'

'You didn't ask.'

The traffic made them late and Mills went straight to her desk where the post had already arrived. Most of it was addressed to the Director but it all came to her in Brenda's absence. She left her own mail until the end: just one envelope containing information relating to her impending appearance as an expert witness in the crown court at York. She felt a sudden anxiety as she considered the enormity of what she was going to do in less than a fortnight.

When she told Glyn that the dreaded letter had arrived, she was surprised how understanding he was. He'd appeared many times and offered to give her the benefit of his experience there and then. The rest of the morning was spent in role play and Mills was astonished by Glyn's sympathetic manner, most unlike his usual attitude to her and everyone else. When she made a mistake or responded in an unprofessional way, he simply smiled and suggested she try it again differently. When he eventually checked his watch and declared it was lunchtime, Mills thanked him.

'That's all right. I know how it feels when you've never appeared before. My first time was a bit of a disaster,' he admitted.

'Oh I'm sure it wasn't.'

'Yes it was,' he said grimly and walked away.

Mills searched for Alex, who had brought sandwiches from home for them both. He was in the tiny office he shared with Donna and Timothy.

'I've left yours in the box,' he said through a mouthful of food, while looking at his computer monitor. 'I'm just checking an email from my friend at Teesside University. He's got much better software than me and might be able to improve the images you gave me.'

Mills spent the afternoon checking and signing reports. Her suspension from the university was a blessing in some respects because it allowed her to do a proper job at the laboratory. By the end of the day she was up to date with her paperwork and was ready to go home. Unfortunately Alex did not return from Teesside University until after six.

'I'm sorry!' he said as he burst into her office. 'The traffic was horrible.'

'Worth going?'

'Too right! D'you want to see?'

They went down to his computer and he set up the "before" and "after" photos. The difference in the clarity when the photo had been enhanced was quite remarkable.

'D'you see?' Alex asked. 'The figure and the bike are obviously sharper but it's what's happened to that white blur.'

'It's a vehicle all right,' said Mills.

'We reckon it's a van. Don't you think?'

Mills wasn't so sure.

'Well, look at the second picture.'

It was much more obvious this time. The sharp angle defining the engine and windscreen. 'That is definitely a van,' Mills said.

'Just shows what you can do with the right software.

Shame it's so expensive.'

'Well, if it produces the results.'

'So what happens now?' Alex asked.

'We go home and get something to eat but I guess I'll send the results back to Ruby and she'll decide. It certainly looks as though a vehicle was involved in Jack's accident. She was interested in the guy who was found with Jack's bike in his van.'

'Was it a white van?'

'I believe it was,' she said with a smile.

Virginia Bassett had been at her son's bedside for much of the weekend. Over that time he'd had several units of blood but he was as pale and lifeless as he'd been when in a coma. It was the waiting that was driving her to distraction. As she approached the ward, she prayed that something positive would be going on, now the weekend was over. She was told he was resting, so no change there, but she demanded to see someone who could tell her what was happening.

Eventually a senior nurse arrived, who took her into a tiny office and sat her down.

'As you know we've been giving Jack some blood to keep his red cell count up,' she began. 'He is very poorly and we're worried about how well his body can cope.'

'Yes, I know.'

'The blood is helping but we still can't find the cause of the aplasia.' She typed on the keyboard in front of her. 'The good news is that there are no signs of any tumours.'

'I know. The doctor told me that last week. They were doing a bone marrow biopsy, he said.'

She consulted the screen again. 'And that showed no

abnormal cells, so that's all clear.'

'So what is causing the anaemia?'

'You'll have to talk to the consultant for more information. I can only tell you the results of the tests.'

'So is there any other treatment besides giving him blood?'

She looked down the sheet in front of her. 'You need to ask the consultant but he's ordered an erythropoietin test.'

'What's that for?'

'It measures the amount of erythropoietin in the blood. It's a hormone that tells the stem cells in the bone marrow to make more red blood cells.'

'Wait, let me write that down so I can tell my husband.'

The nurse found a piece of paper and wrote down the name for her. 'It's called EPO for short. They treat people with kidney failure with it – EPO is made in the kidneys.'

Virginia took the paper, folded it carefully, thanked the nurse and left before she could see her tears. In the corridor she stopped to open the piece of paper and stared down at the neat letters "ERYTHROPOIETIN" – possibly the means to her son's survival.

Ruby was ecstatic when she received the enhanced photographs from Mills. She printed them out on high quality paper together with the original copies and waited to see who would arrive in the office first. To her relief, it was Nina. She laid them out on her desk and asked her to look.

'What do you see?' she asked.

'They're the photos that girl Tamsin took of Jack Bassett's accident. You showed them to me before.'

'Look at this one and then at the enhanced version,'

Ruby commanded.

Nina peered closely at them in turn. 'This one's better,' she said, pointing at the enhanced version.

'Yes and you can see the white van.'

'Is it a van?' Nina asked. 'It could be a car.'

'It's too square.'

'OK, so it's a van. What is your point?'

'The van is really close to the bike. I think it ran into him and knocked him off the edge. Then, he put the bike in his van and drove off.'

'Hold on there, Ruby. Are you suggesting this van belongs to the man who found the bike?'

'It's too much of a coincidence.'

Nina looked back at the photos for a while then up at Ruby. 'I seem to remember you talking about another coincidence – a white car or van nearly causing an accident in the same place. I hope you're not suggesting he's making a collection of bicycles?'

Ruby couldn't tell if she was making fun of her or not. 'No, it may not be the same van. It may just be a coincidence.'

'My point is that white vans are very common and although the photographs are very clear and it probably *is* a white van, there is no proof that it is the van belonging to the man who was found with Jack Bassett's bike.'

'But there might be some damage on his van, paint from the bike perhaps.'

'Perhaps but we would need more than that to begin an investigation.'

'You agree that it's a "hit and run" though?'

'I've got to see Mitch now anyway, let's see what he thinks.'

She picked up a couple of files, took the pictures from her, and disappeared, leaving Ruby feeling deflated. She knew Hazel would want an update on the C.A.T. meeting on Saturday and started on her report.

'Right, girl. How did it go?' Hazel breezed in half an hour later in a cheery mood, for once.

Ruby gave her a breakdown of the event, stressing the fact that once she'd challenged the committee, Stephen Grainger had only one supporter left. 'I honestly think that the group will disband now. There's no way most of them will do anything to threaten the lives of the cyclists or other people.'

'Sounds like a success then. Well done.'

Ruby glowed. She knew better than to tell Hazel about the enhanced photographs or what she'd said to Nina. She just hoped that Nina would be able to persuade the DCI to start an investigation into the "hit and run".

The next few days were a nightmare. Virginia arrived at visiting time the following day to find Jack's bed occupied by a stranger. Her son had been moved back to the critical care unit. Just so we can keep an eye on him, the nurse had said. He had low blood pressure and they wanted to be able to administer oxygen if necessary. Everyone was very busy and she'd wanted to talk to the consultant when Ray was with her so he could understand the ins and outs. Eventually, after another two days of uncertainty, the registrar responded to her request to see him. This time she forced her husband to take time off to accompany her.

'Thank you for coming in,' the young man began.

Virginia waited.

'When we got Jack's results back, they presented us with

a puzzle. We wanted to check and they've just been confirmed.' He was poring over the notes in a blue folder. 'He doesn't appear to be producing any EPO, which explains why he has such a low red cell count. There's no obvious explanation yet but we're doing some more tests.'

'Can you fix it?' Ray asked.

The registrar shut the file. 'Yes, that's the good news. We've already begun giving him artificial erythropoietin. It's the treatment we give patients with kidney failure when they can't produce the hormone naturally.'

'How long does that take?' asked Virginia.

'We should see a response in a few days. We'll monitor the erythropoietin levels regularly and we should see an increase in the red blood cells as it starts to work.'

Virginia couldn't control the tears of relief as she left the registrar's room. At last they seemed to be doing something positive. Ray put his arm round her shoulder and steered her towards the exit.

'I want to go back to see Jack,' she protested.

'It's time to go home and have a good night's sleep. He's in good hands.'

Chapter 16

Every afternoon, as she approached the high dependency unit, Virginia prayed there was an improvement in her son's red blood count. She calculated the days since they first treated him with the drug that was going to make him better. Today it would be exactly a week and so far there had been no sign of recovery. They let her in but warned her that he wasn't really communicating. Jack lay quietly, just as he'd done when he was in a coma. She supposed he was sleeping and crept away to find someone to ask about his progress.

She was willing to wait as long as necessary until his consultant was free but, when he arrived, the news wasn't good.

'We're puzzled by Jack's lack of response. I've treated a number of kidney patients with artificial erythropoietin and never failed to see an improvement.'

Virginia, who couldn't think of anything to say, searched the man's face for something to hang on to.

'However,' he continued, 'I am aware of rare – very rare – cases where the body rejects artificial erythropoietin. Usually it's after quite a long period of treatment though.'

'So why has it happened to him? He's only been on it for

a week.'

'We don't know. We're doing tests on his blood, looking for antibodies. He's also had a bone marrow biopsy. We'll know more when we get the results back.'

'So what happens until then?' She was fumbling in her handbag for a tissue.

'We're assuming that he has anti-EPO antibodies for now and giving him an immunosuppressant.'

She wiped her eyes. 'What's that for?'

'Jack's immune system appears to be fighting the production of EPO which is why he's unable to produce red blood cells. We think Jack's body is producing antibodies called anti-EPO which is preventing the artificial EPO we are treating him with from working. If we're right, it explains his anaemia. We call it PRCA or pure red cell aplasia.'

She couldn't stop the tears.

'Please don't be upset Mrs Bassett. We're getting the tests done now and we'll soon know if that is the problem. Then, hopefully, the immunosuppressant will stop the body from producing the antibodies that prevent Jack from making EPO.' He smiled encouragingly.

She thanked him and, once he'd left, sat down to pat her eyes dry. She hadn't understood much of what the doctor was saying and Ray would be asking her to explain it all later. Once she had checked her make-up, Virginia went back to sit by her son's bed. She was nearly asleep herself when a nurse tapped her on the shoulder.

'A young man was just asking after Jack. I told him he can't come in and that you were with him. He's waiting outside.'

'Who is he?'

'A university friend I think. He says he knows you.'

Curious, Virginia followed the nurse to the visitors' room. Matthew Watson jumped up when he saw her.

'Mrs Bassett!'

'Matthew.'

'How is he?'

'Quite poorly. They don't know what's wrong with him but they're doing more tests. He's had three blood transfusions and they're treating him with something but it doesn't seem to be working.'

She sank onto a red plastic chair and smiled at him but was too exhausted to make further conversation. 'I'm sorry. Jack's not awake now.'

'I know. I wanted to speak to the medics but they won't talk to me. I need to explain something to them.'

Virginia wanted to leave. 'I'm sorry. I really must get home. It was nice to meet you.' She lurched to the door and left before he could ask her anything else about her son. She really couldn't cope with any more today.

Ruby had been starting work early and staying late, ever since Nina had said she could have a look at the possibility that Jack Bassett's accident was actually a "hit and run". She was warned to keep it low profile by Hazel, although since the public meeting fiasco, C.A.T. seemed to have gone very quiet indeed. Much to her force colleagues' amusement, Ruby had cleared a whiteboard and divided it into three sections vertically. The first section, labelled Jack Bassett, contained the enhanced photographs and the date of his accident. The next section, for Anna Rycroft, was empty except for the date she was last seen and when she was found by Ruby. The right-hand side of the board carried the title "Near Miss". She had written the name of the woman who had witnessed a white van or car nearly knocking a cyclist off his or her bike at Buttertubs.

Ruby surveyed the board with satisfaction. Today she'd received a photograph of Anna Rycroft, provided from the records that Nina had compiled when the girl went missing. Ruby removed it carefully from the file. She was dressed in cycling gear, posing proudly with her bicycle – the same one they'd discovered when they rescued Jack Bassett after his fall. Ruby stared at the figure dressed in the distinctive red and white cycling kit, her hair hanging thick and dark round her smiling face. How strangely Anna had changed over time as she remained undiscovered, transforming into the empty bundle of clothing and hair that Ruby had seen when she literally stumbled over her body.

Now she needed a good likeness of Jack Bassett to go on her wall and she knew where to look. Jack was in a cycle team so she looked on the university website and was rewarded with a shot of him accepting a trophy for the fastest time in the university road race challenge cup. She printed it out and placed it at the same level as Anna's picture.

She had no equivalent photograph of the cyclist who was nearly hit by the white car or van. She only knew the date and time it happened. Ruby wondered if she could appeal for the cyclist involved to come forward but decided it might be too "high-profile". With the run-up to the Grand Départ, cyclists came from far and wide to experience the course and so a local appeal might not be adequate.

Hazel arrived just as Ruby was putting her finishing touches to the board. The words "white van" now appeared on the first and last sections of her display.

'What in heaven's name is this? "Crimewatch"?' she asked with a laugh.

Ruby blushed. 'I find it easier to think if I've got some visual inspiration, like mind-mapping.'

'Do you?' she asked as she wandered over to examine the photographs. 'I thought Anna Rycroft had left university,' she observed.

'Yes, she was a teacher.'

'So this was taken while she was still on the UNYCYLE team?'

Ruby looked again at the picture. Anna had the name emblazoned across her chest. 'I suppose so,' she said. But it was the same bike and the same clothes. 'No, she was still using the kit. She was wearing it the day she died. Why?'

'Just asking,' Hazel said and wandered over to her own desk.

Ruby sat down too, using a notepad to scribble her ideas and connections at her desk, too embarrassed to use the board while Hazel was in the room. But every now and then she stared up at the word "UNYCYCLE" replicated on both cyclists' jackets. When Nina appeared, she too went up to the board and perused it then returned to her desk without a word. But she did smile across at Ruby before settling down to work.

'Nina?' Ruby asked when Hazel had left the room. 'What happened to the guy with the white van?'

'Jo Richie?'

'Yes.'

'He'll have his day in court for pinching the bike, I suppose.'

'What if we think he might've cause Jack Bassett's accident?'

'We'd have to ask him about it.'

'We?'

'Well, technically *me* but you could come, I suppose.'

'Awesome!'

Nina looked round. 'Ruby, please don't do that. It's a serious matter, if you think he might have been involved.'

'Sorry.'

Ruby spent the rest of the morning working on how to identify the person in the "near miss". If she couldn't make a wide appeal for the cyclist to come forward, she would have to be cleverer. She went over the intel the woman had given her. A white car or van, she'd said. The cyclist was dressed in red and white. She stared at the empty space then drew a frame where the photograph of the mystery cyclist should be, with a little figure and a bicycle. She coloured the jersey in red. Hazel laughed when she saw what Ruby had done and asked why she hadn't put a UNYCYCLE logo on the sketch.

'That *would* be some coincidence!' declared Nina.

But it made some sense to Ruby. If she narrowed her search to the university cycle team, she could ask if anyone had been on the route that day. She waited until the office was empty before making the call. Eventually she was told to ring the coach, who was most helpful and offered to email the team with her question.

The family room on the high dependency unit was busy when Matthew arrived with Will. He waited until the door swung shut on the last visitor and they were alone.

'You've got to tell someone now,' he said.

'I know. I'm going to, when someone will listen. What do *you* suggest?' he asked angrily.

'Go and try the nurse again. Tell her it's important. Tell her we won't go until we see someone.'

Will left and Matthew waited. Five minutes. Ten minutes. At fourteen minutes he reappeared.

'They told me to wait. They said someone would come along to talk to me.'

They sat staring at the floor until Will broke the silence. 'I was gutted when I saw your email. I didn't even know Jack had been in an accident.'

'Well you weren't around, were you?'

'You could've let me know.'

'I didn't know how to contact you until Spence said your old email was still working. Everyone assumed you'd left for good.'

'Spence knew that wasn't true.'

'I heard you were avoiding the BUCS, that they wanted to talk to you about the drug business.'

'Did you? Who told you that?'

'It's just what people were saying.'

'People, eh?' He was rubbing the stubbly hair on his chin. He changed the subject by asking Matthew about his own cycling season.

'It's been OK,' Matthew replied. 'I did all right in the Etape du Dales. I suppose Jack would've been faster but then…'

'He was taking EPO. Is that what you were going to say?' Matthew nodded.

'I know it was a mistake, a bad mistake, Matt. That's why I'm here now. I can assure you there'll be no more drugs at UNYCYCLE after this.'

There'll be no more Will Humphreys, thought Matthew but said nothing.

Eventually the door swung open and a dumpy man in theatre scrubs marched in. Matthew and Will jumped up.

'Sorry, not much time. You wanted to see me about Jack Bassett. Are you family?'

'No,' admitted Will. 'I was his cycle coach, before the accident. I need to talk to you about… about what he was taking.'

'D'you mean medication?'

'Yes, well not exactly. More of a pick-me-up.'

'I don't follow you.' The medic was looking at his watch.

'Jack was taking something to improve his cycling performance.'

'I see. Do you know what it was?'

Matthew held his breath as Will hesitated.

'It was just to keep up his stamina,' Will began.

'EPO.' Matthew interrupted.

'Erythropoietin?' The physician appeared shocked. Will looked at Matthew, who nodded his head. 'How much? Has he been taking it for long? Subcutaneously?'

Matthew could hardly believe what Will told the medic. He'd been supplying Jack with enough EPO for him to inject himself weekly for over a year. The physician looked increasingly perturbed by Will's confession. When he'd heard it all, he made for the door.

'I don't have the time to explain it all now but you may have put your friend's life in jeopardy,' he said and left.

Will flung himself on a chair and put his head in his hands. Matthew watched him. He could only feel an intense anger with the coach for his stupidity, realising that his own life could have been affected had he accepted

Will's offer to "help him improve his performance in the road races". Fortunately he'd been more sensible than Jack.

Nina had been giving Ruby the news that Jo Richie would be available for interview the following week, when she received a call from Mills.

'Hi Nina. Last year you asked me where to find Will Humphreys.'

'Did I? Who is he, again?'

'He's the cycle coach at uni. He was abroad but he's back.'

'For good or just visiting?'

'No idea. I just know he's around at the moment.'

'Really?'

'I've got his contact details if you want.'

'OK.' Nina grabbed a pen and noted down his university email address. She was still trying to remember why she'd been keen to see him.

'Before you go, Mills. Good luck with the case next week. Let me know how it goes.'

Nina racked her brains to identify why she wanted to see the cycling coach from the university. In the end the clue was facing her on Ruby's board: Anna Rycroft in her UNYCYCLE vest. Will Humphreys had been the man doing up Anna's helmet in Hawes, the last person to talk to her before she disappeared – before he went off to France. She sent a brief message asking him to make contact, curious to find out why he ran away for nearly a year on the day of Anna's accident. Until Ruby had set up the whiteboard, Nina had been content that Anna's disappearance was simply due to an accident on

Buttertubs. Now, as she stared at Anna's photograph, she wondered whether Will's disappearance on the same day that she went missing was a coincidence. She told Ruby that coincidences can happen but perhaps there were beginning to be too many.

Ruby had disappeared while Nina was on the phone but returned a little later with mugs of tea and chocolate biscuits.

'What's this in aid of?' Nina asked.

'Just a minor celebration.' Ruby was looking smug.

'What?' Nina couldn't help laughing at the girl.

'I've had a response from the university cycle team.'

'About…?'

'The "near miss". I know it's a mega coincidence but the cyclist is in the university team. The coach asked if anyone had been in an accident on that date and this guy said he'd been knocked off at Buttertubs. He wasn't hurt but he was pretty angry about it because the driver didn't stop. I'm going to meet him to see if I can find out more about the vehicle.'

'He didn't report it then?'

'Apparently not.'

'When are you going to see him?'

'Tomorrow.'

'At the university?'

'Yes.'

'I might come with you. There's someone I want to see in the sports department myself.'

Chapter 17

'Professor Green!'

The old man had arrived unannounced and was standing in the doorway clutching his briefcase to his chest. He appeared short of breath from climbing the steep stairs up to the laboratory.

'I've read your report and it's a load of nonsense,' he announced when he'd regained his composure.

Mills was lost for words. She put down the file she'd been reading and stood up. 'Please have a seat. Would you like a coffee?'

He seemed taken aback by her civility.

'No. I came here to tell you what I think of your work on this… this trumped-up baloney. The man is clearly guilty; you're simply trying to refute my technique and make a mockery of my long years of forensic work!'

He was red in the face and a fine spray of spit flew as he spoke.

'I'm simply doing my job for the solicitor who requested my services.'

'Services? As an *expert* witness? How long have you been qualified? No – don't answer, I looked you up. Four years, isn't it? What have you learnt in four years compared to my forty?'

What could she say? Should she try to explain where he was going wrong? Was it going to be like this in court? She tried to compose a reasonable response as he continued his tirade.

'I suggest you think very carefully indeed before going into that witness box. In fact you need to consider whether to go to court at all. The prosecution barrister will make mincemeat of you, young lady.'

'Someone has to appear for the defence.' It sounded weak and pathetic as she said it.

'Not if there's no evidence to support it,' he argued. 'You need to see that before you make a fool of yourself.' He was beginning to calm down and was sounding more rational. 'I don't want you to be humiliated on your first appearance in court, Dr Sanderson,' he wheedled. 'Take my advice and wait until you've got more experience under your belt.'

Mills was exasperated. Unsure how to respond, she simply told him that she was sure her results were correct. He snorted with disgust and turned to leave as the door opened and Alex came in bearing two coffee mugs.

'Oops, I didn't know you had a visitor. Would you like one?' he asked.

'No, I'm leaving,' he muttered, pushing past him.

Mills listened to the old man struggling down the stairs.

'Who was that?' Alex asked, putting her mug on the desk.

'Sydney Green. He's the one who got me suspended.'

'He's the expert witness in the rape case?' Alex looked sceptical. 'He looks too old to be working at all!'

'He's horrible,' said Mills returning to her desk and sipping her coffee.

She couldn't prevent tears from forming as she described their conversation.

'You mustn't let him upset you,' Alex said. 'It's probably against the law for the prosecution witness to even discuss the case with you.'

'You think? If that's an example of the way it'll be in court, I'm not sure I can face it, Alex.'

She felt a little better after their chat and rang the solicitor. Alex had suggested it, to give her reassurance, but Mills was still in a mood to withdraw.

'You're saying that the expert witness for the prosecution has been to see you, to discuss the case? That really is not on!' Rajani sounded irate.

'Is it not allowed?' Mills asked.

'It's not ethical. There's no reason why there can't be discussion of conflicting views but not in that sort of *ad hoc* fashion. And it sounds as if his manner was not one of consensus.'

'He was being a real bully, to be honest,' Mills admitted.

'Well, if he has issue with what you put in your report, he should say so. If he tells us what the problem is, you can address it and decide whether he has a point. That is how it is supposed to happen. If any difference of opinion can be sorted before the trial, it should be.'

'I think it's a bit more than a difference of opinion, Rajani. I believe he is wrong and he thinks I am. It's not just a matter of interpretation. He's using old methods that aren't accurate enough for the purpose.'

'Look. I'll let the prosecution lawyers know that he's been to see you and taken a bullying tone. I'll ask them to tell us what he has a problem with.'

'He thinks I've not got sufficient experience.'

'But you have enough for this work, Mills.'

'And he got me suspended from university for taking on the case.'

'What? That's outrageous! How did that happen?'

Mills explained while the solicitor listened in silence. At the end, she expressed serious concerns and said she would speak to her colleagues.

'This needs to be sorted and the air cleared before the trial, otherwise it may have a disastrous impact on the outcome. Professor Green does have a very well-established profile as an expert witness working for the prosecution – we don't want to jeopardise the outcome.'

'Perhaps it would be better to use someone else, instead of me.' Mills felt a sense of relief.

'No! We can't do that. The case is dependent on your evidence. You have to attend.'

'What if I don't want to?' Her mind was made up.

'We'd subpoena you to appear.'

'Seriously?'

'Yes.' Rajani's tone was grave. 'We're not playing at this, Mills. You must understand. The case rests on your report, in the absence of any other evidence.'

Her hand was shaking as she put the phone down. There was no way out. She would have to face the ordeal in court, with Sydney Green determined to discredit her to save his reputation.

Nina was waiting in the office before anyone else had arrived for work. She'd offered to drive Ruby to the university, for their respective meetings. Ruby was seeing the student who'd been knocked off his bike while she planned an unannounced visit to Will Humphreys. Even if he wasn't there, her trip wouldn't be wasted; Ruby had asked her to lead the interview with the cyclist, which Nina agreed was probably for the best.

Ruby arrived looking unusually business-like. She'd exchanged her skinny jeans and baggy T-shirt for a neat skirt and blouse. Nina wasn't going to comment but Ruby twirled round.

'Ta da! See, I can be professional if I need to,' she remarked.

'You look very… smart.' Nina hoped she sounded suitably impressed. 'A very appropriate outfit for interviewing a witness.'

Ruby beamed. 'Time for a coffee?'

'No,' said Nina, checking her watch. 'The traffic might be bad still. We'd better go.'

As it turned out the roads round the university were quiet. It was exam time and lectures had finished. Term would soon be over for the summer. It was the period when Nige would normally be preparing for field work with the postgraduates and Nina wondered whether he had anything planned since he hadn't been at work during the term. Soon the boys would be ready for nursery and their lives would revert to the constant juggling that was the norm if she carried on working full-time.

'The sign for the university was that way,' said Ruby suddenly, pointing behind them.

'It's OK.' Nina had missed the main gate but she wasn't going to let Ruby know that she'd been distracted. 'We'll use the East Gate.'

The security staff recognised the car and waved her in without apparently realising that it was not Nige driving. She parked in the staff car park outside her husband's department, unsure where else was permitted. The sports centre was a short walk across campus and she led the way confidently with her young companion trotting obediently beside her.

'Can we slow down a bit?' Ruby asked after a few minutes. 'These shoes are killing me.'

Nina stopped and looked down at her companion's feet. The heels on the black patent shoes were quite low but the toes were very pointed. She could see how they might pinch. By the time she reached the large new building, Nina had waited for Ruby to catch up several times. They entered the spacious entrance hall at just after ten o' clock and the young cyclist was waiting to greet them.

'This is my boss, Detective Sergeant Nina Featherstone. She's going to interview you, if that's all right.' Ruby explained. 'Nina, this is Patrick,' she added unnecessarily.

'I thought we'd go for a coffee,' he offered. 'There's nowhere else and it'll be quiet at this time.'

'Thank you, that'll be fine,' Nina agreed.

They followed him down a long corridor and into a glass-walled cafeteria. It was empty except for a young woman who was tidying behind the counter. Nina guessed it had only just opened for the day.

'Let me get them,' offered Nina, aware that the lad was looking around anxiously. She watched them as they hovered for some time before finally settling on a table by the window. It was a good thing that she'd come with Ruby, thought Nina. She was going to have to take the lead.

They were silently staring at the view when Nina arrived with the tray. Admittedly the reed bed was quite interesting but Nina was surprised how quiet Ruby had become now she was faced with the reason for her visit.

'So,' began Nina, 'you had a contretemps with a car up on Buttertubs Pass?'

'Yes, I went up there to get a bit of training on the long ascent.'

'Would you like to tell me what happened?' Nina went to take her notebook from her handbag. Ruby was watching her. 'Do you want to take notes, Ruby?'

She nodded and opened her own bag to remove a large notepad and pen. Nina suppressed a smile.

'Were you on your own that day, Patrick?' Nina prompted.

'Yes, I went out for the whole day; no-one else wanted to spend the time before exams. I left quite early.'

'What time did you reach Buttertubs Pass?'

'I'm not sure. It was around lunchtime because I decided to stop after I came off to have my sandwiches. I was shaken up a bit to be honest. It's a long drop down there and I was pushed onto the wire. If I'd gone over, I could've been in the same situation as Jack – or worse.'

'That's why it's important we investigate it.' Ruby had finally begun to take part in the discussion. 'What can you remember about the car?'

'First, I'd like some more background to the events leading up to the incident,' Nina said. She preferred to let a witness build up to the main action. She felt it helped jog the memory to start slowly. 'Was it a sunny day like today? Were there many people about?'

'It was cloudy, I prefer it like that. Good cycling weather. I passed a few cyclists on the route and obviously lots of cars passed me.'

'Anyone on the road up to Buttertubs?' Ruby asked, after

a quick glance at Nina.

Patrick thought for a few seconds. 'I didn't see any other cyclists. No, definitely not. There were a few cars on the road going the other way. Perhaps one or two going my way – I don't really remember.'

'Any white cars?' Ruby asked, leaning forward.

He shook his head. 'I really can't remember, sorry.'

'So you climbed the long hill to the top,' offered Nina. 'Did you stop at all on the way up?'

'No.'

'And then you began the descent?' Nina prompted him.

'Yes. I came down towards the bend where people stop to look at the sinkholes. That's when this car cut me up.'

'Cut you up?' Ruby asked.

'Well, it seemed to come from nowhere. It wasn't coming up the road or I would have seen it. It just roared up on my left and pushed me towards the edge.'

'I suppose it was behind you?' asked Ruby.

'It was level with me before I heard it. The only thing I can think is that it was parked on the side of the road.'

'It pulled out without looking?' suggested Nina.

'It's the only explanation.' Patrick agreed.

'What d'you think?' Ruby asked as she tottered along beside Nina.

'About what?' she asked. She was busy watching the room numbers descending as they walked along the corridor.

'Patrick. He seemed a bit vague.'

'Yes. He wasn't an ideal witness.' She stopped at a half open door. 'This is it.'

She knocked and pushed the door open gently. It was

empty.

'Damn, he's not here.' She fumbled in her bag for a pen and tore a sheet off a notepad on the desk. 'I'll leave him a number.'

She sat at the desk while Ruby examined the books on the tall shelf.

'Hello!'

A man stood at the doorway with an amused grin. 'What have we here? How can I help you girls?'

Ruby was blushing as Nina stood up and flashed her ID. 'DS Featherstone,' she said. Before he could speak, she continued, keen to regain control. 'Will Humphreys? I would like to speak to you about Anna Rycroft.'

He seemed to deflate as his grin disappeared. He went to speak but changed his mind.

'Is there somewhere we can all go and find a seat?' Nina asked, indicating the lack of chairs.

They followed him to a sort of common room. 'The students won't use it until lunch-time. It'll be quiet in here,' he said, seating himself carefully on one of the plastic chairs.

Ruby placed herself at the edge of the room and Nina sat opposite Will.

'We tried to find you last year,' she began. 'You were the last person to speak to Anna before... before she disappeared. At the time we didn't know she'd fallen to her death. There was a big investigation and you were a key witness.'

Will nodded apologetically. 'I didn't know. I was shocked when I heard. I didn't find out until I was back in the country.'

'When was that?' asked Nina, getting her notebook out.

'Only a couple of weeks ago.'

'Where have you been?'

'I took a sabbatical.' He was staring at the floor.

'Really?'

'Well, it wasn't planned but… well, I wanted some time out.'

'OK, so can you tell me what passed between you and Anna when you met her in Hawes that day? Was it planned?'

'Oh God, no! I just wanted to speak to her.'

'It must have been important to go all that way for a few minutes chat.'

'It was at the time. I wanted her to come to France with me – for a holiday.'

'I see.'

He looked up angrily. 'I don't think you do. We were close once. I thought that we'd renewed our friendship when I saw her at the alumni do.'

'And you hadn't?'

'Apparently not. She told me to piss off.'

'You gave her something to drink.'

'Did I? I suppose. Just an energy drink. She was doing a long ride.'

Nina leaned back in her chair, deciding what to do next. She wanted to keep him on side. 'Is there anything you might be able to tell us that will help us find out what really happened to her?' she asked with a polite smile.

There was a pause. Will looked at her with his head on one side. 'What d'you mean? What are you saying? Wasn't it an accident?'

'You tell me,' Nina replied. 'Why would an experienced cyclist leave the road?'

'You mean someone collided with her?'

'We don't know.'

Will looked puzzled. 'Jack came off at the same spot,' he said slowly.

'We know.'

'Patrick had a near miss up there too.'

'Yes,' said Ruby.

'Is there a problem with the road surface?' he asked. 'Has someone done a survey? They've been repairing it in preparation for Le Tour.'

'Could the surface be a factor?'

'Of course. If the tarmac is very smooth… and it was a hot day!'

Nina let it go, wondering why he was making such a good case for Anna's death to have been an accident.

When they left the building, it was Nina's turn to ask Ruby's opinion.

'He seemed genuine enough. I think he was quite upset by her death,' she said.

'I wonder if he really didn't know about it until he came back from France,' Nina led the way across the car park.

As they drove back to HQ, Nina went over the case with Ruby. As far as she was concerned, there were just two possible explanations for Anna's death. The simple one was that the tarmac had become slippery and she slid off the road. The alternative was that she became ill or was drugged and veered over the edge herself.

Ruby was quiet for a while. 'I was wondering if there is a connection between her accident and what happened to Patrick.'

'Anna's accident was last year,' Nina replied as she turned

the car out of the university entrance. 'A coincidence, that's all. But I've been thinking, we could get a board put up on Buttertubs, asking for witnesses to Jack's accident.'

Chapter 18

'I can come in with you if you want,' Alex offered, as Mills climbed out of his car.

'I told you, I prefer to do it myself. Anyway, the court is probably rammed,' she added. 'It's a high-profile case, apparently.'

'Good luck then.'

'I'll probably need it,' Mills muttered as she walked towards the station building.

The journey to York passed too quickly. She emerged into brilliant sunshine and looked around. It was supposed to be a fifteen-minute walk from the station, something she would normally have enjoyed. However, this morning she was in her black trouser suit, already feeling sweaty from the packed compartment and she was carrying a heavy briefcase. She found a taxi and sat peering forward anxiously as they waited in heavy traffic.

'Visiting the museum, are we?' the driver asked.

'No. Actually I'm appearing in court.'

There was a pause. 'Never mind, love. You'll be all right.'

Mills contemplated whether he thought she was up before the judge herself and if she should correct him. Before she could reply, he was turning into the Castle entrance. It wasn't the first time she'd visited the imposing building that housed the crown court. When she'd begun working for Yardley Forensics, Brenda had insisted she did the training course and attended some hearings in York with her. Brenda had spent time explaining the proceedings to assure herself that Mills would be familiar with the court should the need arise. Mills hadn't expected it to arise quite so soon.

The receptionist directed her to wait and Mills found a seat in the public area. She had no idea who the people around her were, or whether they were involved in the case. She'd read about there being a special waiting room for defence witnesses and sat anxiously, wondering if she was supposed to be in one. Time went by slowly. People sitting around her disappeared into one of the two courtrooms. Mills was desperate for a coffee but wasn't sure if she could slip away to find one. After an hour of waiting, Rajani came out of courtroom one and made for the reception desk, where she remained in conversation for a minute or so. Then she turned and strode over to Mills.

'Dr Sanderson.'

Mills jumped up and grabbed her briefcase.

'I'm afraid we're not ready for you yet.'

She sat down on the bench and indicated for Mills to join her. 'The prosecution are dragging out the examination of their last witness. I don't think you'll be on until later this afternoon, possibly not until tomorrow, we can't tell yet. If it gets too late the judge may adjourn after we finish with their witness.' She looked at Mills. 'Are you OK?'

'Just dying for a coffee,' she replied.

'Well there'll be plenty of time for that this morning I'm afraid. Can I see you at lunch time? There are a few points

I'd like to go over with you, if you don't mind?'

'No problem.'

The solicitor jumped up. 'Excellent. I'd better go. They've only adjourned for a few minutes.'

Mills found a coffee in the cafeteria. She'd had nothing so far that day and knew she should eat something. The delay in her appearance had taken the pressure off and she settled down to go over her report while she munched her way through three digestive biscuits. She had no idea what the prosecution would ask her. Rajani had assured her that the defence lawyer would draw attention to her excellent qualifications and the relevance of her research. The solicitor had also convinced her that as an expert witness she was not there to be humiliated. Mills hoped she was right.

When Rajani found her, Mills was still in the cafeteria.

'Have you had lunch?' she asked.

Mills indicated the empty biscuit wrapper.

'You must have something substantial; it might be a long afternoon,' the solicitor ordered. 'We don't want our expert witness fainting in court.' When she laughed her eyes wrinkled up and Mills guessed she was older than she appeared. 'You haven't done much of this before, have you?' she asked.

'No,' Mills admitted. 'It's my first time.' She blushed.

There was the slightest hesitation, hardly there but Mills recognised it.

'No problem.' Rajani's eyes remained unwrinkled as she smiled at Mills. 'Have you had any…'

'I did the course,' Mills offered. 'I know what to do.'

'That's fine then.' The woman leaned across the table. 'I have just three questions. The first one is why the expert witness working for the prosecution didn't use *your* technique to analyse the soils?'

'That's a good question. I presume because he didn't have access to the instrumentation or the knowledge to use it. But I'm guessing.'

'OK. Number two: if he identified the minerals as being identical in the soil samples, why did you find such variation in the elements you measured?'

Mills considered the question. 'Because the trace elements can vary in the same minerals from different locations,' she said. 'To be honest, the mineralogy of soils can vary. We can have sandy soil, peaty soil, clayey soil but it wouldn't be soil if it varied too significantly. The soils we analysed were quite sandy, meaning they contained silicate minerals and that is what Professor Green saw. The mineral phases were similar in the soil samples. But when we analysed those silicates, we found quite different trace elements in them, meaning they weren't from the same source.'

Rajani had been nodding. 'That's what I understood.'

'So what did he say?' Mills asked.

Rajani ignored her. 'The last question is about the laboratory where the work was carried out.'

'Yardley Forensics?'

'No, the university where Professor Green does his work.'

Mills waited.

'What is your opinion of the environment where he carries out his forensic investigations?'

Mills was taken aback. She thought of the chaotic laboratory where Jack sat preparing samples. She doubted the benches had been cleaned in years, there was no proper ventilation. In no way was it a clean area meeting the scrupulous requirements for forensic work.

'You're hesitating.' Rajani said. 'Why?'

'It's awkward.'

'Why?'

'Because I work in the same department. I know the laboratory. It's… difficult.'

'Do you mean there's a problem with the laboratory or the fact you work in the same department?'

'Both.'

'I see.' She looked at her watch. 'I'd better be going but thanks for that. I may see you later. If not, tomorrow.' She picked up her handbag and went to leave.

'Are those the sort of questions I might expect from the prosecution?' Mills asked.

'No, those are the questions our defence team had.'

Mills watched Rajani leave then made her way back to her seat in the public area. At least she had her report to read, although she'd gone over it almost too many times. She was beginning to feel less confident of her findings than before. The time went slowly and she became increasingly anxious as the afternoon wore on. Eventually, a crowd of people emerged from the courtroom, closely followed by Rajani who was accompanied by a man a few years her senior in a wig and gown.

'This is Mervyn,' Rajani said, as Mills stood up to meet them.

They both said "Hi" in unison. He took her hand and held it for an uncomfortably long time.

'Great to meet you. Sorry you've had to wait. We've adjourned for the day, which means you'll be first on tomorrow. Anything you want to ask?'

Mills hesitated. There were so many things but she was embarrassed to show her inexperience.

'No? OK then.' He grinned then turning to Rajani said, 'Back in a minute.'

They watched him striding across the hallway.

'He's OK when you get to know him,' Rajani said to Mills. 'We've got some stuff to discuss so I'll let you get off home. And don't worry – it'll be fine!'

'So how did it go?' Alex asked when he met her at the station.

Mills ripped off her jacket and flung it into the back of the car along with the briefcase before answering. 'I've not been called yet.'

Alex wanted to hear about her day but her head was throbbing and she just wanted to get home and into a cool shower. 'I'll tell you later,' she said and lay back in her seat with her eyes firmly shut.

She was woken by someone gently calling her name.

'Mills, we're here.' Alex was holding the car door open for her.

She stumbled out and allowed him to bring her things in for her. She stood waiting for him to unlock the front door, still slightly dazed.

'Mills! I need to see you!' This time the voice was loud, the tone urgent. Her neighbour was at the gate. 'Stephen's calling an emergency meeting tonight. We've all got to come!'

'Not tonight, Muriel.' Mills didn't turn round.

'But he said we have to.'

'I can't. Sorry.'

'Are you out?'

'No. I'm going to bed.' Mills pushed past Alex into the cottage.

She could hear him apologising to Muriel, telling her she'd had a bad day. Maybe she'd feel better later. When he came in he told Mills the meeting was at eight.

'I'll cook some pasta; you must want something to eat,' he offered.

'Not really. I'm going to have a shower.' She went straight upstairs and into the bathroom, peeling off her sticky clothes before standing under the cool water. Afterwards she lay on the bed wrapped in a towel and listened to the sound of a curlew calling across the dale. When she woke the smell of cooking was drifting from downstairs and she realised that she actually felt hungry for the first time that day. Pulling on her dressing gown, she went downstairs, the stone steps cold on her bare feet.

Alex gave her a kiss and ushered her out of the kitchen. 'It's nearly ready. I've poured the wine. Your glass is on the table.'

Mills didn't want to drink. It was a big day tomorrow, she needed a clear head, but Alex told her it would help her relax. The glass was empty by the time he came in with the dishes.

'Want another?' he asked, picking up the bottle.

'No,' she said as she began eating. 'I mean, no thank you.'

Alex topped up his glass and took a sip. 'Nina rang while you were upstairs. I said you'd ring back.'

'What did she want?'

'I didn't ask. I assumed she wanted to know how it went in court today.'

'There's nothing to say. It went on longer than expected and I wasn't needed.'

After their meal, Mills took the phone upstairs and rang Nina.

'Before you ask, I wasn't called today,' Mills said when her friend answered.

'Oh, hello. Thanks for ringing back. I just wondered… you know…'

'I was there all day and they didn't need me.'

'It's sometimes like that, Mills. They can't always tell how long things will last. When will they need you?'

'Tomorrow morning. I'm dreading it.'

'Well worrying won't help. You know your stuff. Have an early night and forget about it. Remember, you are working for the court not one side or the other.'

'You're right, as usual.'

'I was at your place of work today, Mills.'

'Yardley's?'

'No, the university. I had a meeting with Mr Will Humphreys. Did you know he was back in the country?'

'No, I didn't. Is it about the BUCS business?'

'BUCS? What BUCS business?'

'Oops, I just thought…'

'Come on Mills, what is it?'

'I don't know. The British University Cycle thing or Sport thing. It regulates the university competitions I think.'

'So what does it have to do with Will Humphreys?'

'I think they were investigating him. I don't know how true that is, Nina. I just heard…'

'Investigating him for what?'

Mills sighed. 'Performance enhancing drugs. Allegedly.'

'Well that's interesting – although it's not why I was seeing him today, as it happens.'

'Oh.'

Mills could hear a baby crying in the background.

'Look, I'd better go,' Nina said. 'Have a good sleep, Mills and I hope it all goes well tomorrow.'

'I will – and thanks.'

Mills could hear car doors banging outside and went to the window. Arthur and Colin had arrived for the meeting. Stephen's car was already parked outside Muriel's cottage. She considered whether she should go. An emergency meeting sounded ominous and she was surprised anyone had turned up after the fiasco at the public meeting. Has Stephen concocted another outrageous plan to sabotage the race? She thought of Ruby and reluctantly began to dress.

Alex was watching a film and hardly acknowledged her announcement that she'd be next door. Muriel's front door was wide open and she stepped inside, pushing strands of damp hair away from her face. Stephen was deep in conversation with Catriona in the tiny hallway, his back against one wall, his hand on the other, trapping Catriona inside the house, and Mills outside.

'Oh, good evening. We weren't expecting *you*,' he said pointedly, straightening up and lowering his arm.

There followed an awkward manoeuvring to allow Mills past. Despite the open door, the cottage was hot and airless.

'We heard you were appearing in court and had been detained,' he continued in a sarcastic tone.

'Are you in law?' Catriona asked, pleasantly enough.

'Er, no.' Mills moved to open the dining room door. The buzz of conversation indicated everyone had already gathered.

'You're not in the police?' Stephen was clearly perturbed.

'No. Forensics.'

She pushed open the door and took her place beside Arthur.

'Hello stranger.' He smiled. 'We missed you, didn't we Colin?'

She grinned at them both and waved across at Muriel, who also seemed relieved to see her.

'Do we know why we're here?' she asked Arthur under her breath.

'Another master plan by our leader,' he replied.

'I thought the group had disbanded,' she said.

'So did I but Muriel insisted and we didn't want to leave her in the lurch.'

Mills sighed. She supposed there would be no harm done if Stephen thought he had support when none of the group would implement any of his hare-brained schemes.

Eventually Stephen came in, apologising for keeping them waiting. He'd had important things to discuss with Catriona, he explained. They all watched her cross the room to take her seat next to him. Looking anxious, she removed a small book from her bag and sat poised to take notes.

'This will be a short meeting,' Stephen began as he wiped his forehead with a cotton handkerchief.

The sense of relief in the room was audible.

'I thought you'd be pleased. I want to address one key point as we are getting close to the big day, D-Day.'

They waited for him to hear what the D stood for but he continued without explanation. 'We've already discussed the use of tacks so we won't go into that now. I want to add another string to our bow. In fact it is a sort of string, although wire will be more effective – stretched across the road as the riders go through.'

'A trip wire?' Mills couldn't help it. She'd meant to keep quiet, to let the others do the talking, but she was so appalled it had just come out.

Stephen ignored her outburst and went on. 'We're not going to discuss it in detail because Catriona and I can handle it ourselves. We don't need your help, just your support. I trust I can rely on that?'

The question hung there. No-one responded. Mills could feel sweat trickling down her back.

'I'll take that as a yes then.' He was mopping his face again.

Mills looked round the room. Some of them had sheepish expressions, others raised their eyebrows but no-one spoke.

'Well, that's all I wanted to say.' He rose to leave. Catriona was staring at her notebook. 'Shall we go?' he asked her.

She nodded, picking up her bag and following him out of the room. Everyone sat motionless until Muriel finally stood up.

'Anyone for a cup of tea?' she asked, disappearing into the kitchen and leaving Mills alone with Arthur and Colin.

'You know why she follows him about like a lap dog?' Arthur asked. 'I'll tell you. She lives next door to him.'

'I suppose they're good friends then,' Mills offered.

'Wrong. She wants to extend her cottage so she can take more visitors in her B&B. She knows he can stop her if he raises objections again this time round.'

'She's tried before?' Colin asked.

'Oh yes. And he wasn't having any of it. I reckon he's

got her eating out of his hand and that's why.'

'She didn't look too happy this evening,' commented Mills.

Colin agreed. 'Outside her comfort zone I should think.'

Mills left before the tea was brewed – she couldn't bear the stuffiness of the house any longer. Outside there was a little breeze but she went straight in to send an email to Ruby. She needed to warn her of Stephen's latest dangerous plan. A trip wire would be a real hazard on any part of the route but if it was on Buttertubs Pass it could be fatal.

Chapter 19

The train journey to York was as hot and unpleasant as the day before but this time she was much earlier. Unsure when the court would begin its work, she left the house at a ridiculous time, according to Alex.

'I can take you to the station, if you let me get ready,' he'd pointed out as she woke him to say she was leaving. She'd been awake since five and would go mad if she didn't get moving.

'I want to go now. Anyway, I don't know what time I'll be back, I'd rather take my own car.'

'But you'll be far too early!'

'I want to be sure that I'm there in good time,' she argued.

Well she was certainly that. Unsure whether any of the coffee shops in the city would be open yet, she bought a cappuccino at the station and started along the route to the Castle. She'd taken the precaution of packing her shoes in her bag and wearing flats for the journey. Even so, the hard pavement was uncomfortable to walk on and she was regretting purchasing a hot drink when the sun was already burning her back.

In order not to arrive too soon, she wandered across the

bridge and into the area she knew best. It was the quiet period before the start of the working day so she was relieved to find "Caffe Nero" open for business. She sat with her second cappuccino for nearly an hour until she was sure she would be able to get into the court building. At first the coffees had a beneficial effect, her mind felt sharp and alert, but as time went on she developed a dull headache which she put down to lack of food. The walk to the court building didn't help so she headed for the cloakroom to down a couple of paracetamol tablets and change her shoes.

Rajani and the barrister were waiting for her in the entrance hall when she emerged.

'Good morning Mills!' His greeting was too cheerful, the smile forced.

'Feeling better today?' Rajani asked.

'I'm fine,' she lied.

'Good,' said Mervyn. 'You'll be on as soon as the court sits.

'Just wait here until you're called,' advised Rajani. 'He'll ask you some questions about the report and then the prosecution will cross examine. I'm sure they won't take long.'

Mervyn snorted and Rajani looked at him sharply before giving Mills a reassuring smile.

She watched them disappear down the corridor and sat down to wait. It wasn't long before she was following the usher into the courtroom, her legs shaking. It seemed as if everyone was watching her as she entered the witness stand. She was aware of being asked if she would swear or affirm. Her answer sounded thin and shaky as she read the card.

'I do solemnly, sincerely and truly declare and affirm that the evidence I shall give shall be the truth the whole truth and nothing but the truth.'

The judge was speaking and she turned towards him, remembering that she must keep her gaze between him and the jury.

'...and remember she is here to assist the court and that overrides any obligation to the instructing party – in this case the defence.'

He seemed to be addressing the jury rather than speaking to her. Eventually Mervyn rose and asked her to tell the court how she was qualified to give her expert opinion. She knew that would be required and had rehearsed what she would say. She described her training and qualifications, mentioning her role at the university and in Yardley Forensics.

'You call yourself a forensic archaeologist. Could you explain how that gives you expertise in soil analysis?'

He knew what he was doing. Sydney Green was a soil scientist and the case hung on the comparison of the soil on the accused's trousers and the soil from the crime scene. He wasn't stupid and he knew the prosecution would pick up on whether she was sufficiently expert in soil science to comment on the case. To be fair it was Alex who had prepared her for this.

'My PhD thesis concerned the study of bog bodies: corpses buried in peaty soil. As part of that work I had to analyse large numbers of soil types and identify small changes in trace elements found at the sites of the burials.'

That seemed to satisfy him and she relaxed sufficiently to remember to look away from him and back in the direction of the jury. Twelve pairs of eyes returned her gaze.

He then asked her to describe exactly what samples she had received and what was done to them, how they were analysed and how she had handled the data. Now she was back in her comfort zone. She'd gone over the report so many times and now she had the boards that had been prepared for the court in advance. She had no idea how long she spent describing the work but she could see the jury were still attentive.

Then came the difficult question that no-one had prepared her for but that she guessed would come up at some stage. Clearly the defence were pre-empting the prosecution's line of questioning.

'Dr Sanderson, your very thorough and detailed report shows that the two samples of soil are so different that the soil on the defendant's trousers could not possibly have come from the crime scene.'

'That's correct.'

'So how can we explain that the results of Professor Green's mineralogical examination suggest they *are* a match?'

He was smirking and looking round the courtroom. Some members of the jury were leaning forward expectantly. Mills swallowed hard. Her mouth felt dry but this was not the moment to pick up a glass. She took a deep breath and began. She used the same argument she'd given Rajani the day before, explaining slowly and carefully, trying not to sound patronising. The minerals could be very similar but the trace element information would give the definitive results.

He seemed satisfied with her response. He thanked her, told the judge he had completed his questioning and sat down. Mills was feeling a little more confident now and looked round to see who would be questioning her next. It was the first time she'd seen Rajani in court, seated behind Mervyn and then she caught sight of the defendant. He was middle-aged man in a dark suit, smartly dressed. He looked the height of respectability and very uncomfortable beside the dock officer.

She quickly averted her gaze to the jury, catching sight of the public. A handful of people seated in the gallery. Among them was a face she recognised but couldn't put her finger on where she'd seen him before.

'Dr Sanderson.' It was difficult to judge the age of the woman rising to her feet. The white wig probably made her look older, Mills thought. She had a black dress under her gown but Mills could only see the top half of her torso. She could be fifty or even older.

'You told the court that you work at the University of North Yorkshire. Am I right?'

'Yes.'

'I assume that is in your capacity as an archaeologist.'

'No, actually I lecture in forensics.'

'Forensic archaeology?'

'Well, no. I give lectures on modern techniques in forensic analysis as well.'

'And your job title there is?'

'Lecturer.'

'Would that be a permanent position?'

'No. I'm on contract at the moment.'

'So the exact title is Temporary Lecturer?'

'I suppose… Yes.'

'If you were to get a permanent position, I understand it would take some time before you achieved a professorship, a chair?'

'Of course.'

'What exactly would you need to do to achieve that status, *Dr* Sanderson?'

'Carry out research, publish papers…'

'Have you published many papers in the field of soil science, Dr Sanderson?'

'No.'

'I suppose *Professor* Green must have done so?'

'Well, I…'

'Let me help you. He did. He has published forty-five papers on soil science in scientific journals during his career. So I guess he is fairly knowledgeable about the topic.'

No response seemed necessary. The conversation had left Mills feeling inadequate. She looked at Mervyn but he had his eyes on the papers in front of him. Rajani was giving her an encouraging smile.

Thankfully the prosecution had exhausted that line of examination and began on another tack – or so she thought.

'Can I ask you about your position at Yardley Forensics. You are currently the head of the laboratory?'

'Yes, while the owner is indisposed.'

'I see. So you are the "acting" head of Yardley Forensics.'

'Yes.'

'Thank you.' The woman turned to the jury. 'It's helpful to understand the level of responsibilities that the expert witnesses hold, particularly in this case where they hold opposing interpretations of the forensic evidence.'

Mills took a deep breath as she studied the jury and wondered how much of the detail they had absorbed.

'Dr Sanderson, you have given the court a detailed explanation of the analyses carried out at Yardley Forensics. The interpretation was carried out by you?'

'Yes.'

'Have you had many cases where this type of interpretation has been a key feature of the case?'

Mills thought for a moment. 'The laboratory has carried out this type of analysis many times before.'

'No, that's not what I meant. Let me put it more simply for you. Have you personally carried out this type of interpretation to be presented in court before?'

'Yes, I have. I was recently asked to examine soil taken from a murder scene on the North York Moors. We used the same methodologies to locate the crime scene.'

'What about rape cases?'

'No. I've not been involved with a rape case before.' Mills turned to the judge. 'The technique is the same regardless of the crime.' Then she added, 'My Lord.'

He nodded encouragingly at her. 'I think this would be a good time to have a short break,' he added.

Mills left the witness stand and walked out into the public area feelingly dazed. She was immediately joined by Rajani.

'You're doing fine. Let's get you a coffee and something to eat before the next round.'

The courtroom was emptying and the man she'd spotted in the public gallery went past alone. He didn't acknowledge her but he had a strange expression of amusement on his face. Now she recognised him: he was from the university, one of the administrators in her department. She only knew him as Mr Runshaw. No doubt he was there to protect its good name. If the jury found the man guilty of rape, Green would be vindicated and she'd be discredited, along with Yardley Forensics. If they found for the defence, Sydney Green would be gunning for her blood. Either way was not a good outcome for her. As the prosecuting barrister had reminded her, her post at the university was only temporary.

The break was over too soon and Mills was back on the stand, bracing herself for the next round. She had no idea what would happen next and was expecting the worst but this time the woman stood up with a smile, her head cocked sympathetically on one side as she studied her. Mills was distracted by the lock of steely grey hair escaping from under the dirty white wig.

'*Dr* Sanderson.'

She was doing it again: emphasising her junior rank compared to Green.

The barrister tilted her head on the other side. '*Dr* Sanderson, please take your time and let me know if you want a break. We all appreciate how stressful it is, appearing as a witness in front of a jury.'

The bitch, Mills thought. She straightened up and looked directly at the judge. 'That won't be necessary, My Lord,' she said loudly and clearly.

He smiled at her and nodded. 'I'm sure you're right.' Turning to the barrister, he gave her a stern look. 'Please continue.'

'Yes, My Lord.' She turned the pages of her notes, as if deciding to omit some of her line of questioning.

Mills turned to look across at the jury, reminding herself that it wouldn't do to lose control with the woman.

'Dr Sanderson, you said that the technique you use is an inductively coupled plasma mass spectrometer,' she read the name out carefully, making it sound unfamiliar and strange. 'How common is it to use this sort of test in forensic work?'

Mills explained that it had been around for a long time and was becoming a normal means of analysing forensic material.

'So why, do you think, Professor Green did not make use of it himself?'

Mills looked across at the public gallery. The administrator was leaning forward. She couldn't say Green was a dinosaur and hadn't kept up with science.

'Dr Sanderson?' the woman prompted.

'Professor Green is a distinguished soil scientist,' she began, looking at the jury. 'He has his own area of expertise in mineralogy. I have been trained in the modern ways of forensic analysis and ICPMS is the way I have chosen to go.' Oh shit, she thought, and looked up at the gallery for the man from the university. His face showed no emotion.

'You told the court that it is possible for two scientists, carrying out different analyses, to get different information from the same samples.'

'Yes.'

'But surely the facts are the facts. If forensics can give two different answers they can't possibly be used in court, can they?'

'I suppose not.'

'Are you suggesting that the forensic evidence in this case may not be reliable?' She was turning to the jury with a look of mock horror on her face.

Mills deliberately addressed her reply to the jury. 'I'm saying that some methods may be more reliable than others.'

She immediately regretted her feisty response. The barrister swung round aggressively. Somehow Mills had given her permission to pounce.

'So who is right in this case, Dr Sanderson? You or *Professor* Green?'

It wasn't supposed to be like this, Mills thought. On the course they'd emphasised that expert witnesses were respected, that they would be treated as knowledgeable experts, there to assist the court, not one side or the other.

The jury was waiting. 'I can't answer that. It's not straightforward.'

Mervyn was fiddling with his papers, head down. Rajani was looking across anxiously. The court was silent for several seconds.

'I'll ask you again, Dr Sanderson. Who is correct?'

Mills turned to the Judge. 'I believe my findings are accurate, My Lord. I am sure Professor Green is confident of his findings – as far as they go.' She paused.

'Go on,' he encouraged her.

'Well, Professor Green relied on mineralogical analysis of the soils and he found that the two samples contained the same common minerals such as silicates and feldspars, so assumed they had the same origin.' She paused and he nodded for her to continue. Her hands were sweaty and she wiped them on her skirt, surreptitiously before continuing. 'I analysed them for trace elements – the less common ones that occur in the more exotic minerals.'

'For the court,' the Judge asked, 'can you tell us why Professor Green did not see these exotic minerals, if they were in the soils?'

'They could be present in tiny amounts, too small and insignificant to notice – but their effect on certain trace elements is significant.'

She waited to see what would happen next. The judge thanked her and asked the prosecuting lawyer to continue. Mills stiffened, ready for the next attack.

'Just to clarify, are you saying, Dr Sanderson, that you do not agree with Professor Green's evidence?'

'No.'

'No?'

'No, what I mean is, no, I'm not saying that.'

'So you do agree with him?'

Mills sighed and looked back at the judge. 'I'm saying that he found the same major minerals in the two soils but the interpretation that they came from the same site is incorrect.'

There, she'd said it now. Green had made the wrong interpretation of his findings.

The judge suggested it was a good time to adjourn for lunch and Mills stepped down with relief, although she noticed that her legs had now stopped shaking and she was beginning to feel quite hungry. She made for the entrance to the building and stepped out into the fresh air, planning to eat her lunch outside. She'd stood up for herself and she no longer cared what Professor Sydney Green thought of her.

Her mood was short-lived when she spotted the administrator from the university, lighting up a cigarette. He took a long drag and then looked up. He'd seen her and was coming over.

'Dr Sanderson!' His forced cheerfulness irritated her.

'I was just going to have lunch.'

'Perhaps I can join you?' he asked.

'Sorry, I brought a sandwich.'

'Well, have you got a minute?'

Frustrated, she didn't reply but stood waiting.

'The Head of Department sent me,' he explained. 'Told me to follow the case.'

'Why, exactly?'

'He's worried about Professor Green's reputation.'

'Oh, I thought he might be worrying about mine.' It was cheeky but she was feeling reckless. If she was going down, she'd go fighting.

'To be honest, he's getting near retirement and we don't want to shake the boat.'

'Green or the Head?'

No reply. They stood for several minutes while he puffed on his cigarette.

'I should warn you, the Head is on Sydney's side in this. He's got no choice.' He dropped the cigarette and ground it in with his shoe.

'I understand that,' Mills said.

She turned and went back into the building. In the Ladies she splashed her face with cold.

Rajani caught her in the entrance hall. 'I've got to go,' she said. 'I can't spend any more time here.'

'What d'you think?' Mills asked. She needed to know whether she'd made the right responses.

'It's fine,' she replied. 'There was no other way of expressing it, was there? Once the jury understands the scientific reason for your interpretation, they'll get it.'

'You think they don't now?'

'Not yet. Anyway, I must dash. I'm sure they'll be finished with you soon.'

That's the problem, Mills thought. I might be finished for good after this.

Chapter 20

Back in the courtroom, the lawyer remained seated when Mills took the witness stand. The judge explained that the jury had sent some questions relating to the forensics and he would be asking Dr Sanderson to go over some of her evidence again – but this time in more detail.

She presented the description of what she'd measured and how she'd analysed the results by taking ratios. Mervyn produced the boards again, showing how the symbols representing the two soils formed tight groups totally dissociated from each other.

'So, you see, the soil from the defendant has a completely different fingerprint to that from the crime scene.' She considered for a moment. 'They are as different as they might be if one came from Cumbria and one from Northumberland.'

She could see several heads nodding. Mr Runshaw was in the gallery making notes. Mervyn looked pleased.

The prosecuting barrister stood up slowly. 'No further questions, My Lord,' she said and sat down again.

The judge dismissed her with a nod of the head and a smile.

Mills made straight for the Ladies to change her shoes

before leaving. She'd promised herself some retail therapy after it was all over but now she just wanted to get home. What did they say? She'd won the battle but lost the war.

Someone called her name as she left the cloakroom. Mervyn was coming out of the courtroom.

'I just wanted to say thank you. Your evidence has had a significant impact on the case. I hope we can work with you again.'

Mills wasn't so sure.

'Are you rushing off now?' he asked. 'Not waiting for the verdict?'

'Will they decide today?' Mills asked.

'They'll be retiring this afternoon, after the summing up. I don't think it will take too long.'

'I've got to get back to Swaledale,' she said, not wishing to remain a minute longer than necessary.

'Oh, lovely. Whereabouts?'

'Near Gunnerside – well, actually nearer Ivelet.'

'Beautiful part of the world.'

'You know it?'

'Not well.'

'Actually I live in Mossy Bank. It's so small no-one's heard of it.'

'Mossy Bank? Now I *have* heard of Mossy Bank. Why?' He scratched his head under his wig. 'It must've been a case.'

Mills made to leave but he suddenly frowned. 'Yes, a car accident. Sad case. A woman and her grandchild, both killed outright. You probably knew them?'

Mills was puzzled. 'Not from the village, there's been no-one. When was this?'

'Over five years ago I would think. Anyway, must be

getting on. Just wanted to say thanks. I'll get Rajani to call you with the verdict.' He squeezed her arm in a friendly fashion and rushed back in the direction of the courtroom.

Ruby paused on her way back to the office after eating her lunch in the sunshine. Jo Richie was manoeuvring his battered white van into the car park. She was sufficiently certain it was him to wait until he reached the main entrance.

'Jo?' she asked. He seemed surprised she knew his name. 'I'll take you up to Sergeant Fuller.'

Hazel had insisted that she conduct the interview but Ruby had made a special request to sit in. She still didn't know if it was to be permitted.

They didn't speak as they climbed the stairs. Richie seemed out of his depth, looking anxiously around as staff passed them in the corridor. There was laughter coming from the office and Ruby asked him to wait outside.

'Jo Richie's here,' she announced.

Nina, who had been sitting on her desk, hopped down and straightened her skirt. Hazel's expression became serious.

'So can I sit in?' Ruby asked, expecting a negative response.

'OK,' Hazel replied, giving her strict instructions on what she could and couldn't do. Mostly it was what not to do.

Nina was grinning.

Hazel picked up a file and was at the door. 'Well, hurry up if you're coming.'

Ruby followed as Hazel led Richie to the room they'd booked for the interview.

'Don't look so worried Jo,' she began as she opened the file. 'We don't bite. We just want to clarify exactly what happened when you "found" the bike on Buttertubs Pass.'

'I did find it.'

'Do you often travel on that road, Jo?'

'No.'

'How often, then?'

'When I visit my mother.'

'And how often is that?'

'It depends.'

'Depends? Depends on what?'

'When she says I have to go.'

Hazel sighed audibly. 'Have you visited her since you found the bike?'

'No – been waiting for the insurance, haven't I?'

'Oh yes. I'd forgotten that you'd omitted to get insured. So, what about *before* you found the bike, when did you visit her before that?'

'Christmas.'

'Christmas? Not between Christmas and May?'

Richie shifted uncomfortably on his chair. 'What?'

'Just for clarification, Jo. The only time you drove over Buttertubs Pass this year was on that day in May when you spotted the bicycle lying by the side of the road and picked it up.'

He hesitated.

'It's a simple question, Jo.'

'Yes. I went over in the morning, had my dinner with her and drove back in the afternoon.'

'Fair enough.' Hazel shut the file. 'So just for confirmation, you did not go over Buttertubs on any other occasion in May?'

'No – I said. No insurance.' He was slumped in his chair, hands in the pockets of his hoody.

Hazel excused them and asked Ruby to follow her into the corridor. 'I can't keep him any longer. As he said, he hasn't been able to drive the van, so he wouldn't be over there again in May.'

'But he wouldn't admit that he'd been driving while still uninsured, would he?' argued Ruby.

Hazel didn't answer. She was looking at the ceiling, apparently considering what to do next. Then she disappeared back into the interview room, shutting the door carefully behind her. Ruby moved closer; if she leaned her head against the door she could just about hear the conversation.

'…so what I'd like to know, Jo, is where your van was during the rest of the month, after you were cautioned for driving without insurance.'

There was a pause. Ruby pressed her ear against the wood.

'Outside my house.'

'The entire time?'

'Yes, you can see if you like.'

'How's that, Jo?'

'My neighbour's got CCTV set up across the road.'

'I doubt he'll have footage from last month, Jo. However, there is a particular date that interests us…'

'What date?'

'The seventeenth of May.'

'Cup final day?'

'I don't…'

'I was in the pub from lunch time until it was over.'

There was a pause.

'Plenty of people there?'

'Yes. You can ask any of them.'

'The landlord?'

'He knows me.'

'Then write down his name and the name of the pub on this paper while I speak to my colleague.'

Ruby jumped back as the door handle clicked.

'I think we might have confirmation of his whereabouts on the day of the near miss,' Hazel told her.

Ruby nodded.

'You heard?'

She nodded again.

'Well, stay with him,' Hazel instructed, 'while I get in touch with his local.'

Ruby went in and sat down self-consciously. She didn't know whether Hazel's earlier instruction to keep quiet extended to this part of the meeting. In the end she couldn't bear the silence.

'She's just going to check with the landlord.'

'No problem.' He sat up grinning. 'Can I go now?'

'Not until she comes back.'

He slumped back down in the chair. 'She your boss?'

'Sort of,' she said.

'I didn't do nothing except pick up the bike. I thought it was dumped. Was it valuable like?'

'Quite.'

He played with his phone while Ruby waited. It was fifteen minutes before Hazel returned.

'OK sunshine, off you hop,' she said as she came in.

'I can go?' Richie asked.

'Yes.'

He struggled up and pushed past her into the corridor.

They followed him to the entrance hall and saw him out of the building.

'What did the landlord say?' Ruby asked.

'He was there all day, giving him lip.' She laughed. 'He asked if it was about the bike he was trying to flog. Everyone knew it must be bent, he said.'

Virginia Bassett emptied her carrier bag of purchases onto Jack's bed and bent to give him a kiss. She didn't care if it embarrassed him, she was just so pleased to see him sitting up and looking alert. She'd been haunted by thoughts that she would lose her son during the last week and now the weight was lifted, she felt light-headed with the relief.

'The doctor's pleased with your progress,' she told him as she peeled the lid from a strawberry yoghurt and handed him a spoon.

'They do feed me in here, Mum,' he said, taking it reluctantly.

'You've got to build yourself up now. I told your father. The sooner you come home, the better. Then I can give you some proper nourishing meals.'

Jack scooped the contents of the pot into his mouth obediently and handed it back to his mother.

'Your father was so upset when he heard you'd been taking that – what do you call it? – EPO. He was very angry at first. I told him, it's water under the bridge. We should just be thankful that they discovered what it was before… Well, you know.' Her voice wavered. 'But you must promise that you'll never do anything like that again!'

She told him how worried she and his father had been when the treatment took so long to act. He let her witter on, only half-listening, waiting for her to finish. Then he asked her what had been on his mind.

'Did you tell anyone about the white car?'

'White car?' She was busy opening a packet of biscuits and passing it to him.

'I told you, I saw a white car – when I had the accident.'

'Did you? I don't remember.'

'Well I do. A white car came straight at me from the side of the road. I couldn't do anything. It pushed me over the edge.'

'Are you sure? No-one said anything about it to us.'

'That's because I didn't remember at the time. But I can see it now, really clearly: the bonnet in my line of site. It wasn't there one minute then – bang! Will you tell Dad? He can tell the police. Please Mum.'

He made her promise to report what he'd remembered, in case it was important. 'If I was deliberately driven off the road, it should be investigated.'

Virginia, shocked by the suggestion that her son's accident was caused by a careless driver, agreed to ring his father. 'He'll know what to do,' she said as she packed the empty cartons back in her carrier bag and left.

When Hazel and Ruby appeared in the office later that afternoon, Nina was anxious to show them an email. Ray Bassett had been on the phone, saying that his son had seen a car at the time of the accident and believed it had driven Jack off the road.

'Do they say what colour?' Ruby asked.

'White. It confirms what Ruby showed us in the photographs,' Nina said. 'D'you think it *was* Richie's van?'

'No,' Hazel was emphatic.

'But it's still a white vehicle,' said Ruby. 'And so was the one that had the near miss on the seventeenth.'

'True,' said Hazel. 'But there are thousands of white cars on the roads and nothing we can do about that.'

'I was thinking about Will Humphreys… but he was in France then,' Nina pondered.

Hazel was beginning to look irritated. 'More importantly we are only ten days away from the big race. Have you got anything for us, Ruby?'

'Stephen Grainger plans to put trip wire across the road.'

'That'll be tricky, with all the vehicles running up and down the route.' Hazel was laughing. 'He'll have to be pretty quick to set something up between the cars and the bikes.'

Ruby looked hurt. 'Not necessarily. And it could be really dangerous if he goes ahead.'

'We *could* ask Mitch for someone to keep an eye on him during the race,' suggested Nina.

'I don't mind…' began Ruby.

'No, definitely not. We'll put uniform onto it,' said Hazel. 'That'll stop him.'

As soon as Ruby left for the day, Hazel turned on Nina. 'Why do you keep supporting her over this nonsense with the white car or van or whatever it is? She's here to sort out the group trying to disrupt the race. You're only encouraging her to be side-tracked!'

Nina was taken aback by her friend's vehemence. 'She's just a kid, Hazel. I don't like to dampen enthusiasm.'

'It's me who'll get it in the neck if anything goes wrong on the fifth. She'll be gone after the race and I'll have to carry the can.'

'I don't think you should be too hard on her though. There could have been a connection between the cycle accidents.'

'Nina! The inquest found that the Rycroft girl's accident was just that. The near miss was clearly exactly that. You spoke to the lad. And Jack Bassett was run off the road by a car which we have no information for. It's as simple as that.'

'I'm not sure…'

'Aren't you?' Hazel glared at her. 'I suppose you'd just let her carry on, running round like some private detective? Fancy herself as Nancy Drew? The trouble with you is you're too soft. If you want to get on in this game you need to toughen up Nina Featherstone!'

She stormed out, leaving Nina staring after her. Hazel had been her mentor and she always considered her a good friend but she was left shaken and close to tears by the onslaught.

Back in Mossy Bank, Mills went straight upstairs to run a shower. She'd sat through the train journey with gritted teeth. She'd turned up the music to an unbearable pitch as she drove from the station, angry with the injustice of it all. If they found the man guilty, her reputation and that of the lab would be damaged but it would also mean that an innocent man would go to prison, for years perhaps. She let the water run over her head as tears flowed and she howled.

For an hour she sat on the bed in her underwear, waiting for Rajani to call until she could bear it no longer. Pulling on shorts, T-shirt and trainers, she went downstairs. The light on the answering machine was flashing and her heart raced as she waited to hear the verdict. Stupid. Rajani didn't have her home number.

'Mills, it's Fiona. How are you darling? Well I've done it. I managed to persuade your father to come up for the cycle race – the Tour de France, that's what it's called, isn't it? It's so nice of you to invite us and I'm sorry it's taken so long to get back to you. Anyway I'll speak to you soon. Bye!'

It was the last straw. Mills left the house without even combing her wet hair, slamming the door in exasperation.

The sun was hot as she took the lane above the village but a slight breeze made it pleasant to walk in. A curlew was calling overhead. She slowed her pace and allowed the sound to calm her down. She found it impossible to remain mad for long once she was up on the fell. She relaxed as she walked, eventually finding a comfortable stone to perch on, where she remained for a long, long time. She thought about her mother and, if she was still alive, what she would think of her daughter now. Mills would have given anything to be able to talk to her at this moment – she'd always given her such sensible advice. She sighed as she stood up and turned back.

Alex's car was outside the cottage when she arrived back and the smell of cooking was drifting through the open front door. Inside, there was a bouquet of flowers on the table.

'Is that you? I wondered where you were,' he called, coming from the kitchen with a tea towel in his hand.

'What are the flowers for?' she asked.

'To celebrate. There's champagne in the 'fridge!'

Mills mechanically picked up the flowers, taking them through to the kitchen. Alex followed her.

'You don't seem pleased.'

'No, they're very nice. Thank you.'

'I rang Brenda and told her the news. She was delighted.'

'Rang Brenda?'

'About the court case. The acquittal.'

Mills stopped arranging the flowers. The jury had made their decision? 'How do *you* know?' Mills asked.

'The solicitor rang you at the lab. She wanted you to know that the jury found for the defence. It only took an hour. In the absence of any other evidence the man was acquitted.'

Mills was relieved for the defendant. He was innocent and it was the correct verdict. It was good news for Brenda and Yardley Forensics but not for her.

'How is Brenda?' she asked as she poked the rest of the bunch into the vase.

'She's finished the treatment. She sounded OK. She might drop in tomorrow to congratulate you in person.'

'I wasn't going to…'

'Oh you've got to. Everyone wants to see the heroine. Timothy is really excited. He's getting his mother to make one of those big cakes.'

Mills pulled a face as she carried the vase into the sitting room.

'What's the matter?' Alex called.

'Nothing. I'm going to get changed.'

She could hear him preparing the meal in the kitchen below as she sat on the edge of the bed. She was still there when Alex called that dinner was ready. He'd made a pasta dish she liked and had opened the champagne but the food seemed to stick in her throat and she only had a couple of sips of the champagne. She knew she was spoiling the celebratory mood but she couldn't help it.

Eventually Alex asked her again what was wrong. In the end it was a relief to talk about it. She'd kept it bottled up throughout the trial and had told no-one about the threat to her future. Alex put his arm round her as they sat together on the sofa, comforting her when she finally told him about the departmental administrator being in court and how her role in discrediting Sydney Green could mean the end of her academic career.

'So you see I may not have a job at the end of this month.'

Chapter 21

There was a party atmosphere in the lab next morning. It was usual to celebrate when work had been successful in defining the outcome of a case – something Brenda had instigated. But she was quite fussy about when they could congratulate themselves, after all it wasn't their job to assist the barristers but to "help the court get to the truth" as she put it. But this was a clear case where their scientific prowess had succeeded by her definition and consequently there was cake at coffee time.

Mills tried to emulate the jubilant spirit of the team and had joined them in the tea room. When Brenda opened the door gingerly, Mills barely recognised her. The dumpy middle-aged lady with rosy cheeks and wild auburn hair had somehow diminished into a much older woman with a hollow face, in clothes that hung off her skinny frame.

'Brenda!'

'Don't sound so horrified, Mills. I've only come for an hour. I couldn't miss one of Timothy's home-made cakes.'

The others fussed round her and carried her coffee through to the office. They left her with Mills and Alex, perching on the desks while Brenda sank onto the sofa.

'Well that's a relief. Can't stand up for too long before I

begin to get weary.'

'You're looking good,' Alex offered.

'Don't be ridiculous, lad. I look like I feel, bloody awful. And I know it, so none of your nonsense.'

He looked suitably embarrassed.

'Oh don't mind me, lad,' she continued. 'I'm more cantankerous than ever, so they tell me.' She cleaned the crumbs from her plate and took a swig of coffee.

'So it all seems to be going well here without me,' she said, glancing round. 'I hope we've still got plenty of work coming in?' She looked at Mills.

'Not too bad. We could cope with more though.'

'Well, after your success in court, I'm sure we'll find more work coming our way, particularly if you've finally shown Professor Green up for what he is.'

'About that...'

'And the good news is that I've been signed off as fit for work.'

'Really?' Alex sounded genuinely surprised.

'Well, I told my GP that I'd go mad if I stayed at home any longer and he agreed that once the chemo was finished I could start to take on more work. Don't worry, I won't be full-time for a while but I want to get the bit between my teeth again.'

'That's great – isn't it, Mills?'

'Yes, brilliant.' She tried to sound pleased.

Alex was asking Brenda about the imaging software he wanted to buy. It cost thousands and Mills had said the lab couldn't afford it. It also couldn't afford to pay too many senior staff members. Once Brenda was back in charge, there wouldn't be room for all three of them.

She took the crockery back to the tea room while Alex

continued to praise the capabilities of his precious software. She thanked Timothy for his work on the rape case until everyone cheered and clapped, while he blushed. Brenda had left by the time she was back in the office and Alex was busy on the computer.

'I think she finds it harder than she would like us to know,' said Mills.

Alex looked up. 'Well, she's still got her marbles. She's agreed to the imaging package. I'm ordering it now.'

'She what?'

'She said it was a good investment.'

'It costs a fortune!'

'I know. Isn't it great?'

She went over and stared at the screen. The cost of the package would pay her salary for three months. Didn't he understand that she needed this lab job now that the university would be giving her the sack?

Nina was almost relieved when she received an urgent call at work from her husband. The atmosphere between her and Hazel was still rather frosty.

'I'm really sorry, love, but I've been summoned by the Head of Department. He wants me to go in this afternoon.'

'No problem.'

'Really?'

'Honestly, Nige. It's fine. You can pick Rosie up from school on your way back.'

By the time Nina was home, Nige had fed the boys and changed them. He rushed off to the university and she popped them in the yard for their nap while she worked on her laptop. Nina had been hurt by Hazel's remarks but they hadn't prevented her from continuing to puzzle over the trio of accidents involving cyclists at Buttertubs. Hazel had been correct: a death, a near miss and an injury were not particularly remarkable but it niggled away at her. National statistics for accidents involving bicycles in the region suggested it was unusual at least. She searched for cycle accidents on the internet and found that there were three cyclists killed on the roads in North Yorkshire in the previous year, excluding Anna Rycroft who wasn't found until later, and fifty-two injured. She looked for more details on accidents in the Dales, and was trawling through irrelevant newspaper articles and blogs when the words "Mossy Bank" caught her eye. It was a piece in the "Northern Echo" from some years ago. It described a tragic accident that had happened, not at the village as it turned out, but on the road near Hawes. A family had been travelling from Sedbergh when a cyclist shot out of the road from Buttertubs Pass straight into the path of the vehicle. The driver, who came from Mossy Bank, swerved and drove into a stone wall at 40 mph. She was killed outright and her passengers, a daughter and grandchild, died later in hospital. Nina shuddered and left the website. Outside her little family were safe in the sunshine and she went to join them for the rest of the afternoon.

When Nige arrived home with Rosie, Nina was preparing the children's tea.

'What did the Head want?' she asked when he came into the kitchen.

'It was rather odd.' Nige absentmindedly chewed on the crust she'd cut from a peanut butter sandwich. 'He asked if I could go back earlier than planned. They want me to take the field trip to Orkney in August.'

'But Mills is doing that, isn't she?'

'Yes but he said that plans may be changing.'

'Did you ask him why?'

'Not really. He said they were reviewing the arrangements.'

'I hope you told him you couldn't change yours.'

'I said I would ask you.'

'Nige!' Her husband was such a pushover. 'Well you can tell him we've made our plans based on your paternity arrangements and they can't be changed.'

Nige left the room without answering.

'Does Mills know about this?' she called after him.

'I don't know. I don't suppose so.'

'Well, you'd better find out.'

He reappeared in the doorway. 'Should you ring her?'

She sighed. If Hazel thought she was soft, what would she say about her husband?

She took the phone into the yard, while Nige gave the kids their tea.

'Are you still at the lab, Mills?'

'No, we're on our way home.'

'Good. I just wanted to let you know that Nige had to speak to his Head of Department today. Has he been in touch with you?'

'Who? Nige?'

'No, the Head. Nige asked me to call you. He was asked about starting back at the university early.'

'Why?'

'I don't know but they asked if he could take the Orkney trip.'

There was a pause. 'I get it. Yes, it's beginning.'

'What?'

Mills explained how she'd found herself in conflict with Sydney Green. She was still speaking when she lost signal.

'Damn. I've lost her.'

'What's the matter?' Alex asked. 'What's beginning?'

She told him what Nina had said and he told her she should go to see the Head as soon as possible to have it out with him. 'I'll come with you, if you want,' he offered.

'No! I can fight my own battles, thank you.'

'Fair enough, I was only trying to help.'

Mills waited until they were home before calling back. She needed to speak to Nige to get all the information. He repeated everything the Head had said.

'Well, it certainly sounds as though he's looking to finish my contract.'

'But if I refuse to go back early…'

'They'll find someone else, Nige. They want me gone – or at least Sydney Green does.'

Alex was waiting for her when she finished speaking to Nige. He sat her down and handed her a glass of wine.

'Talk to me, Mills.' He looked grave. 'Tell me what's happening. I want to help.'

His voice was so gentle and full of concern that she wanted to bawl her eyes out like a small child. But she swallowed hard and admitted that she feared she would lose both her short-term lecturing appointment and her equally temporary contract with Yardley Forensics.

He sat beside her and took her hands. 'You must go and speak to your Head of Department – as soon as possible.'

'It's no good. He'll support Green against me.'

'You don't know that until you see him.'

'There must be a way of persuading him that you're in the right.'

'Such as?'

'I don't know. Won't any of the other lecturers support you?'

'Nige will but no-one else is really involved.'

'What about people working with this Green character? Are they all on his side?'

'Probably.'

And that was the end of the conversation, although it didn't stop Mills from thinking about what he'd said. Perhaps there *was* someone who could help.

Anxious to change the subject, she mentioned the call from Fiona.

'I don't want them to come,' she told Alex. 'She makes such a fuss and it's a nightmare with the baby.'

'Flora sounds lovely and it will be great to meet your dad. The only thing is how will we all fit in?'

'They'll have the spare room. It's big enough.'

'The problem is…' Alex said slowly. 'When, before, you said they wouldn't be coming… I… that is… I…'

'What?' Mills was getting irritated by his evasiveness.

'I asked my mum and dad to come.'

'What? You asked them without consulting *me*?'

'Well *you* did – invite your parents, I mean!'

'You'll have to tell them they can't come!'

'I can't. It's been a last-minute thing; Dad's taken time off work. And anyway, I asked them first.'

It degenerated into a row that lasted all evening. Neither would back down and the only thing that they agreed on was that they couldn't have both sets of parents staying at the same time. It wasn't the space issue, although it would be cramped, but simply that Mills wouldn't contemplate the concept.

There was no sign of Hazel and Nina had been at her desk for an hour when Ruby arrived.

She explained her absence. 'I was asked to speak to uniform about Stephen Grainger.'

'And?'

'They said they'd "keep an eye", whatever that means.' She looked disappointed.

'I'm sure they will, Ruby. But they do have a lot on their plate on the fifth.'

Nina was unsure whether to tell Ruby about the information that had come in that morning. 'There's been a response to the appeal for witnesses at Buttertubs,' she began.

Ruby looked up, expectantly.

'There's a man who spotted a bike lying by the side of the road that day and it was still there when he returned an hour or so later.'

'At what time?'

'I don't have the details. He's going to give a statement later today, after work. But it seems to show that Jack's bike was there for the taking. I think it probably confirms the story that Richie gave us.'

'That he saw it and thought "I'll have that" – like Burglar Bill.'

Nina often had difficulty following Ruby's conversation but on this occasion she knew Burglar Bill, he was one of Rosie's favourite story book characters.

'So I don't think we can go any further with Jack Bassett's accident, even if it was a "hit and run". We've nothing to go on…'

'But…'

Nina held up her hand to stop her. '…and nothing to link it with the "near miss". Hazel wants you to concentrate on your task of assuring no local troublemakers spoil the race on the fifth of July.'

'I know. But how can I, if uniform aren't taking it seriously?'

'Talk to Hazel.'

'She doesn't like me.'

'Don't be silly. She just wants to see you succeed. It does reflect on her, you know. She's responsible for your work. She can be very useful to your career if you give her what she wants, Ruby.'

The poor girl looked crestfallen.

'I tell you what I'll do. I'll go to the hospital this afternoon and talk to Jack Bassett to get any details he can remember about the vehicle he mentioned. Then we'll draw a line under it all. Agreed?'

'Thank you, Nina. I wish you were my boss.'

Nina ignored her and began working on her emails.

Nina was pleased to learn from his mother that Jack Bassett had left intensive care. Nige had spent many weeks there after nearly dying from hypothermia and the place brought back bad memories. She found the appropriate men's ward, and the nurse indicated where he was sitting, fully dressed, beside his bed concentrating on an iPad.

'Jack Bassett?' She introduced herself, explaining that she'd heard he had remembered something of his accident. She also mentioned that Nige taught at the university, hoping to put him at his ease.

'I told Mum to tell you before, when I first remembered,' he said. 'It was a white car and it drove straight at me.'

'Do you think it was deliberate?'

'Either that or he was a really bad driver.'

'He?'

Jack seemed to consider for a moment. 'I don't know why I said that… unless I saw him. I don't know.'

'And are you sure it was a car?'

'What d'you mean?'

'Could it have been a van, or a minibus?'

'Yes… and no. I only saw the front. It could have been a van but not a bus.'

He was unable to provide any further information, so she thanked him, wished him a speedy recovery and prepared to leave. But he stopped her.

'If I write a note, could you give it to your husband?'

'Of course.'

He pulled his locker round and rummaged in the drawer, eventually pulling out a notepad. 'Do you have a pen I can borrow?'

She handed him her biro.

'It's just that he was my tutor last year and I need to talk to someone about something. I think he'll understand. I've put my mobile number. I don't want to bother him but it is really important. My whole career could be at stake.'

Chapter 22

Mills was in the back garden when the phone rang. She let Alex answer it but he called her inside.

'It's Nige, for you.'

She turned off the hose and wiped her hands on her jeans before taking the receiver.

'Mills? Sorry but this is important, right.'

'Hi Nige, how are you?'

'Mills, Jack Bassett got in touch with me…'

'Is he out of hospital?'

'No, listen. He called me about Sydney Green.'

Now Mills was paying attention.

'Are you still there?' Nige asked.

'Go on.'

'He's had this email from Sydney – the lad is still in hospital. He's putting the pressure on to back him up in this thing between you and him.'

'What d'you mean?'

'I'll read you the email – he forwarded it to me, right? I'll just read the relevant bit: *It is possible that you may be asked about some analyses you carried out for me earlier this year. I do not expect you to divulge any information regarding work carried out for me at any time. If you disregard my request, there may be consequences that could affect your final qualifications.'*

'What is he threatening? What can he do? What did Jack want *you* to do?' Mills asked.

'Green will be marking parts of his final exam papers and he'll be on the Board of Examiners. That's threat enough. Jack wanted advice.'

'So what did you tell him to do?'

'I told him that his views would be very helpful and suggested he might be needed to resolve the issue between Sydney and a colleague. He knew I meant you. Matthew had told him about the court case… and the verdict. It's all over the department.'

'Do you think he could help?'

'I don't know. He's a bright lad and should see that Sydney can't hurt him, if you're proved to be in the right.'

'It's a gamble for him.'

'Why don't you call him? There's nothing to lose.'

Not for me, thought Mills as she copied down Jack's number, but to ruin someone else's life as well, that was different.

She could see Alex was expecting an explanation but ignored his quizzical gaze. Eventually he asked if she'd made an appointment to see the Head, as he'd suggested.

'Yes but they said there was a meeting already planned to discuss "the issue". I got an email about it this afternoon. It's on Tuesday at eleven.'

'Did they say who would be there?'

'No.'

'You should get legal advice.'

'Really?' What did he know? Why was he interfering? She went back into the garden to think. Next door, Muriel was taking her washing in.

'Hello, love. How's things?'

'OK.'

'You don't look OK, Mills.'

'Just tired.'

'Well, I'll tell you something to cheer you up. Arthur's written a letter for Stephen, saying he wants nothing more to do with C.A.T. and we're all going to put our names on it. Would you sign it too?'

Mills looked up and nodded.

Muriel rushed inside and reappeared with a sheet of A4. The letter consisted of four typed lines of text stating that the undersigned no longer wished to be associated with the Campaign Against the Tour (C.A.T.) "because of the extreme nature of the tactics that are being implemented and the possible danger they present to the public".

'What about Catriona?' Mills asked, as Muriel handed her a pen.

'I don't think Arthur is asking her, she seems too much in Stephen's pocket.'

'I hope this will be the end of his antics,' Mills said, signing before handing back the paper and pen. 'And good riddance.'

Later that evening, while Alex was busy watching television, she sent an email to Jack, asking if she could visit him in hospital.

Mills was in the reception area, studying the list of wards when a familiar voice called her name. She turned to see Matthew Watson coming towards her.

'He's in the coffee place,' he said with a grin. 'I had to bring him down. He wanted a coffee.'

She followed him along the corridor to where Jack was

sitting in a wheelchair at a table.

While Matthew fetched a coffee, she thanked Jack for agreeing to see her.

'I should explain,' she began. 'I've recently been an expert witness in a rape case that...'

'I know. Matthew told me, it's all over the department. That's why I spoke to Dr Featherstone.'

'He said.'

She waited as Matthew placed a mug in front of her.

Jack looked at Matthew and then back at her. 'Did he tell you about the email from Professor Green as well?'

'Yes, he did.'

Jack was obviously waiting for her to take the lead and so she took a deep breath and began the spiel she'd rehearsed on the way.

'As you know, Professor Green and I presented evidence on opposite sides of the case. We interpreted our results and came to different conclusions, which is not unheard of.'

The two young men were listening attentively.

'The jury accepted my interpretation of the evidence and came back with a verdict of not guilty. There shouldn't be a problem but...'

'Professor Green thinks there's a problem.' Jack's tone was level but he looked troubled. 'He's pressurising me to keep quiet.'

'But why is that, Jack?' Matthew asked. 'What's it got to do with you, anyway?'

'Because I analysed those samples for him using the microprobe and showed him that his mineralogical data was misleading. He just ignored me.' He looked at Mills. 'But you knew that because I gave you my report.'

'Yes, although I wasn't sure they were the rape case samples at the time. Obviously I didn't make use of your results and I've never mentioned your work to anyone up to now.'

Matthew leaned forward. 'I told Jack he should give it to Nige Featherstone. He'll know what to do with it.'

Mills looked across at Jack. 'It's not an easy decision is it? I understand that Professor Green is being "difficult"?'

Jack nodded. 'Yes. He could mark me down if I do.'

Mills finished her coffee. 'I appreciate you talking to me, Jack. Particularly with you being so unwell. Obviously I can't expect you to put your future on the line for me. I don't want you to, honestly.'

Matthew was nudging his friend but Jack sat looking dejected.

Mills smiled at them both. 'Get well soon, Jack. Thanks for the chat and keep in touch.'

She walked away, disappointed but certain she didn't want the young man to get into trouble on her account.

Matthew grabbed the wheelchair and shoved it along the corridor. 'You said you'd help her,' he muttered. 'Surely you're not scared of old Green. I told you, he can't change your exam results now – they'll be announced in a couple of weeks.'

He steered the chair into the lift and pressed the button. 'Don't you want to do the right thing?'

'Yes, but…'

'You owe me.'

The lift stopped, the doors opened and Matthew heaved the chair round in the direction of the ward.

'What d'you mean: "you owe me"?' Jack asked.

'If I hadn't got Will to come in and sort out your illness,

you could be dead now.'

'That's a bit steep.'

'No, it's true. You owe me. I think you should let Dr Featherstone use all the emails Green sent you. Let the department know that he's past his sell-by date.'

Matthew manoeuvred the wheelchair next to Jack's bed.

'OK, I'll think about it.'

'Make sure you do. And then do the right thing.'

Mills usually had a pleasant sense of familiarity when she drove onto the university campus but not today. The feeling of dread heightened as she took the lift to the Head of Department's office. She rarely visited the top corridor that housed administration and senior academics. The carpeted corridors and large offices were a sharp contrast to the lower floors.

'D'you want to go in?' His personal assistant offered her coffee and waved her into the inner office.

Professor Cole and Mr Runshaw were in conversation at a large table.

'Come in Dr Sanderson. Were you offered a drink?'

She nodded, sat down in the nearest leather chair, opposite the two men, and waited.

'Thank you for coming,' the Head went on. 'We just wanted an informal chat, following the end of the… erm… trial.'

She waited.

The Head looked at the administrator, who coughed. 'Professor Green has put in a complaint,' he said. 'It is under the general heading of research misconduct.'

'Oh.' Mills was unprepared. 'What does that mean?'

Runshaw referred to a sheet of paper covered in spidery

handwriting in front of him. 'He states that you stole his student's results and used them for your own ends.' He looked up. 'I should explain, he is referring to a report written by one of his students.' He looked at the page again.

'Jack Bassett,' she prompted.

'That's right.' He sounded surprised that she knew. 'He says you used his report to oppose his evidence in court.'

Mills closed her eyes. It was becoming almost comical… if her contract hadn't been in jeopardy.

'I didn't, use Jack's report,' she responded. 'I did see the report but I didn't use it in the case. My evidence was based entirely on the work at Yardley Forensics.'

'Professor Green is contending that without Mr Bassett's report, his evidence would have been accepted by the jury....'

'No!'

'…and Mr Bassett's work was that of an undergraduate student, full of flaws and, frankly, erroneous.'

It was a nightmare. The man was making it all up and clearly they believed him.

'He's lying!'

'Why would he lie, Dr Sanderson?' The administrator glanced at the Head.

'I don't know. Perhaps to cover his inadequacy.'

'What was that, Dr Sanderson?' Professor Cole looked shocked.

'To cover his own mistake?'

'How do you think he was mistaken?' Cole asked.

Mills pointed at Runshaw. 'Ask him. He was at the trial. Ask him about the evidence.' Her voice was shaky and she wanted to leave.

The Head continued as if she hadn't spoken. 'The purpose of this meeting was to let you know the details of the complaint. There will be a formal hearing in due course.'

'When?'

'I'd like to get it sorted as soon as possible. The Dean is off to the States next week. Perhaps we can arrange it for Thursday?'

'We'll email you with the details,' offered the administrator.

Mills was too shocked to argue. She just wanted to get away and fled from the room without further discussion, almost bumping into the PA, who was bringing in her coffee.

It was unusual for Mills to visit the campus without calling in to see Nige on the way home but this time she hesitated. She was unsure whether she would be able to keep her composure after the bruising she'd received. She sat in the car trying to make up her mind. Even when she reached the house, she waited for several minutes before getting out of the car.

'Mills, I've been calling you. Your phone's off.'

Nige opened the door wider to let her pass.

'Sorry, I was with the Prof Cole.'

Nige had just finished giving the boys their lunch and she helped him settle them down for a nap.

'So what were you doing this morning?' he asked as they came back downstairs.

She gave Nige a full account of the meeting while he made them a sandwich and a mug of tea.

'You ought to have someone with you at this formal hearing,' he said.

'Should I?' Mills hadn't had time to even think about it.

'Or at least a friend, if you wanted.'

'Would you. Nige? Would you really?'

'Of course. You must give me all the background but when we've finished eating, I'll get you a copy of what Matthew has sent me.'

To her surprise, Nige had been sent a copy of every email that Sydney Green had exchanged with Jack regarding his work on the soil samples. He handed her a sheaf of paper.

'How did Matthew get this? Jack won't let me use it; he's scared it will affect his grades.'

'He's changed his mind. Matthew says that he persuaded Jack to do the right thing.'

'Are you sure?'

'Yes, Jack sent them to Matthew to forward to me, you can see his message at the top.'

Mills read Jack's email but it made no sense. It talked about repaying Matthew for getting the help he needed by sending these emails on to Dr Featherstone. She shrugged, admitting that Jack had obviously given them to Matthew after she'd asked for his help.

Nige sat quietly while Mills read the messages. They began with Green asking Jack to do some simple analyses of two soils for him. Jack responds by pointing out that the microprobe would give him much more detailed information and Green tells him to go ahead. In the next relevant message, Jack sends the preliminary results indicating that they are probably soils from different sources but Green comes back, telling him that he is wrong. Jack offers to do further analysis but Green tells him it won't be necessary.

Mills looked up.

'Have you got to the bit where Green starts getting nasty?' Nige asked.

Mills shook her head and continued reading.

Jack's next message shows he has disobeyed his supervisor's instructions and reanalysed the samples in more detail. This time he is adamant that the soils are different. And then Green's tone changes. He demands that Jack gives him the soils and all his results. Jack politely replies that the work is forming part of his dissertation so he has to compile the results but points out that the nature of the samples will be anonymous, as discussed earlier.

On a separate sheet was the message from Green that Nige had read to her over the phone.

If you disregard my request, there may be consequences that could affect your final qualifications.

'He makes it very clear,' Mills said.

'I think that should convince the Dean.'

'We can't show him this!' Mills protested.

'Why not?' asked Nige. 'It shows what a bully Sydney is.'

Nige was still trying to persuade her that it would be all right when the boys began to stir upstairs. The next hour was spent keeping them occupied while Mills filled Nige in with the details of what had happened during the trial. Mills had never thought of Nige as a particularly strong, dependable type but now he was taking the lead and laying out how he thought they should approach the university hearing.

By the time Nina arrived home with Rosie, they had decided on a plan of campaign. Initially she reprimanded Nige for not having the children's tea ready but soon apologised when she heard how they had spent the afternoon. Before Mills left, Nina thanked her for the help she'd given Ruby over the Campaign Against the Tour.

'No problem. Actually, you can tell her that everyone except Stephen and Catriona have left C.A.T. in disgust. They don't like his tactics.'

'I will. She's done a good job and I'll be sorry to see her go, although I'm not sure Hazel feels the same.'

'No?'

'She thinks she's been spending too much time on the various accidents befalling cyclists over your way. Incidentally, did you know someone in your village lost three members of his family in an accident caused by a cyclist?'

It meant nothing to her. 'Must've been a long time ago.'

After Mills had left, Nige asked what she'd been talking about.

'I saw it online. It was in the papers – six years ago, I think. A man in Mossy Bank lost his wife, his daughter and grandson. Three generations. All caused by a cyclist not looking where he was going.'

'Strange you didn't hear about it at the time.'

Later that evening, Nige looked up from his laptop.

'I found that article about the driver from Mossy Bank who was killed with her family. It *was* six years ago and spookily the cyclist was one of our old students.'

Nina looked up. 'Not a member of the cycling team?'

'It doesn't say but I could find out. Funny I didn't hear about it at the time.'

'That was when you were in hospital. I'm not surprised it passed us by.'

'True. We did have quite a lot to think about.'

Nige tapped away on his laptop for several minutes while Nina washed up.

'Here it is,' he called triumphantly. 'The team for that year.'

'And was he on it?'

'Yes, *she* was.'

Nina went back into the sitting room and looked over his shoulder.

'Another member of UNYCYCLE,' she said. 'Let's hope Ruby doesn't get carried away with this.'

'What d'you mean?'

Nina told him about the young researcher's obsession with the trio of team members involved in accidents on Buttertubs Pass.

'That road is notorious,' he agreed.

'I suppose it is a coincidence.'

Her husband, a physicist and mathematician, insisted on working out the odds of so many accidents or near misses occurring in the same place and concluded that Ruby could be right in thinking it was more than a coincidence.

'Perhaps there's a bad patch of road – or it's just a dangerous corner,' he suggested. 'It could be worth investigating in order to avoid any more accidents.'

Later, while they were watching television, Nina moved closer to Nige, who put his arm round her.

'I was thinking about when you were in hospital, Nige,' she said. 'Mills was a massive help then. You will make sure she's OK, won't you?'

'Don't worry. I'm going into that meeting with her and I'm not leaving until they give her back her old job.'

Chapter 23

'*You* were supposed to be cooking today.' Alex was chopping onions when Mills walked in.

'Sorry, I had a meeting with the Head.'

'Yes – at eleven o'clock.'

'I went to see Nige. He's been helping me with the hearing I've got to attend.'

'I wanted to show you the new software. It arrived today. I've been trying it out on all sorts of things,' he announced. 'You should've been there. I enhanced a photo of the office and you could see all sorts of detail. Timothy was so impressed!'

Mills left him to it and went upstairs but she could hardly get into the bedroom for furniture.

'What's been going on?' she called.

'Sorry,' he shouted back. 'I was rearranging the rooms, ready for the parents.'

She went downstairs and relieved him of the chopping board. 'Go upstairs and sort it out. I'll do the dinner.'

She banged the frying pan on the stove and murmured to herself as she fried onions and peppers. Not once had he asked how the meeting had gone; all he was interested in was his stupidly expensive software. Didn't it occur to him that she might be losing her job while he crowed about his ridiculous enhancements? She threw in the rest of the vegetables and stirred them furiously. When they were done, she called Alex.

'I won't be long. Just want to finish this.'

Suit yourself, she muttered and put the plates on the table. She'd nearly finished eating when he finally appeared.

'Sorry, I was moving one of the bedside tables from our room into the guest room. I thought my parents could have it.'

'What about Dad and Fiona?'

'I assumed you'd want them to have our room. They'll have the baby as well and the room is bigger.'

They hadn't talked it through and now it dawned on Mills that he seriously intended to house both sets of parents under one roof.

'So where do *we* sleep then?'

'Here.' He pointed at the sofa. 'It turns into a bed, I've tried it.'

He jumped up and flung the cushions to one side. He hauled on the seat and it turned inside out exposing a flimsy-looking mattress and base. He lay down on it and bounced about.

'See. Perfect!'

Mills didn't answer. It was going to be totally awful. In three days she would be entertaining Alex's mother and father, who she'd not met before, and worse, Dad and Fiona would be descending on them with baby Flora. Both situations would be difficult but all in one go was intolerable.

'I think we should cancel,' she said. 'Tell them we can't

do it.'

'Don't be silly, Mills. It'll be fun. I can't wait to meet your dad, and Flora and Fiona – or is it Fiona and Flora?' he joked.

'Then tell your parents there isn't room. They can come another time.'

'No. We invited them all and we'll cope.'

'You do realise we'll need to do a big shop and before we can do that we have to decide what we need. I haven't got time. I've got this hearing with the Dean and everyone. It's too much. I can't do it!'

Her voice had increased in volume and pitch. She left the room and retreated to the bedroom before Alex could see her tears.

The furniture had been re-arranged, presumably to make room for a cot to fit at the foot of the bed. Alex doesn't realise what Fiona is like, thought Mills. She won't cope in a small bedroom. Dad will be driven mad and Flora will cry all the time. Alex's parents will think they've come to a madhouse. She slowly realised that she was embarrassed and that was why she didn't want Alex's family to meet them. She wasn't proud of how she felt but just at the moment it was a problem she could do without.

On the day of the hearing, Nige met Mills at the entrance to the department.

'It's all in here,' he said, patting the file under his arm. 'I've made copies. I hope there's enough.'

They made their way to the top floor and along to the meeting room. It was empty except for a tray of coffee in the middle of the polished table.

'Chocolate biscuits,' observed Nige, helping himself.

'They certainly know how to live.'

'Nige!'

'What? D'you want coffee?'

'Shouldn't we wait?'

The Dean arrived as they were deciding.

'Good, you've found the coffee. Help yourselves.'

Nige served them and they stood awkwardly waiting for whoever else was going to attend. First it was the Head, who explained that Professor Green was on his way. Before he arrived, Mr Runshaw appeared. They were all seated when Green finally burst through the door carrying a pile of papers and thumped them on the table. The Dean took the lead and urged him to sit down so they could proceed.

'I hope we can keep this short and to the point,' he began. 'In a nutshell, Professor Green here has raised a complaint against you, Dr Sanderson, in that you took results from one of his students and used it to your advantage in a high-profile court case. Is that a fair representation of the facts, Professor Cole?' He turned to the Head, who nodded.

'Would you like to explain why you felt it was necessary to raise an official complaint, Professor Green?'

The old man coughed and stood up.

'You can remain seated.' The Dean smiled at him. 'But please keep it brief.'

His submission was far from brief. He began by explaining exactly who Jack Bassett was and why he was assisting him in the forensic work. 'It was part of his dissertation on the microprobe analysis of soils with different mineralogy. I proposed it as a project especially so we could build up expertise in modern forensic methodology.' He smiled at the Dean in an obsequious manner.

Green described the trial at great length and Mills could see that the Dean and the Head were getting irritated by the unnecessary detail. After a while, the administrator intervened.

'May I suggest we cut to the verdict? It seems to me that it is the most relevant part of the case.'

'The jury was misled by Dr Sanderson's evidence, which I must point out depended heavily on Jack Bassett's thesis. I have it here…'

The Dean raised his hand to prevent him distributing copies. 'We don't need to read it, Professor Green. We just need the gist.'

At this point Nige asked if he could speak. They agreed.

'Jack Bassett is unwell and remains in hospital but he's given me some documents that *are* relevant to the case.' He passed the papers round the table.

Green grabbed them and turned crimson as he read the contents. 'These are private emails,' he said angrily.

'Jack wanted me to use them to demonstrate that he had tried to tell Professor Green that his results were not corroborated by the microprobe.'

'Is that right, Sydney?' the Head asked.

'They've been taken out of context,' he remonstrated.

Mills watched the proceedings like a spectator at a play. No-one referred to her or asked her opinion but somehow that didn't upset her. Her friend was defending her and they would pay more attention to him. She had very little clout amongst the present company, a mere temporary lecturer. She listened as the arguments bounced backwards and forwards until suddenly, she and Nige were being asked to step outside. They sat side by side on a low windowsill in the corridor, listening to voices being raised in the meeting room. Finally the administrator emerged to join them on their perch after giving Mills an encouraging smile.

Another ten minutes before the door opened and Sydney Green stormed out, glaring at them before striding down the corridor and out of sight. The Head asked Mills to come back into the meeting room, shutting the door behind her.

He ushered her into a seat and looked at the Dean before speaking. 'Dr Sanderson, we'd like to treat this hearing as an informal one. You may wish to dispute that but, before you decide, I'd like to make two points.'

Mills waited.

'The first is that Professor Green has been considering when to take his retirement and has recently indicated to us that he is willing to finish at the end of the summer term.'

Recently, thought Mills, like five minutes ago? She nodded.

'Secondly, we would like to continue your contract for another year, if you're happy?'

She nodded again. She wanted to know what had happened but that wasn't how it worked in the university. Ranks closed and the whole affair would be glossed over. She wasn't about to complain.

Out in the corridor, Nige gave her the thumbs-up and Mr Runshaw said she'd done a good job. When he'd gone, Nige told her that he knew the outcome.

'Old Runshaw was beside himself,' he said. 'I thought he was going to burst into song.'

'D'you think Green will continue to do forensic work?' Mills asked, as they waited for the lift.

'What do *you* think? No-one will touch him with a bargepole now.'

Nige looked delighted but Mills wondered what the old man planned to do. She'd been responsible for him leaving the university; he may have left voluntarily but everyone in the department would be aware of the truth or put two and two together.

'Come on,' said Nige. 'We need to celebrate.'

They called for Jake on the way and went to the cafeteria for tea and cakes.

'I suppose you'll be taking over some of Green's lectures now then?' Jake asked when she'd explained that her contract had been extended beyond the point when Nige was back full-time.

'Possibly.' She hadn't thought. She could cover his forensic courses, that was certain. But soil science? Perhaps not.

The conversation turned to Jack Bassett and the role he'd played in the downfall of Sydney Green.

'He'll be out of hospital soon, I imagine,' said Mills.

'He won't be cycling for the team again from what Matthew Watson's been saying,' Jake said. 'He's quite excited about taking over as the key man – although gutted for Jack, of course.' He grinned.

'Do either of you remember a girl in the team called Sally something?' Nige asked. 'She caused a big accident; it was in the papers at the time. About six years ago.'

They shook their heads.

'I'm surprised you don't know about it, Mills,' Nige went on. 'The driver lived in your village.'

'What happened?'

He described the news report. 'Apparently she was hardly scratched but three generations in the same family died.'

'They seem accident prone, these racing types,' Jake said. 'Going too fast I expect.' He stood up. 'Got to go, bye.'

'That's what I told Nina,' said Nige. 'Travelling at high speed on narrow roads. Not a good combination. But Nina thought there might be a connection between what happened and Jack's hit and run.'

Mills was thinking of the photographs that had been sent to Alex for enhancement. 'There was definitely a vehicle involved in Jack's accident,' she said.

'Yes but this time it was the cyclist who came off worst.'

She refused his offer of a pub lunch and headed straight home. She was sure the lab could manage without her and she wanted to enjoy the rest of the day. Anyway, she had to visit the supermarket if she was going to cater for four additional adults and a baby over the weekend.

Muriel counted three hand-written posters between Mossy Bank and Hawes. She was on her way to work so she was in a hurry but she slowed down at the first one, which read "STOP THE RACE". The second said "KEEP THE ROAD OPEN" but it was the last one that made her stop all together. The paper was splashed with red paint and the letters were in jagged black handwriting: "DEATH TO THE CYCLISTS". He'd even included the initials C.A.T. It made her feel quite ill and she tore it down, screwed it up and flung it in the back of her car. In her mind it confirmed that Stephen had gone off the rails and as soon as she was in the office, she rang Arthur. Eventually he answered his mobile, informing her that he was in Leyburn and wouldn't be back until later.

'Why don't I give Stephen a ring?' he suggested. 'Try and reason with him?'

She distracted herself with the monthly accounts but found herself watching the minutes go by. Eventually the phone rang and Arthur reported the conversation he'd had with Stephen.

'The man's not in his right mind,' he began. 'He says he's got more posters to put up between Grinton and Leyburn. He's working his way slowly over Grinton Moor as I speak. I'll probably see him on my way home. I'll try to make him see sense.'

'You can take the posters down, if he won't.'

'We'll see. I'll ring you when I've had a chat with him.'

Good luck with that, thought Muriel as she went back to the figures.

Arthur spotted Stephen's car parked beside the track to Grinton smelt mill. As he slowed, he could see a familiar figure disappearing round the bend in the road where it crossed a bridge. Arthur parked his car carefully off the road and followed. Stephen hadn't gone far – he was trying to fix one of his posters to the stone wall, and having some difficulty by the looks of things.

'Want some help?' he called as he came within earshot.

Stephen looked round sharply, seeming to relax when he saw Arthur. 'Hello! Come to give me a hand?'

Arthur stood back. Muriel hadn't exaggerated when she described the venomous nature of the posters.

'I say, they're a bit extreme, aren't they?' he asked.

Stephen carried on tying strings to the stonework. 'I don't think so. It's a direct message. To the point.'

Arthur waited until Stephen had finished fixing the offending artwork and had stepped back to admire it.

'There. I think that makes the views of C.A.T. perfectly clear, don't you?'

'It could land you in trouble with the police, old boy.'

'No matter.'

They started back up the hill to the cars. 'The important thing is to get the message across.'

'At least it's better than putting tacks on the road or trip wires,' laughed Arthur. 'That would have been madness!'

Stephen turned slowly and looked him in the eye. 'What do you mean?'

Arthur shrugged. 'Well, you don't want to put anyone in danger.'

'Why not? It's the only way we'll get to stop the race. Extreme measures, Arthur. Extreme measures.'

He watched Stephen leave then climbed into his car and drove slowly to the bridge. He wanted to remove the offending poster before setting off back to Mossy Bank but there was a line of cars behind him and he drove on with a sigh.

Mills had unpacked the shopping and was drinking a well-earned cup of tea in the garden when Muriel appeared on the other side of the hedge. She relayed how Stephen had been pinning inflammatory posters round the countryside and despite Arthur's best efforts, he wouldn't see reason.

'Arthur and Colin are coming round in a minute to discuss strategy,' she said importantly. 'Have you got a minute? I'll give you a knock when they arrive.'

Mills agreed reluctantly. She'd wanted to go out to celebrate keeping her job but judging by the traffic, all the pubs would be rammed that evening. It seemed as if everyone had already arrived for the race on Saturday. Instead she'd sent a text to Alex to pick up a takeaway.

'I can't stay long though,' she warned Muriel.

Worried that she'd had no response from Alex, she rang him but it went to voicemail. The explanation was soon clear when he came through the door ten minutes later.

'Got the food?' she asked. He was only carrying his laptop bag.

'What food?'

Mills didn't answer but went back into the garden.

Yes, she was sulking but there *was* a reason. She explained about the text, which apparently he hadn't received because he was driving, and told him about the hearing.

'So it's all OK?' Alex laughed.

'Yes, except there's nothing for dinner… and there's the knock. I've got to go next door now.'

Arthur and Colin were at Muriel's front door.

'Come through to the garden, all of you,' Muriel ordered. 'It's too hot in here.'

Arthur immediately took control of the meeting.

'I know we told Stephen we've washed our hands of C.A.T. but I feel it's our civic duty to remain close to him, if only to see what he's getting up to. There's very little time before the race.'

'With so many people about, it may be difficult to keep tabs on him,' said Colin.

Mills agreed.

'Well, I don't mind spending a few hours shadowing his movements,' said Arthur. 'I've nothing else on.'

Mills suspected he was rather enjoying the buzz of

excitement over it all.

'Colin,' Arthur went on. 'You aren't working tomorrow are you?'

'No but…'

'Well then, don't you worry, ladies. Colin and I will keep an eye on him to make sure he doesn't do anything stupid.'

Muriel spoke up for the first time. 'He's already done that. Those posters put shivers down my spine. I hope you're getting rid of them?'

'We'll do our best to remove the worst of them,' Arthur assured her. 'The more important job is to stop him sabotaging the race itself.'

He turned to Mills. 'Muriel says you know someone in the police. Can you give them a nod and a wink?'

'Yes, dear,' Muriel added. 'That friend of yours, the exotic looking one.'

Mills assumed she meant Nina. She promised to contact "her exotic friend" as soon as she was back home but actually planned to call Ruby instead.

In the kitchen, Alex was surrounded by pans and dishes.

'What are you doing?' she demanded.

'Making you a celebration meal. I didn't expect you back so soon; it'll be another hour before it's ready.'

She opened the oven and slammed it shut. She took a deep breath before peering in the 'fridge.

'You've used the fish – all of it.'

'They'll be some left over.'

'It was for your parents tomorrow!' she yelled. 'We didn't have anything for tonight. That's why I asked you to bring something in!'

Alex looked upset then annoyed. He threw the knife on the work surface and marched down the passage. Mills heard the front door slam. She checked the oven again and went to call Ruby.

'Are any of the others involved?' Ruby asked when Mills told her about Stephen.

'No, quite the opposite. The members of the team – or at least ex-members – are keeping a watch on what he's doing.'

'Well, thanks for letting me know. I've tried to get someone to monitor him up until the race but I haven't heard anything. I'll keep you updated if you can do the same.'

'Sure.'

Alex had made a fish pie with her beautiful pieces of lemon sole and there was nothing she could do about that. She would be serving it to them tomorrow. Meanwhile there was a tin of beans and plenty of bread so, when Alex returned looking miserable, she was able to present him with a supper of sorts as a peace offering. He forgave her and found the bottle of champagne she'd rejected previously. By the end of the evening he'd persuaded her that the arrival of his parents as well as her father and Fiona wouldn't be so bad – honestly.

Chapter 24

Nina waited until Hazel had left the office before telling Ruby about the traffic accident near Buttertubs Pass six years previously.

'It's just a coincidence, of course,' she said. She didn't mention her husband's statistical analysis. She wasn't sure why she was telling Ruby, except there was a nagging feeling that somehow it was tied to recent events. 'I've sent you the newspaper report from the time.'

'But the cyclist *was* in the team, just like the others?' Ruby paused while she opened the link to the report. 'So she would've been wearing the team colours: red and white?'

'I don't know. Perhaps. There isn't a photo of the girl; just the old man whose wife was driving.'

'Imagine losing your wife, daughter and grandchild,' said Ruby.

Nina had; it would be unbearable.

'That's weird,' Ruby was staring at the screen. 'He's a member of C.A.T. Now that *is* a coincidence.'

'Ruby…' Nina warned.

'This guy loses his family in a tragic accident and the cyclist leaves in one piece. She isn't even charged. Maybe he has a grudge.'

'Nonsense, Ruby. What about the cyclist? Surely he would target her specifically if he wanted some sort of revenge, not the Tour de France.'

However, by the time Hazel returned, Nina was sufficiently swayed that the connection was worth investigating, that she insisted on Hazel listening to what Ruby had to say.

'Go on Ruby. Tell her what you found.'

'This cyclist who caused the car crash moved to Australia with her family soon afterwards. To get away from it, I should think. Make a new start? Anyway, no longer about.'

'So?' Hazel was tapping her foot impatiently.

'What if he wants to get his own back; avenge his wife's death?'

'Bit dramatic.' Hazel moved across the room.

'He runs another cyclist off the road just to show them?'

'Too random.' Hazel sat down at her desk.

'But it's not random,' said Nina. 'Not at all. You see they are all members of the same team. They were all wearing the same cycling gear.'

'UNYCYCLE,' added Ruby. 'Red and white.'

Hazel was listening.

'Statistically it's more than a coincidence,' Nina added.

Hazel raised an eyebrow.

Nina looked at Hazel. 'Three attempts to knock a cyclist from the UNYCYCLE team off their bikes on the Buttertubs Pass after he's lost three members of his family nearby. It's got to be worth investigating.'

'And there's another reason why *I've* got to,' said Ruby, standing up and walking towards the door. 'He's in the campaign to stop the Tour de France. That's my job.'

*

Alex left for work early on Friday. He told Mills he'd be back in the afternoon. His parents were due to arrive early evening and he wanted to be sure the cottage was ready for them. Mills was going to clean the place and prepare more meals in advance. Alex knew he could have taken the day off. Very few people were coming in because there was too much excitement about the following day, with Harrogate being an important location in the Grand Départ. But he wanted to have another trial with the new software without distraction.

The lab was eerily quiet and as he went down the corridor, peering into the laboratories, he only spotted Glyn and Timothy. He carried his mug back to the office and switched on the monitors. He had just about mastered the enhancement program and so far had only played with some shots he'd taken indoors. Today he wanted to look at the photographs of the cycle accident, to see if he could do as well as his contact at Teesside University. There were numerous options to try and time flew by. He grabbed another coffee and continued by trial and error until he was seeing an improvement in the discrimination. There was definitely a clear outline of the vehicle now and there were still some possibilities to try out.

He was interrupted by a call from Mills.

'Hi, I didn't know if you'd left already.' She sounded flustered.

'D'you want me to pick up anything on the way?'

'No, it's not that. Muriel just rang. She asked me to go to Hawes. I don't want to but I did say last night…'

'No problem. I'll be leaving in an hour or so.'

'But Dad will be here soon.'

'Don't worry. I'll be there.'

Mills grabbed her bag and car keys, slamming the front door behind her. Muriel had sounded frantic. She was at work in Hawes but Arthur had rung to say he'd driven over Buttertubs Pass following Stephen's car. Stephen had stopped at the top by the cattle grid so Arthur had parked further down the road and was watching him, in case he was spreading tacks or setting wires. Colin was due to contact him so he could take over from him but he wasn't answering his phone. Could Mills see if he was at home and, if not, could she drive over to watch Stephen for a bit?

'Can't Arthur stay until Colin arrives?' Mills had asked, anxious to get on with the vacuuming. 'My dad's coming this afternoon.'

But Muriel had pleaded with her. 'There are people arriving up there already. If he's putting tacks on the road there'll be an accident before the race even starts. Arthur thinks that might be what he's planning and he doesn't want to confront him on his own; not up there. He's keeping an eye on him but he's got to go soon.'

Mills hammered on Colin's door but there was no answer. She rang the number Muriel had called her on but it was engaged and Muriel's mobile was switched off. She was on her way to her car when, to her relief, Colin's van turned the corner and stopped outside his cottage. He returned her wave but carried on up his path.

'Colin! Wait!' she shouted as she ran back down the road.

It took a while for the old man to understand what she was telling him.

'Does Arthur want us to meet him up there?' he asked. 'I was on my way to take over from him. We agreed I'd do the afternoon.'

'He didn't want to tackle Stephen on his own,' she explained.

'And nor do I. You'd better come too, in case he turns nasty.'

Mills wasn't keen to get involved if Stephen was going to "turn nasty" but Colin was not going to be deterred.

'He'll behave if he's in the company of a lady,' he insisted.

In the end, just to get it over with, she agreed to accompany Colin to meet Arthur.

'He can give you a lift straight back here afterwards,' he suggested.

Reluctantly she opened the passenger door and waited for him to remove his white coat and clipboard from her seat. Behind her, in the back of the van, were rows of egg trays neatly stacked and piles of egg boxes.

'Do you have a wide area to cover with your deliveries?' she asked for something to say.

'Not too far. I only go out three times a week. I should be retired really but I need something to take me out of the house.'

He drove slowly and carefully.

'Have you been doing it long?' Mills asked absently.

'Six years now. Ever since… well, since I've been on my own.'

He was a widower, like Arthur of course.

'I hope we can sort Stephen out quickly,' said Mills, changing the subject. 'I've got to get back. My parents are coming this afternoon.'

There was no response as he turned the van right onto the main road.

'Do you have any family coming for the race?' she asked.

'No family. Since I lost my wife and daughter the rest of them don't have anything to do with me.'

Alex was conscious that time was passing and he should have left a long time ago. It was just that the software was doing such a brilliant job and there was only one more run to do. The white blur had been transformed into a vehicle, and not just any vehicle. It was definitely a van, a white van. That was already clear but there was something else, a black smudge on the side of the van. He was certain it was a logo of some sort. If he could just enlarge it and improve the quality, he might be able to provide a description to the police.

The phone on the other desk rang and he leaned over to pick it up.

'Mills? Is that you?' It was a woman's voice.

Alex explained that she was out of the office. 'Can I help?'

'I don't know. I'm Ruby. I'm calling from Newby Wiske. I wanted to ask Mills about something.'

Alex recognised the name; it was the girl who'd sent the photographs for enhancement.

'Is it urgent? Only she won't be back in before Monday. Or I could call her. She's at home.'

'No, I've tried her home number. She's not there. Don't worry. I'll try again later.'

'By the way, Ruby. I've been doing more work on the photos you sent over for enhancement.'

'Oh.'

'And I've got an interesting result. It is definitely a white *van* and I'm looking at a very blurry logo on the side of it.'

'A logo? What does it say?'

'I can't make it out. It's not words. It's a picture I think.'

'If you can see what it is, please let me know or send a copy,' she asked.

He sat back down at the screen and selected several new options. One more run.

'I didn't get on very well with my father's girlfriend when they first met, after my mother died,' Mills told Colin. 'But it got better in the end. They're married now and have a little girl.' She thought it would help.

'My daughter died in a car accident with my wife. Her little boy, my grandson, was killed too. His father has never forgiven us… me… for that. It wasn't her fault.'

He'd slowed right down and Mills thought he was going to stop the van but gradually he seemed to pull himself together and carried on.

'I lost everything on that day six years ago. My wife, my daughter, my little grandson.' His voice was croaky.

'Have you any other children?' she asked.

'Oh yes, I have a son but he won't speak to me. He said I should've brought a civil action against the girl that caused the crash. I couldn't face it.'

'What happened to the girl?'

'She walked away hardly a scratch on her. Inquest said it was an accident.'

A pile of egg boxes fell over as he swung the van left onto the road to Buttertubs Pass.

'Anyway, there are other ways of getting even,' he muttered.

Mills was thinking fast. She'd already made the connection. Colin was the widower from her village whose family had been wiped out in an accident caused by a cyclist. Nina's suggestion that he might be connected with Jack's accident hadn't entered her head. Now she wondered exactly what he meant.

'Getting even?' Mills prompted.

'More than one way to skin a cat? Isn't that what they say?' He laughed. A quiet humourless laugh.

They were climbing slowly now with cars flashing past in the other direction.

In retrospect, Mills wished she hadn't asked the next question. 'What do you mean?'

Alex had had a breakthrough and was ringing Ruby with the good news. Come on, he muttered to himself as he waited for her to pick up.

'Hello?'

'Nina? It's Alex, is Ruby there?'

'No, she's not. Can *I* help?'

'The white van that ran into the student at Buttertubs, it's got something on the side.'

'Go on.'

'It looks like a bird.'

'A bird?'

'Yes.'

'OK, I'll tell her.'

As soon as Ruby came back, Nina gave her the message.

'A bird?' Ruby repeated. 'Jo Richie didn't have a bird on his van, that's for sure.'

'What about this Colin Norton? Do we know what he drives?' Nina asked.

Ruby shrugged. 'I'm still waiting for it to come through.'

Colin's reply to her question was unexpected.

'What would *you* do if three of your family were killed by a cyclist?' he asked.

'I don't know – what did *you* do?'

'I waited for the pain to go away but it didn't. So I decided to do something about it. That's what they tell you, isn't it? Revenge is a dish served cold. I read that somewhere.'

He'd slowed the van down until it had almost stopped.

'Revenge?'

'A life for a life.'

'The girl last year?'

'I didn't know if it was a girl but it was a lucky choice.'

'She was wearing the team colours.'

'That's right – red and white, just like the bitch that killed my Jenny.'

He was crying. The engine was running but the handbrake wasn't engaged so his foot must be on the brake. She didn't move.

'Let's find Arthur,' she said. He was still shaking with emotion. 'Colin, listen to me. We need to find Arthur.'

He wasn't listening. A car overtook them with the horn blasting and several cars followed. Mills could see the passengers staring in at them. To her left was the long drop below, the taut wire preventing her from opening the door.

'You want to know the truth?' he sobbed. 'The one last year, she was for Jenny. But then it seemed only fair there should be one for Lizzie. After that I tried but I couldn't go on with it. I can't face it anymore.'

He revved the engine and they shot forward into the middle of the road. A car coming the other way nearly hit them, swerving and sounding its horn. Colin pulled the steering wheel sharply to the left and trays of eggs went flying in the back. The van scraped against the wire fencing, the only protection between them and the drop below and he steered sharply to the right, stalling the engine.

Mills took her chance. She flung the door open and jumped out as he started the van again and disappeared out of sight. She crossed the road and stood beside the Buttertubs viewing platform, her heart racing as she tried to gather her thoughts. She started running up the hill to see if she could find Arthur, keeping close to the side as cars appeared at regular intervals. Then she saw Colin's van reappear, careering round the bend, travelling far too fast. She jumped out the way as he sped past, his face white and tense. She watched in horror as he drove straight on, hitting the wire fencing. The van flipped, as if in slow motion, and was gone. She ran back down and across to the edge ignoring the cars as they screeched to a halt around her. Not so very far below the white van was engulfed in a ball of fire.

Chapter 25

There was no sign of Mills when Alex reached Mossy Bank. Her car was there but she had vanished. There was no note and her mobile went to voicemail. He only knew that she was dashing off to Hawes. The lane was empty of cars, so he assumed she'd left with Muriel but he had no way of contacting their neighbour. He flipped through the numbers on the landline phone and found Nina's.

'Nina? It's Alex. Do you know where Mills has gone?'

She couldn't help him.

'She said she was going to Hawes but she hasn't taken her car. She must've gone with a neighbour,' he explained.

'Oh.'

'Oh? Oh what?'

'Well, we've had a report of a vehicle fire on the road over to Hawes this afternoon. I don't mean to worry you; it's just they might have closed the road.'

'Damn. It would help if I knew who she was with. I don't suppose you have a number for Muriel, our next-door neighbour?'

'Afraid not. I'm really sorry Alex but I need to go.'

'Thanks anyway.'

'Wait! Hold on!' Nina called.

He waited while there was a muffled conversation and excited voices.

'Alex? Can you do something for me? We're trying to locate a Colin Norton who lives in your village.'

'Don't know the name.'

'He's in his sixties and drives an egg delivery van.'

'I know the man but his van's not here. I guess he's out on his rounds.'

'Possibly. What's that, Ruby?' There was a pause.

'Alex, Ruby says that Colin Norton's van has a hen on the side. Does that make sense to you?'

'Yes it does. Tell her the bird in the photograph could be a hen.' And then it clicked. 'Colin Norton's delivery van? Is that what's she's saying.'

'Yes. It's all a bit confusing, but it looks like it may be the vehicle involved in the fire on the Hawes road.'

Alex had to do something. 'I'm going up there. I don't know what Mills was doing but I know Muriel asked her to go and the chances are the reason involved those idiots threatening the race.'

He slammed down the phone and made for the door. As he started the car he saw the ancient family Ford Focus coming up the lane towards him. His father slowed down but Alex just waved, continuing at speed to the main road and joining a steady stream of cars making their way through the dale. But he didn't get far. A police car with its blue light flashing was blocking the turning for the Hawes road.

As Alex jumped out, a young officer in uniform opened his car door.

'Can't get through,' he said. 'There's been an accident at Buttertubs.'

'My girlfriend may be up there!' he explained. 'She may be in the van that caught fire.'

The officer looked concerned and his hand went towards his radio. 'Why do you think that, sir?'

'Because the egg delivery man lives in our village. He could have given her a lift!'

'I don't have any details yet, sir. Bear with me.' He shut his door and spoke on the radio for several minutes.

Eventually he opened the door again. 'My colleague's coming down to escort you up there, sir.'

Alex stood staring up at the empty road imagining the worst. Finally a police car appeared in the distance. The car turned round at the junction, drawing up alongside the other police vehicle and the officers spoke to each other. After a short exchange Alex was ordered to get in and they began the ascent.

The officer explained that they were still trying to ascertain how the vehicle had gone over the edge. It had burst into flames on impact and the driver must have died instantly; he'd made no attempt to escape.

'Were there any passengers?' Alex asked, not wanting to hear the answer.

'No.'

'Are you sure?'

'Oh yes, sir. The young lady climbed out, just moments before.'

'Short red hair?'

'That's right. Know her?'

Alex sighed. 'Yes. Talk about nine lives.'

It was chaos as they reached Buttertubs. Cars were parked all over the road and groups of police and paramedics were standing around. Alex followed the officer to where Mills was seated in the back of an ambulance.

'Are you hurt?' Alex called above the general hubbub.

'No, I'm fine,' she shouted back. 'They wanted me to hang around to give a statement.'

'I thought you were in the van,' he said, shaking his head.

'What's that? I can't hear you. Why aren't you at home? They'll all be there soon.'

He waited until they'd finished with Mills and then Arthur dropped them back at Alex's car. The old man had been watching Stephen's car at the cattle grid above Buttertubs and saw his friend arrive alone. Before he could speak to him, Colin had turned the van round and was racing back down the hill at full speed. By the time Arthur had started his car and followed him, the white van was flipping over, disappearing into the valley below. He nearly hit Mills as she raced across to the edge. Together they watched the inferno. To their surprise they were joined by Stephen Grainger. He was clearly as shocked as they were by the sight. Arthur was still puzzling over the comment Mills made at the time: *Been analysing some tacks covered in DNA; I hope we don't have to use them, Stephen.* It was barely audible but it was clear that Stephen heard.

At Mossy Bank the lane was lined with cars, including a flashy Audi that Alex assumed belonged to Mr Sanderson. Muriel flew out of her door and ran over as he was squeezing his car into the remaining space.

'Are you all right, love?' she asked Mills. 'We were so worried. I saw the road was blocked and I knew it wasn't supposed to shut for the race until this evening. There's been an accident, they said. I thought… well, best not think… I told your stepmother…'

'Have you seen her?' Mills asked.

'Seen her?' she laughed. 'They're all in with me. I said to them, I'm sure it must be something important that's detained you.'

Alex and Mills followed her to find members of both their families drinking tea in Muriel's sitting room. It was a strange introduction but Alex was pleased to see that they all seemed to be getting on very well.

Mills listened as Alex explained to the group how he'd gradually learned that the man living down the road was probably responsible for a series of deliberate attempts to kill young cyclists.

'But why?' asked Muriel. 'He seemed such a nice old boy.'

'It was because of what happened to his wife and family.' Mills went on to tell them about the car crash caused by a cyclist from the university. 'That's why he chose cyclists in the team colours.'

When they asked how he came off the road, Mills explained that he'd deliberately gone into the barrier. She felt he probably wanted to die. She didn't mention that she'd been in his van a few minutes earlier.

'But why were *you* up there?' her father asked.

Muriel admitted it was her fault. She'd wanted Colin to help Arthur confront Stephen, who was definitely planning something up on the top there.

'Well, he won't be able to do anything now,' Mills said. 'The road is closed until the race is over.'

Mills thanked Muriel for looking after everyone and led her visitors next door. It was only then that she realised there was no sign of the baby.

'Fi, where's Flora?' she asked.

Fiona blushed and mumbled that Hugh had gone back for her – she was sleeping on Muriel's bed. Alex led his parents up the narrow stairs to the back bedroom and Fi went out, ostensibly to unpack the car.

'What a beautiful cottage!' Alex's mother was making her way carefully back downstairs. 'I hope you don't mind but I've brought a casserole. I know you're a busy girl and I thought I would prepare something for supper – as there is such a crowd of us.'

'That's great. Thank you.'

'Philip!' she called up the stairs. 'Can you help me get the hamper from the car?'

'Does your mother do a lot of cooking?' Mills asked Alex when his parents were outside.

'Yes. I told her to bring some things; you don't mind?'

'Not really.'

Fi and Hugh appeared with Flora, who became the centre of attention until it was her bedtime. Stephanie's boeuf bourguignon just needed heating up and was delicious, although she brushed aside the compliments, admitting that she had done a cordon bleu cookery course in the past. Fiona was unusually quiet and later surreptitiously slipped a few packets of biscuits and a bought cake into the kitchen when Hugh was unloading Flora's baby food.

The evening went more easily than Mills had imagined. Fortunately Philip and Hugh had similar interests.

'I wouldn't have put your dad down as a football fan,' Alex said when they were washing up.

'Nor would I,' admitted Mills. 'I think he's making a special effort. Like your mum – I can't imagine she's *that* interested in Flora.'

When the phone rang, Alex went to answer it, bringing the receiver into the kitchen. 'It's Nina.'

'Mills, are you all right? I heard what had happened but I didn't realise you'd been involved.'

'I'm fine, really. I got out of the van in time.'

'You were in the van?' she sounded horrified. 'What if? It's too horrible to think about!'

'Yes.' To be honest Mills hadn't had the time.

'It all happened so fast,' Nina went on. 'When Alex told us it was a bird on the side and Ruby had identified Colin Norton, we sent uniform over immediately. Obviously it was too late, he'd already left home.'

'I gave a statement,' Mills explained. 'He admitted he'd driven Anna Rycroft off the road – and Jack Bassett. When he missed the third one, he began to regret his actions. I suppose he realised it wouldn't bring his family back.'

'Poor man. It makes you realise how important family is.'

Mills agreed and went back into the sitting room, where she squatted on the floor next to Alex and listened to more embarrassing stories about his childhood. His parents were a proper couple, like her mother and father had been. It was a very long time since she'd felt part of a real family.

Stephen Grainger sat alone watching a rerun of an old detective series. The road through the dale was closed now, in preparation for the race, but he could hear vehicles moving past his house at regular intervals, no doubt police and race officials preparing the route. He peered through the curtains again to check the car parked across the green. He couldn't be sure but earlier, when it was light, he swore it was the girl with the big hair who'd challenged him at the public meeting. He couldn't be sure she was watching *his* house but whatever she was up to, she'd been there a long time. Well, she was wasting her time if she was after him because he wasn't budging – not even when the race went past. He'd set up a giant poster on his gatepost expressing what he thought of the race. When Catriona rang, he'd told her it was all over – the cyclists won. She was shocked when she heard about Colin.

'It wasn't… please don't say it was your trip wire!'

He'd reassured her that it was nothing to do with him and he had no plans to take any further action to stop the race. The image was imprinted on his mind: the familiar egg van flipping over and over then disappearing out of sight. Flames turning the white van black.

'Apparently he was responsible for the death of a young woman cyclist on Buttertubs last year. We don't want any more accidents, do we?'

He put on his coat and went outside. The girl in the car sat up. He tore down the poster and, turning in her direction, ripped it into tiny pieces, letting them flutter away in the wind. As he went back inside, he heard a car engine start up and the vehicle moving away down the dale.